Love Edy

Shewanda Pugh

Razor's Edge Edition

D1316373

Love Edy
Published by Razor's Edge

1st Printing
Razor's Edge: trade paperback, June 24, 2014
Printed in the United States of America

ISBN: 0692027149
ISBN-13: 978-0692027141

Cover art by Claudia McKinney
Book design by Ian Thomas Healy

Dedication

FOR CALEB, WHO RENEWS ME DAILY

"Whatever our souls are made of,
his and mine are the same."

Emily Brontë

One

Friday night. The sky hung heavy, seamless, with heaven's stars blotted out by overbearing skyscrapers. Shrieks and a cacophony of cheers rang out, hysteria supreme in a microscopic stadium rocking on the edge of Boston's South End. Thin and buckling bleachers rattled with the stomps of impending mania, shrill whistles and hefty shouts: those were the true sounds of redemption. Fourteen years and not a single touchdown against Madison High; fourteen years, but no more.

It had come at the hands of a freshman running back who couldn't stop moving, a last-minute, fidgeting substitution. To others, his appearance must have seemed a concession, but Edy Phelps knew better. Edy Phelps knew *him* better.

He was hunger and discipline, jittery and ravenous, so rattled that nerves kept him shifting and stretching and pacing along the sidelines. Obsession fueled him, and kept him keen on an opportunity unwilling to come. Except that night, *chance* came to Hassan Pradhan. His chance. Finally.

It happened in a breath. A snap of the ball. A fake pass and Hassan thundered downfield at a speed only fear could sustain. His moment. His only moment. Take it. Take it. Run. *Fly.*

He could hear *her* thoughts—no, *feel* her thoughts.

Edy was sure of it. They'd always had a connection. And it was in that way she aided him. Fists pressed to her lips, teeth slammed together, screaming with her soul. *Soar. I know you can do it.*

Just as the clock whittled to nothing, Hassan vaulted into the end zone.

A collective roar swallowed Edy and the crowd leapt as one. A win. Few would recall the last.

On her left, Hassan's parents cheered: mother in a starched linen suit and pumps too prim for a game, father in a white button-up, belly pressing the fabric, sleeves rolled to the elbow. His mother, Rani, was without the brilliant red bindi she couldn't do without, giving her forehead that naked look. On Edy's opposite end were her parents, their absolute best friends, in the long-sleeved alumni tees reserved for football season, mother free of the skirt suits that dictated her days. Edy abandoned them all for the sidelines, for Hassan. She weaved round patches of shrieking upperclassmen, hopped over rows of empty benches, apologized to the fat man whose cocoa she sloshed, and ignored the slice of a sudden, early winter wind.

He'd done it.

All those nights, all those talks, round and round about the possibility of getting in a game, the two of them in bedroom shadows, careful to keep their voices low. Some nights he thought a chance would never come; others, he insisted it had to. Either way, he always said that if it did, *when* it did, he would do something worth remembering. And he had.

At the sidelines, Edy's gaze swept a team clustered so thick, so honeyed together with the sweetness of victory, that she worried she might never find her neighbor, her best friend.

Ice cut the air, and the glare of stadium lights had her like an ant under a magnifying glass in the noonday sun. She remembered the way the Dyson twins would burn insects and snicker, and she thought no, she'd be hot if she were a tortured ant, not cold. The fog of her breath seconded her motion.

She spotted him.

Edy had come to hug someone already occupied, someone surrounded by sweeping blonde curls, dark curtains of perfect hair, nestled by an endless supply of short skirts. Hassan draped an easy arm around a cheerleader with shimmering flaxen locks, mouth curling into a grin when a brunette of with pouty lips cried foul and claimed him as her own. Soft tans and the curves of certain womanhood donned them both. Edy looked from them to her own angular body and knew what she would find: all edges and sharpness, slender, muscles sculpted from a life of dance. The baggy jeans, football jersey, and sloppy poof of a ponytail she wore didn't give her much to run with either. That hair used to be the brunt of Hassan's endless jokes. Big enough to tip you back," he'd say, before tugging it in absentminded affection. She fingered that hair with the same sort of absent--mindedness, before looking up to see a blonde plant rosy lips on Hassan's cheek.

Ugh.

Edy didn't care about the movies, the books, the popular culture that insisted football player and cheerleader, jock and pretty girl, were a natural sort of fit. It wasn't. *They* weren't. It absolutely couldn't be.

A girl like that couldn't understand what made him *him.* So what if he was . . . obscenely gorgeous, with sun-licked bronze skin, silken black locks, and eyes an ever-glimmering, gold-flecked green. He had a quiet sort of beauty, made for old Greek sculptures and timeless works of art. Not that he was quiet. *He* was explosive, with good looks and athleticism. But beyond that were pleasures and disappointments, what he loved and could not bear. Imprinted on Edy's mind were the crinkles at the corner of Hassan's eyes when he smiled, the clench of his jaw when irritation set in, the rich and sonorous laugh that had slipped octaves lower in recent years. A girl like that blonde could be nothing to him—could know nothing *of* him. She knew a moment and a touchdown. That was it.

Edy's hands made fists.

The blonde moved in to kiss his cheek again, just as a teammate shouted his name. Hassan jerked back, only to be caught at the corner of his mouth by her lips.

A whoop rang out from the guys.

Heat flushed Edy's veins and her fingernails dug, digging, digging, until tears blurred her vision.

Wait.

He was her best friend, family really, if you considered the way they were brought up. So, she really had no reason to—

The blonde threw her arms around Hassan. The team swarmed and the two disappeared from sight.

They were kissing, weren't they?

Edy closed her eyes, forcing back the hottest tears and the bitterest taste of sudden envy.

She loved him. Dear God, she loved her best friend.

It fell down on her at once, uncompromising truth and the weight of reality like a cloak too heavy to bear.

The boy that had grown by her side, promised to another in a tradition as old as marriage itself, another girl of his ethnicity, religion, beliefs: that's the boy she loved. A single line existed between Edy's family and his, between the Pradhans and Phelps, who otherwise acted as one.

But Edy loved him.

And, of course, there was no recourse for that.

Two

Friday night. Three weeks since the Madison win, two hours since annihilating Charlestown. Another victory at Hassan's hands. Time to celebrate, Edy supposed.

Edy slipped the door of her home library closed behind her, tucked their oversized family medical guide under her arm, and gripped the front of her fuzzy pink terry robe in a fist. Her gaze swept left, then right, before dashing straight to her bedroom—a short scurry down the hall and up the stairs. She had minutes to spare before the party, maybe less.

Once inside, she locked the door and tossed the book onto her bed, joining it with a bounce. Edy flipped to Chapter Sixteen, "Sexual Development and Puberty," and took a deep breath, then another.

Moments ago, she thought she'd felt a small, tender lump while thumbing around in the shower. It should have been the first sign of breast development, but at fourteen, she'd jetted a full four years past the average age for debut. So she aimed to look now, with a pseudo instruction manual in sight. Edy patted her chest; thumbed, jabbed, grunted, and let her arms drop in defeat.

Nothing. Flat as a freaking tortilla.

Seven signs of puberty existed, six of them absent in her. Edy's chocolate skin ran smooth and hairless, her body curve-less and acne-free. She had no period to speak of and were it not for her distinct need to double up on Secret antiperspirant before ballet, she'd swear herself relegated to childhood forever.

Edy sat up and folded her legs Indian style—*Native American style?*— on her bed, frowning at a diagram claiming to be her insides. Since ten, she'd been squinting at books like this, books that told her first to be patient and later that something had to be wrong. Girls began puberty at ten or twelve, finishing at sixteen, seventeen at the latest. Even if she did begin that year, the year she'd turn fifteen, it would mean she'd still be developing at twenty or twenty-one according to the pace of these charts. Was it possible? Or was she broken, faulty in some way?

Edy took a peek at her body. Stuffing her bra could be an option. If she didn't move around much, it might hold. Chloe Castillo had stuffed her bra for close to a year, stopping only when breasts grew instead. In doing so, she'd left Edy as the only girl in the ninth grade with a washboard chest and hips as attractive as a spine. When coupled with owlish brown eyes and only the slightest swell of a bottom, she wasn't exactly runway material.

The bedroom door rattled and Edy started. Heart athump, she chucked the book under her bed, turned a circle in search of clothes and squeaked at the sound of Hassan Pradhan's bark.

"You walk in four minutes! Twins said it, so you know it means three."

Edy jumped into matchstick jeans, struggled into an unassuming white turtleneck, and cracked the door open with forced indifference. Hassan raised a brow at the creak she made, paused, and then nudged the door further with two fingers.

"We lock doors now?" he said.

No. Yes. *Definitely yes.*

He pointed a finger at her chest.

"Something on your shirt," he said.

Edy shook her head, slow. No way. She knew the trick. Knew it well.

"Really," he insisted. "It's right there."

She refused to look down. Nothing could be there and both of them knew what would happen if she did hazard a glance.

"Fine." He laughed. "Go out looking like that. Don't stand near me."

And he turned for the stairs, giving her an inkling of opportunity.

She looked and Hassan snapped back, faster than the thought that followed, the one telling her she knew better. Even as the laugh burst from her, his finger snapped up, zipping over her chin, mouth, and nose before flicking the space between her eyes with its dampness.

He whirled for the stairs, dismissing her as a non-threat, only to have her foot plow squarely into his backside. Hassan stumbled for a stair or two, grabbed the railing, and broke his fall.

He turned back to face her. "You lock the door on me again and I'll tell you kicked me."

With Edy's pacifist father the threat had serious consequences—if he meant it, which he didn't. Never mind that Hassan elected to take pummelings on the football field far more severe than any her dancer's foot could render. Telling her father she'd hit him meant enduring hours of him reading aloud about the philosophical beliefs of Mahatma Gandhi, Martin Luther, Jesus, and Henry David Thoreau.

Satisfied at having reprimanded her, Hassan bounded downstairs, down stairs he'd chased her endlessly on, everyday, since learning to walk. His shoulders were broader than she ever thought possible, back straight, waist wasp narrow. At fifteen, he stood eye-to-eye with his father and a head above her, body hard, and kept by the assurance of athletic grace.

He ran a hand through limp black hair, damp and clinging to perfect skin.

Edy exhaled and hurried after him.

Downstairs, they threw her father a pair of cursory hand waves. He rose from his favorite arm chair to hurl an avalanche of restrictions meant for them both. They ranged from returning home at a respectable time to resisting the urge to sample ecstasy, heroin, and cocaine. When Hassan scoffed at the latter, her father followed them, all the while citing a recent Columbia University study that said one in three teens would have the opportunity to sample drugs at a party.

"Well then," Hassan mumbled, low enough for Edy's ears only. "I'll be sure not to miss my chance."

She grinned.

Outside, a gleaming black Land Rover inched forward, slowing past Edy's house. When they stopped, it stopped. When they started, it started again. Finally, Hassan let out a snort, grabbed Edy by the wrist, and hurried down the walkway.

The Land Rover continued its creep, moving slow enough for Hassan to throw open the back door and wave Edy in. The moment she lifted her foot, however, the Rover shot forward, only to jerk to a halt. When she tried again, it did the same. Edy couldn't help but giggle.

"Would you stop before she falls?" Hassan yelled. "Friggin' clowns."

The front window slid down and a pair of snickers greeted him. The driver's head emerged.

"If all the beer's gone, Sawn, you'd better morph into Sam Adams and brew more," Mason Dyson warned.

Mason, one half of the Dyson twin freight train that lived two blocks away, swiped a swath of perfectly managed dreadlocks from his eyes and grinned. Edy seized the opportunity to jump into the SUV. Once inside, she mumbled hellos to Mason and his identical, Matthew, who thumped her on the forehead in greeting. Edy settled in next to their younger brother Lawrence. Hassan climbed in behind her and slammed a palm into the driver's side headrest, jarring Mason before settling in behind him. Mason, seemingly oblivious to the assault, adjusted the low rumble of hip hop drifting from the speakers, let up his window, eased off the brake of the factory-fresh Land Rover, and tossed a wave to Edy's father, who stood in the doorway. He, in turn, lifted his hand absentmindedly, thoughts no doubt far and away on some strand of research. She didn't know *why* she expected any different, but it would have been nice for her dad to pretend his daughter was the least bit . . . desirable and therefore worthy of serious distrust.

Oh well.

In the front, the twins broke out into a hand slap tournament over the radio. Mason wanted Pitbull and Matt, Justin Timberlake, thinking it would "entice the girls." Though Edy's father had ventured to the door to see them off, he'd been distracted enough to bring a newspaper. A lift of his head froze the action. In the end, Pitbull reigned victorious.

Edy sighed. There she sat, seconds from the "it" party of the moment, with not one or two but four of the school's star football players. The Dyson twins were upperclassmen, defensive teammates that had shown talent even in South End's worst days. Their younger brother, Lawrence, was a wide receiver just beginning to come into his own. Then there was Hassan, of course, the Boy Who Beat Madison, an accomplishment that sprouted legs and run away of its own accord, growing with every step it took. Since then, there had been more wins and more touchdowns. At school, in the corridors, *these* were the boys to know. These were the boys that girls whispered about, watched, and wanted. There were times when she overheard one girl or another, spazzing out on fantasies and trysts that involved Matt and Mason. Edy warmed, pushing back thoroughly unwanted images. Everyone knew not only what the Dyson boys did, but that they did it often and well. Nonetheless, Edy's father stood in the doorway, waving as his lone and virginal daughter made off with a car full of jocks.

She was safe. Woefully, painfully, unquestionably safe; as secure as a Victorian-era maiden out for a stroll with her beau, watchful chaperones at the ready. With the Dysons, with Hassan, she was but one of the boys—or worse, a little sister suffered out of obligation.

As if to illustrate, Matt thumped her on the forehead once more as Lawrence elbowed her over, claiming to need more space. There could be no doubt that Edy Phelps was safe from the clutches of male temptation, even if she wanted it any other way.

As if on cue, the Land Rover tracked backwards.

"What's wrong?" Matt said.

"Castillo. Six o'clock." Mason shot a look in the rearview mirror.

Six o'clock, just over Edy's shoulder. Chestnut curls sweeping in the wind, makeup runway dramatic, glamour girl Chloe Castillo—in no need of bra stuffing these days—had the attention of three Dysons, Hassan, and, to her own dismay, Edy.

"Party?" Mason wondered aloud.

"Gotta be," Matt said.

"Well, then. We certainly can't have her out here all alone. Not in the mean streets of Boston."

There were mean streets in Boston. Edy's mother, the district attorney, could attest to as much. But those streets never pierced the tree-lined affluence of their posh enclave.

"Gonna give her a ride, Lil' Dyson," Mason said to Lawrence. "Try not to pitch a tent."

Lawrence winced, ears reddening at their snickers. Edy looked from one to the next for clarification. Only when Matt flicked his pointer finger skyward that she could make sense of the comment.

Aroused. Try not to get aroused.

Warmth crept over Edy's cheeks. She ducked her head, wishing herself away.

"Matt—" Hassan warned.

"What? I didn't *say* it! And anyway, she's a big girl. She knows what we're talking about." Matt shot Edy a mockingly suspicious look. "Somehow."

Suddenly she, instead of Chloe Castillo, had the attention of the entire car. They were so full of crap that way. Still, Edy stiffened under their looks and took an interest in the back of her eyelids instead. Long seconds passed where her heart simmered down to a slow beat. She stole a peek at Hassan, who glared back at her, foul as a bare mouth mule gumming on thumb tacks.

The SUV screeched to a stop near Chloe, reminding Edy that they were moving at all.

"You must be heading to the party," Matt said. "You should be riding with us."

Chloe peered into the Rover.

"Is there even room?"

"Sure. You'll just have to, uh, squeeze onto Lawrence's lap. No biggie, right?"

Chloe took a step back, face a shade pinker than her makeup allowed.

"I guess not," she said.

She peeked at Lawrence, whose head snapped left, treating her to his back instead. Matt shot his little brother a look of impatience before jumping out and opening the back door. He flexed arms that were the subject of schoolgirl whispers and lifted Chloe up in a show of bravado, making her giggle. Edy pursed her lips and looked away. For a girl with apparent reservations, Chloe Castillo settled into Lawrence's lap easily enough.

Edy looked up to discover a silent head-jerking argument underway between Mason and Lawrence. It grew wild as the seconds ticked on, with the older boy eye popping, neck jerking and wheel barrowing emphatically, urging Lawrence to put his arms around Chloe. When the younger Dyson lifted his hands in slow surrender, he placed them ginger as two broken limbs at her side.

They ventured six blocks over before Mason whipped a U-turn in the middle of the street. He parked at a three-story Victorian the color of a setting sun. Teens pressed into the yard fence to fence. Lights and bass-laden hip hop spilled from yawning windows and a wide-open front door, as a gyrating rainbow of adolescents crowded round a keg on the northwest side of the house.

Chloe eased out the Rover, followed by the boys, who were met with an uproar of shouts and greetings. Football players swarmed, swallowing them in an intricate exchange of handshakes. They disappeared into the crowd, and Edy hung back, unsure of what to do in a melee of testosterone.

Long seconds passed, and Edy exchanged a look of quiet awkwardness with Chloe. The two hadn't had words since sixth grade. No reason to change that now.

Chloe's lips parted just as the team's quarterback slipped between them, dividing the space between the girls with his back to Edy. *Great.* She counted the moments with her gaze on his broad expanse, knowing that her view would be brief.

"Oho! My QB, the man I've been looking for." Mason Dyson swept an arm around the smaller boy's shoulders and whipped him in an arc away from Chloe. His twin appeared in the quarterback's place.

"He smells," Matt announced, then blinked as if just noticing Chloe. "Thinking out loud. Sorry. But he's not your type, is he?"

Edy smirked. Of course he is. Of course, *they* were. For all the obvious reasons.

"You mean Jeff?" Chloe said. She hesitated as if still trying to figure out if the quarterback had B.O. "I don't really know him. I—"

Matt flicked an impatient hand. "Tell me what you think of Lil' Dy—er, *Lawrence*," he said.

"Think?" Chloe echoed.

Oh Lord.

"You do *think* of him, don't you?" he said.

Matt smiled as if he knew some well-shrouded secret. Chloe blushed, though whether from his presence or some homed-in thought was impossible to tell.

Edy supposed it made no difference to a girl like Chloe Castillo. It made no difference whether she won over Matt or Mason or Lawrence. Lawrence, like his brothers, was a starter. He could talk to Chloe or any one of the mindless girls that infested their high school, and he could snag her with minimal effort. She, in turn, would be hysterical with glee.

"Coming?" a voice at Edy's ear said.

She lurched at the sound of Hassan, then scolded her skittering pulse. He was close, close enough to dampen her ear with his lips. Edy yanked the reins on her runaway heart, urging it to steady. He was the same boy he'd always been, and she, the same girl.

But her buck wild heart begged to differ.

He startled me, that's all.

Edy turned to face him a moment too late. She spied the top of his hair amidst a second rush of teammates as they swept Hassan up and into the house.

Eventually, Edy made her way in, ushered by the cold. In a living room that stood grand even while defaced with the presence of drunken teens, she had her back to the wall, eyes on a solid mass of dancers rocking to hip hop. A decade of professional instruction in ballet made it no easier for her to go out there and join them. She wasn't trendy, nor did she keep up with the latest dance fads. They moved with the jolts and jerks of the untrained.

But it wasn't just that. For Edy, anything not intricately choreographed belonged to the theater of her bedroom. So, she would keep to the wall, watch and wait. For one song, two songs, ten.

Only then did she see the slender redhead ascending the stairs, hand laced with Hassan's.

Edy's heart stilled and her lungs flattened, waiting for him to pull away.

When they disappeared from view together, she fled.

~~~

Matt and Mason were at the center of a crowd, executing a series of jerking and improvised shuffle--steps. They perfected grinds and lurches, stopping only to consult each other, before pulling out a pair of giggling girls to regurgitate their choreography.

It was easy for them. Little more than a double dose of nonsense, Matt and Mason could get serious about nothing but football. Tall and dark, lean and athletic, lithe and dependable, somehow, Matt and Mason could make a girl want them even when she shouldn't, even when she ought to know better.

Hassan took a sip of beer—his first ever—and cringed at its rankness. He imagined his father catching him just then, voice thick and rippling with the accent of his homeland. He'd rage for an hour and smack him upside the head to make sure that the message stuck. It wouldn't. What he did with the beer afterward would depend on whether or not Hassan's mother was around. If so, Hassan's father would toss it away. If not, he'd tackle it in a mouthful of enthusiastic swallows.

Hassan made eye contact with a red-haired girl that was older and definitely staring. She licked lush, wet, pink lips, causing him to look away. Was she putting on a show for him? A second glance said she was.

"Aimee," Matt announced, and Hassan jerked as if caught. "Aimee Foss, a junior."

He took the beer from Hassan, gulped it, and handed it back.

Hassan risked another look. Weeks ago, before he made the game-winning touchdown against Madison, he would have found it hard to believe that a junior would look in his direction, let alone have interest. But twenty-two days of post-Madison fervor had shown him teachers who shrugged at late homework, girls who kissed him on dares, and all the back slaps, handshakes and fist pounds he could stand. He hadn't made up his mind how he felt about any of it yet.

"You're a coward," Matt announced. "I'm gonna talk to her for you."

Hassan choked. "No! Matt—"

Too late. Already, Matt parted the crowd.

Rushing over would make Hassan look stupid, especially if he wound up crashing an otherwise harmless conversation. Staying put might result in humiliation, considering embarrassment was the Dyson twin specialty. He had speed and could bolt for the door, but leaving would mean he ran from a girl.

Hassan gulped the bitter brew and waited. He shifted, resisting the urge to fidget. One second, two seconds, three.

She made her way over. Head high, gaze even, confident in her stride.

They could've been in a beer commercial. Him standing there, looking dumb, with some specialty brew in his hand, her parting the crowd in slow motion, hair fluttering from the blast of an A/C vent. This was the part where he discovered she wanted the beer and not him.

"Hassan." She made his name sound like a whisper of silk against satin, the rustle of imported fabric. There it was again. A dip of the tongue, subtle. She smiled at him and his cheeks grew hot.

"Aimee," she offered.

She surprised him by extending a hand, ultra-formal for a bunch of teens. He took it, and she didn't let go.

"Will you come with me?" she said. "Upstairs?"

His Adam's apple bobbed, thick in his throat. She didn't mean anything by the offer. After all, lots of things were upstairs. He just couldn't think of any.

"Alright," Hassan managed. He cleared his throat and set the beer on a table.

Aimee led him by the hand through the crowd. Upstairs and a single left later, they arrived at a bathroom, large and luminous. Hassan blinked. Aimee pulled him in and shut the door behind them.

"Number twenty-seven" she crooned, just a hint of slur in her voice. She stepped forward, copper curls spilling into damp, hooded, and shadowed green eyes. "Ninety yards against Madison. Two touchdowns against Southie. Three against Charlestown," she announced. The girl leaned forward, lips parted, and ran a red-tipped finger from Hassan's nose downward, eyes never leaving his mouth.

"Kiss me," she said.

He froze. Had the girl never heard of small talk? Already, he'd forgotten her name. Even if she wanted to . . . *do things*, it seemed to him that she should wait for his advances. Maybe he was old fashioned. How many guys did it take for a girl to do away with the formalities?

She turned her back on him to flip out the light switch, bathing them in darkness. Hassan opened his mouth, only to find that words wouldn't come. Soft lips and the nip of teeth grazed his ear. Her mouth dragged lower, paused, and devoured.

She kissed hard, punching her tongue between his lips, blazing the cinders of cigarettes there. He'd kissed before, easy, meaningless flirting that was never so demanding, and never with a girl that made him feel smothered, or made him feel like he needed to reach out and grab a buoy. Before he could get the hang of it though, she'd backed away. Now she had fingers at his zipper. Fumbling.

The beer muddled what was already a jumble of confusing, contrary thoughts: that he should *say* something, that he didn't really *know* her, that he was sorry if he was supposed to, that he couldn't even recall ever having seen her. And what the *hell* was her name?

He shoved her back, then snatched for her when she pitched, only to ease her clumsy head crash to the door. He'd never put his hands on a girl and hadn't meant to that time. If he'd hurt her, he didn't think he could deal with that.

The redhead clutched the back of her head and let loose a stream of gutter rude insults, before finding her footing enough to slap him and barge out the door.

What the hell just happened?

He splashed water on his face and pushed the image from his mind, before forcing himself out of the bathroom. Once at the top of the stairs, his gaze swept the crowd and met that of a slender Asian girl who blushed in response. Her smile made him think of Edy.

"I see you met Hungry Hungry Hippo," Matt said, appearing at his side.

Hassan started. "What?"

"Hungry Hungry Hippo. Come on. You must have seen that mouth work."

When shrugging into his shirt didn't work, Hassan buried his embarrassment in an attentive sweep of the crowd. Obviously, Matt had expected something to happen upstairs with the redhead. He wouldn't give him the satisfaction of confirming or denying it.

"Where's Edy?" he said instead.

A casual question, yeah, but even as he asked it, he realized that he hadn't seen her for awhile.

"Seriously, I don't see her." His gaze began to comb the crowd methodically.

He ventured downstairs. Two, three dozen kids grinding on the dance floor, but he knew better than to look among them. Along the walls, she wasn't there. In the kitchen, not there either. So, he backtracked, winding through the dancers on second thought.

"Sawn?" Lawrence asked, appearing with Chloe by his side.

"Edy," Hassan answered and kept moving.

He thought about the girl and the bathroom and how easily that had happened. He thought about the teammates all around, guys who poured beer down the throats of girls and shrugged at the outcome. *Edy had better not be drinking*, he thought, knowing it to be hypocritical and not caring.

He weaved his way back to Lawrence just as Matt showed up, then Mason. All three wore the same worried expression. They split up, with Mason heading out front to search the yard and Matt upstairs. Hassan and Lawrence searched the bottom floor in vain.

The twins returned empty-handed, leaving the boys to ponder what would happen should they go home without Edy. Once, they'd lost her in the old Jordan Marsh downtown at Christmas time. All four boys had abandoned her for a WWF Wrestling display with authentic replica belts. They were halfway through an improvised bout when they upturned a row of mannequins and realized she was no longer at their side.

It hadn't mattered that they'd been found, safe and playing in a clearance rack of plus size blouses. It hadn't mattered either, that she had had no interest in wrestling. They were like a family, each responsible for the other. Edy's father had seen fit to remind them. No faux gold, glitter, or cheap enticement should ever make them forget it again, he'd said.

The sight of Lorenzo Carpenter descending the stairs jarred Hassan from the memory. Lorenzo was the team linebacker, party host, and guy most likely to slink away to dip Liquid X in some girl's drink. Dudes like him had a way of sensing diminished capacity in a six-mile radius, or helping it along, at any rate. If he knew what was best for him, he'd turn up Edy unscathed and on demand.

The Dysons beat Hassan to Lorenzo, minds with him, on one accord. Together, the twins seized him by the collar and slammed him into the wall. They were backed up by Hassan on the right and Lawrence on the left. So much as a flinch from the linebacker would bring down a fury of fists.

"Edy," Matt demanded. "*Now.*"

What the hell were they thinking, bringing her to this guy's house and letting their guard down? They had *pakhana* for brains. Shit, to be exact.

Lorenzo stared back at them with eyes too far apart.

"Edy *Phelps*?" he said and choked on a laugh.

Matt cocked back his fist.

"Wait! Hold on," Lorenzo hollered. He struggled against the hold on him, face twisted in irritation, limbs grappling, flailing, before coming to a final, frustrated rest. A look left and right confirmed that no teammates would come to his aid. Instead, they watched, as if the party finally kicked up a notch.

"I saw her," Lorenzo said. "Earlier."

"Where?" Hassan said.

Mason slammed the boy into the wall.

"Stop screwing around and tell us where she is," Mason said. "Drunk? Upstairs? You know better than to touch her, don't you? If you so much as—"

"Yeah!" Lorenzo said. "I mean, no. I didn't touch her! Like somebody would even bother."

"What's that supposed to mean?" Hassan said.

Lorenzo turned to him, wincing.

"Come on, Sawn. We all know—"

Matt shoved him again.

"Face *forward*. Talk to *me*."

"Fine!" Lorenzo grinned. "What's the problem, anyway? If Edy wants to give a little something something to somebody—"

He choked on the rest. Mason caught him by the throat, squeezing, then releasing, just enough to warn. Just enough to slide the smile off his face.

"Where is she?" Matt said, calm despite the elevating assault.

By Monday, they'd all have to find some semblance of normalcy on the practice field. They'd deal with Monday when it came.

"Gone, you idiots!" Lorenzo yelled. "And she's been gone! She walked right out the front door. Now get off me."

Lorenzo's arms battered the wall of bodies around him. But Matt and Mason released him on hearing what sounded like the truth. The group exchanged an uneasy look.

Gone.

And they hadn't even noticed.

~~~

Mason muscled the Land Rover over a bed of shrubs and into the street, knocking his passengers left then right with the hustle. Just as Matt yelled for him to head in the opposite direction, Lawrence demanded to know if he could possibly hurry up. Hassan's eyes kept to the street, desperate for a glimpse of a just-departed Edy.

He supposed to an outsider their panic looked silly. But none of them cared. Edy was one of *them*, and they didn't need her father to remind them.

"Why would she leave like that?" Mason said, halting at a red light and chewing on the side of his thumb.

"Maybe someone tried something," Lawrence said.

"Tried something?" Matt echoed.

Silence filled the cabin.

Hassan's face tightened, teeth sealing with the weight of wet cement. That image didn't work for him. It didn't work for him one friggin' bit.

"If someone had tried something, Edy would've come to one of us," Mason said.

Chloe, who sat wedged between Hassan and Lawrence in the center backseat, cleared her throat. "Maybe she didn't want to," she offered.

That had everyone's attention.

"And why wouldn't she want to?" Matt snapped.

"I don't know," Chloe said. "Maybe . . . if she liked it." She looked from one face to the next, each cold, hard, unappreciative.

"Maybe you oughta be quiet," Lawrence muttered and turned to face the window.

Hassan rode with the company of his thoughts, now violently intruded on by Chloe's assertion. Meanwhile, he kept dialing Edy's cell and it went to voicemail each time. Tension hung like a threat in the air.

"Who saw her last?" Mason demanded.

"Oh, don't start that again," Lawrence said. He turned to Hassan, eyed the cell in his hand. "Keep trying. Keep calling."

Hassan sighed. He pushed away a thousand crazy thoughts: that Lorenzo Carpenter had been lying to them, that Chloe had been telling the truth, that Chloe had been talking about Lorenzo when she told them the truth.

"We have to check her house," Mason said. "It's the only place left."

"Right," Matt sneered. "We just walk into her living room and ask Nathan if he's seen the daughter he left with us."

"Not us." Mason said. "Sawn."

"How?" Hassan said. He looked up from the phone.

"You've got a key," Matt pointed out. "Use it and walk up to her room."

"Like Nathan isn't up? Waiting?" Hassan said.

"Window," Lawrence said. "Climb up. Look in. See if she's there."

Her window. Their secret rendezvous place since Hassan had learned to climb trees at six. It was a decent idea. He could only hope that her father wasn't sitting on the bed, waiting for his now-late daughter.

They parked on the tail end of Hassan's street, Dunberry, behind a cluster of oaks and a stop sign. All four boys climbed out, hunched low, and scurried covertly to 2260, Edy's address, while Chloe waited behind in the car. On arrival, the Dyson brothers clustered around a sweeping, aged, and red-tipped chestnut, squinting upward as Hassan scaled it. They watched with a nervous eye for Edy's parents, or his, next door.

Hassan made it to the thick "V" of limbs that split half toward Edy's house, half toward his. He hoisted himself up, grabbed a gnarled branch for balance, and found a knot of familiar footing to stand on. A square of darkness stared back at him. He reached forward and yanked up Edy's window.

"Edy!" Hassan hissed. "You in there?"

Silence.

"Ed—"

She emerged from the shadows, hair in an oversized ponytail, pajamas ultra-pink and wrinkled, the epitome of a been-sleeping girl. Only, he knew better. She stared back at him, evenly, eyes wider in the night.

"What are you doing here?" he said. "Why aren't you answering your phone? We've been looking for you. We didn't know what to think."

"I'm here because I live here. You can go back to your party now."

"What? I can go back—" Hassan flared. "Why didn't you say you wanted to leave? Mason would've taken you. Or Matt. I would have walked you, if nothing else."

"I don't *need* anyone to take me. Now if you'll excuse me, I'm tired."

But he couldn't excuse her. Not like that. Her anger, whenever he earned it, sat with him, needling like a shoe that didn't quite fit.

"Cake?" he said uncertainly.

His name for her. It had always been his name for her. But she jerked as if the word itself burned.

He needed to *do* something. To fix whatever was happening. Only . . . he hadn't the faintest idea what was happening.

"Edy, please. If I did something, just tell me. "

She ran fingers along the sill. They were long, slender, curving beauties that had climbed trees with him, and been laced with his a thousand times.

He had an urge to make it a thousand and one.

"Good night, Hassan," Edy said.

She looked up at him with puffy eyes and closed the window between them.

"Night, Cake." He whispered it to darkness.

Three

The next morning, a Saturday, Edy watched her father's pearl-black BMW ease out the driveway, windows down to conserve energy. With no traffic in either direction, his speed matched that of an old lady's scooter. Once out and facing Mass Avenue, he offered her a curt wave. Edy waved back, keeping up the motion as her father rolled away, apparently without the use of gas. Hassan's dad always did say that his best friend drove as if headed to select his own grave.

Hassan.

Edy had earned the indulgence of last night's tears, but she would permit no more. Instead, she told herself that the party had been an awakening of sorts, about Hassan, about herself, about the parameters of their relationship. After all, she had been the one bleeding through the line that divided friend and more. Last night, he had only made clear what he expected "more" to look like, and it was not much.

She could live with that.

She would have to live with that.

Edy took her eyes off her father as he turned the corner and a massive moving truck across the street caught her attention. Washboard white, peeling, with sun-stripped letters on the side, it proclaimed itself to be the property of Joseph & Son. Odder still was the house it sat at. Unlike the reserved Queen Annes and Victorian relics of their block, the pink Painted Lady of 2265 Dunberry was lavish to the point of gaudy. Empty since the departure of Widow Meade, the nauseatingly fanciful dollhouse had whole sections of ruby paint chipped from its bulbous towers and fanciful pearl trim that stood thick like the twisted icing of a wedding cake. It beckoned in some misguided bid for attention, like the sinister home in a Brothers Grimm tale. It was a cheap imitation of the charm and splendor around it.

The truck's back doors flung open, and a spindly white boy backed out, shoulders hunched, the edge of a navy couch in his grip. Lengthy and paler than a ghost in winter, only his hollowed cheeks had splotches of red. Blond hair plastered to a hard skull with a wayward bit blowing free in the wind as his mouth clamped with the weight of his burden. Edy stood, curious. The couch was a plain thing draped in simple fabric, no wood carvings as far as she could see, and certainly not new, imported, designer or antique. In fact, its lumps were so prominent she could see them from across the street.

The other end of the sofa emerged, and with it, a middle aged, beer gut of a man, and the reason for the boy's struggles. The man's end of the couch rode low, nearly to the ramp they moved down. He fumbled in his pocket for something, and Edy caught snatches of the boy yelling. The man shot him a look of exasperation, but picked up the slack anyway. Hair sandy brown, skin oyster white, his five o'clock shadow, pouting belly, and Dickey blue pants confirmed Edy's suspicions. They were hired help. But for whom?

The Pradhan's front door swung open, and Hassan stepped out. Clad in a fitted, long-sleeved ribbed sweater and fashionably tattered jeans, he hopped the fence that separated his house from Edy's and made his way across her yard.

"I can't believe someone's moving in that circus tent," Hassan said.

He planted a kiss on Edy's forehead—habit—then paused—not habit—before giving her a once-over as if to see how she'd taken it.

Edy couldn't help but wonder if those lips had been on the redhead the night before.

"Could be a family of architects," she said, turning away. Edy heard the raspiness in her voice and hesitated. *Get it together.* "With plans to fix the place up."

She looked from the house across the street to him. Still, she had his attention. Too much of it. His gaze searched her face as if committing it to memory.

"Cake?" he said. She blistered with thoughts of the night before, of fingers entwined, of ascending to privacy, of a place Edy couldn't follow. She had expected to fool the one person she'd never been able to, to be nonchalant. And now that she couldn't, she hadn't time for a plan B. He was looking right at her.

"You okay?" Hassan said.

"Fine." *Find something else to do.*

"You don't look fine," he said.

She looked at him. "Well, I am."

Hassan exhaled. Contemplated. She could *feel* him thinking. "Listen, Edy. Last night—"

"Last night I decided to go home. End of story."

His mouth clamped shut, opened, then shut again. Finally, he turned to the scene across the street. Minutes ticked by. "What do they look like?" he said.

"Not sure. I've only seen the help."

Hassan grinned as the pair emerged again from the house. "Hired help? They must not charge much."

As if to underscore his point, the pot-bellied man dropped down on the porch and lit a freakin' cigarette. Jeez. She couldn't believe people still smoked.

Edy's mother strode from their house, clad in a stiff and layered Armani suit of runway perfection. It cut and flared where it needed to.

"Oh. Hey, plum," she said to Hassan. She paused long enough to mess his hair and fuss and say whatever mothers said to the child they wished was theirs. Whatever warmth radiated from her evaporated when she turned to Edy.

"Today's Saturday," she said. "That means study your Latin, brush up on the biology, and *then,* if there's time, make it to ballet."

She started off for her Lexus.

"Shut up," Edy and Hassan chimed under their breath in unison. She hadn't kept her mother's impossible schedule since the day she realized no one made sure she did. That had been a year ago, thank God.

Hassan led the way into her house, shoving open the door and heading straight for the kitchen. Once there, he snatched a plate from the cabinet, grabbed a fistful of pancakes, and stuck his head in the fridge for more food. When he came away again, it was with a carton of strawberries and a can of whipped cream. He stacked that on his plate and took a seat.

"Your dad's going over some stuff with me this week. He's been studying film and working out theories. Something's got him wired. He thinks we can make a run for a state championship, if you can believe that."

Hassan rolled a pancake, toppings and all, and jammed half of it in his mouth. "West Roxbury's the monster to fear, though."

Edy's father was a professor by trade, but football was his lifelong passion. A former kicker for Harvard with a talent too short of his love, it had been her dad who'd bought Hassan his first football, taught him game fundamentals, and sat huddled for hours with him, cultivating an understanding and philosophy so nuanced that only the two of them could make sense of it.

"We start this morning," he said apologetically. "I'm heading up to Harvard Yard in a bit. He has a break he wants to spend with me."

Of course. This was the way it started. And he probably wasn't even meeting her dad. Maybe he was meeting the redhead. She would know by Monday in any case. Toenails didn't get clipped without making the South End High grapevine.

"So. You're not walking me to ballet."

She'd meant to say it with more indifference, with a slice that cut him instead of her. Instead, the words only depressed her, a reminder that three years of a ritual could disappear in an instant.

He reached over and yanked on her ponytail.

"Hey, long face," he said. "I've been walking you there forever. Don't I get credit for time served?"

Time served.

When she didn't answer, he snorted and returned to his pancakes.

"What are you in for today?" he said in that oblivious way that belonged only to boys. "After ballet?"

Edy unclenched her teeth. "I don't know. Bake some cookies and bringing 'em to the newcomers. Extend the Suzy Homemaker welcome."

"Like hell," Hassan said, surprising her with his fervor. "This isn't 1950, June Cleaver. And I don't like the look of them, anyway."

"You didn't even see them."

"That's what you think."

Edy raised a brow. It was his habit to assume the role of big brother, taught to him by their parents, perfected with practice, despite them being exactly the same age. Nonetheless, he had little room to talk, after boinking the redhead. "Funny. Turns out I can ignore you as easily as Mom."

"Listen to me," he said. He stared at her, stared until her outrage, her annoyance; her urge to defy him began to melt—because hard feelings between them always did. Edy snorted at the trick. He then rose, loaded his dishes in the dishwasher, and planted a kiss on her forehead in what had to be goodbye.

"Stay away from the new neighbors."

He disappeared.

~~~

Edy didn't get a chance to venture across the street until the following morning. Ballet practice ran long, and afterward, she spent the evening making chocolate chip cookies for the new neighbors, only to roast them to a fine, thin crisp.

Instead of marching over empty-handed, she waited for an opportune time to visit. Sunday morning, Edy plopped down on the porch with a fresh glass of mango *lassi*, her dancer's feet creaking in protest as she watched her father back out the drive. The *lassi*, a sort of Indian yogurt smoothie, had as many variations as imagination allowed. Edy, who'd made her first with the aid of a stool and Hassan's mother, had an arsenal assortment of the drinks under her command. Though she could make them, she preferred his mother's *lassis* still. Hassan's mother had a way of adding special touches just for Edy—flaxseed for energy, ginger for pain, and extra honey when her sweet tooth raged.

Shaded from the heat of a persistent sun in ambivalent hot-then-cold-then-hot autumn, Edy waited for the new folks to make an appearance. A baby blue Dodge F-150 sat in their drive, chipped, rusted, and slumped to one side. Next to it was yesterday's truck. The old beat up Dodge, she figured, must have belonged to a carpenter or contractor of some sort.

When the front door opened, yesterday's pair stepped out. They crossed the yard and disappeared into the back of the moving truck, emerging later with odds and ends. They retreated and returned again and again, bearing assortments on each turn—a lamp, small boxes, garbage bags stretched full and misshapen by who knew what. When the boy came out alone and with an oversized CVS bag, hanger jutting from the bottom, Edy knew the contents wouldn't hold.

He struggled with it, even as the man brushed past him and went inside the house, content with muttering at his own burden. Edy was on her feet without knowing it.

"Your stuff!" she hollered and broke into a trot as the plastic bag began to seep clothes. "It's gonna fall!"

She crossed the street, threw open the gate, and scooped up the pile of fallen fabric, dashing to his side as his bag tore completely, vomiting shirts and old Converses, tattered boxers and ripped jeans right onto her feet.

They stared at each other, him red-faced, her cringing, before Edy decided to pick up the escaped clothes and be done with it. Except when she did, her hand brushed Swiss cheese underwear and she jerked in revulsion. Resolve melted under the fury of a blush they both shared.

"Please!" He puked the word. "Let me do it! I can—" He snatched the clothes from her and shoved them into his bottomless bag, so that they fell to the ground at once. He looked straight at her, at her as if every item was exactly where he intended it to be, and he had amply proven his point. He looked at her as if all those shirts and pants and shoes, weren't piled right on their feet.

Edy's cheeks inflated on a laugh she wouldn't let go. She *couldn't* let go. She held it until her insides ruptured and the dam burst, and oh, it broke free. He eased her a reluctant grin, cheeks aflame, before sliding into a grin himself. They dissolved into eye watering silliness. Underwear on their feet and instant friends somehow.

"I'm Edy," she said when their laughter died down.

He let the bag drift to the ground. "Wyatt Green."

"I live across the street," Edy said. "At 2260."

They stared at each other.

"Well, then," she said. "Guess I'll see you around."

She began to back away.

His face pinched. "Wait! I mean—"

He glanced back at the house, just as the front door swung open.

"Thanks for your help," Wyatt blurted. He scooped the fallen clothes in a single swoop and rushed to the door, leaving Edy to frown in confusion.

Four

Edy saw the boy named Wyatt Green the next morning and blushed with the recollection of touching his underoos. Even as she leaned forward for a better view from the center backseat of the twins' Land Rover, two thoughts occurred to her.

Wyatt wasn't hired help.

He was headed to their school.

"Stop!" Edy cried, so loud that Matt stomped the brake. He looked around as if expecting to find an animal, car, or child in the road.

"What? What happened?" he said.

All eyes were on her. Mason, Matt, Lawrence, Hassan, and even Chloe Castillo, with them once again.

"I know him," Edy said, indicating the tall and rawboned guy standing on the curb and muttering to himself as he adjusted the strap on a battered backpack. "Give him a ride."

Every male set of eyes turned on the figure, collectively sizing him at once.

"No room," Matt announced and stomped on the gas.

The sound of screeching tires jerked Wyatt's head up. Edy ducked in horror.

There they were, piled door to window, squashed to make room for Princess Chloe. The boys shoved each other to make allowances for her, barking commands to slide over, nudging Edy if she wasn't quick enough. She was never quick enough.

"You guys aren't being fair," Edy said. "Why *can't* we give him a ride?"

Already, Wyatt Green was out of view, left behind on a corner they'd long since turned.

"I told you," Matt said and shot her a look of warning in the rear view mirror. "There's no room."

Edy met Chloe's gaze evenly. She was a pretty and sparkling thing who'd only noticed Lawrence when the sureness of his hands and the quickness of his step emerged. Six years of elementary school, three years of middle, and Edy could no more place a conversation between Chloe and Lawrence than she could between herself and Abraham Lincoln. There was room for tinsel and glitter and falseness in the Rover, but none for anyone she knew.

"If there's no room" Edy said, "then maybe she should get out."

"Maybe you should chill out," Matt said.

Edy sat back in a huff. Defeated. Pissed. Outnumbered.

She could feel Hassan's eyes on her. Fire, Edy thought. More golden in fury, like flames.

"That dude just moved here the other day," Mason said. "So, you don't know him. And if you want to get to know him, you sure won't be doing it in my car."

"Hear, hear," Matt said.

Hassan continued to stare. Edy looked straight ahead, unwilling to meet his glare just yet.

South End High had the look of old New England: three stories of blood red brick, stately, old and resolute, stretching out for half a block. A sweep of concrete stairs led to its heavy oak doors, propped open before and after school. On its front, a legion of old, fogged, single pane windows stared out like blinded black eyes. The above-door placard that greeted them every day said what had been drilled into every South End student at orientation: That the school grounds had three centuries of history, it was a former meeting place for a chosen few plotting against the British Crown on the eve of the Revolution, and that the building had official recognition from the National Historic Registry.

They arrived just as the old fashioned liberty bell shrilled its ten minute warning. Ten minutes till every tardy kid could count on a nose full of Principal Rhinecorn's sour breath, plus two days of detention.

Out of the Land Rover and scrambling across the parking lot, Edy, the Dysons, and Hassan melted into the crowd. Around them, conversations swarmed as a thousand angry bumblebees all jammed in the same hive, and all buzzed the same buzz: party, clothes, sex, someone dumped someone, new boy, new boy, *new boy.*

Edy wondered if Wyatt Green had found the school okay, if he knew where to report, if he knew who to avoid. Caught in the upward stream of students, she careened enough to catch a glimpse of the open doors and the walkway of overflowing peers, before the hand at the small of her back pushed her on.

Hassan.

Edy split from the boys at the start of the day, taking homeroom with the jackal-faced Mrs. Rhodes. A trembling surly old woman who could neither see through windowpane-thick spectacles, nor hear on the days she forgot to power on her hearing aid, she marked present people absent and absent people present while conversations carried on unchecked. "Last year until retirement," she promised them every day.

Edy took a seat towards the front and against the far wall, out of range for Rhodes' blurred vision. Behind her was Eva Meadows, the once plump, dark haired girl who'd summered in Greece and came back for high school lean, sleek and svelte. Even her eyes had darkened from apple green to emerald. Rumor had it that 25k in plastic surgery had done most of the work. But kids didn't get lipo, did they?

"Name's Wyatt Green," Eva said. "He moved into that condemned house across the street from Edy. Daddy says they must be squatters."

"Well he does dress like one," the blonde cheerleader, Sandra Jacobs, conceded.

Her mother, who had also been a cheerleader at South End, was on her third husband, a business magnate who made his home in Milan. People said that Sandra hadn't seen her mother in two years and that her mother and stepfather hadn't been on U.S. soil in three. She got the best sort of gifts from them though, judging by that splash of a Marc Jacobs bag hooked on her chair.

"The new kid looks like he smells," Eva said. "I think I heard someone say he does."

Sandra stiffened, but said nothing. Edy's fingers curled into fists that she wished were bigger. She knew these girls, knew their meanness from earlier days, younger days, when their sting and the bitter dismissal were hers to own. She could hit one, she knew, and put some real power behind the blow. A lifetime of being the only girl in a clan of boys meant she could land a wicked right. Their paranoia had ensured as much.

The flat screen at the front of the room powered on and a freckled, peach-faced girl with rag doll curls smiled till her cheeks reddened.

"Good morning, South End and welcome to another wonderful Monday. I'm your host, DeeDee Bell, here to give you the latest."

Edy pulled out her e-reader. Around her, others reached for similar distractions—cell phones, iPods, an iPad in one instance, as DeeDee started in about the penalty for tardiness. Then meetings. Half a dozen clubs were looking for new members. The Historical Society had begun preparations for its annual spring program and, as usual, needed volunteers. At that, every head in the room swiveled to face Edy, teeth bared in gleeful grins.

Of course. She hadn't expected to go unscathed.

Each year, Edy's father volunteered for the Historical Society's evening production. He'd show up in a powdered wig, monocle and black tights—none of it required—to read a line attributed to his great, great, great grandfather, a freedman named Jebediah Phelps: *"'Tis freedom we seek. Nothing more."* He'd scan the auditorium meticulously, gaze sweeping across row after row, ensuring that the breadth of his message had been digested. Once satisfied, he'd give a soulless lecture on political philosophy, tying the lone words of Jebediah Phelps to the works of a half dozen philosophers. Should jeering interrupt him, as it always did, he'd pause long enough to stare down the culprit and begin again, voice carrying even further than before. With each octave he rose Edy sunk in her chair, all too aware of what would follow. Her dad was Fredrick Douglas at South End High, Morgan Freeman, or Harriet Tubman on a bad day.

It was definitely a Harriet Tubman kind of day.

After a dreary compilation of A.P. classes, Edy headed for her least favorite place, brown bag in hand. The muted, buried dread she saved for lunchtime bubbled up to the surface the moment she entered the cafeteria. She imagined at some high schools, lunch really was just lunch, the place where people gathered for food, a bit of people watching, and the last scratching in of last night's homework, answers borrowed from a friend. But at a place where the children of powerhouse politicians, athletes, journalists, and doctors coalesced, a hierarchy emerged, built on money, looks, talent and parental prestige. People were either in the light or the shadows; they were either someone or no one at all.

"Brown Brahmins" was what the local newspapers called them, a play on the Boston Brahmins, or upper-class elites of the city who could trace their lineage to Mayflower times. Brown Brahmins lived in Sci-Sci, a six-by-six strip of streets that served as the city's Hollywood Hills equivalent for people of color. They shopped at the Sax in the Pru and ordered duck confit at Hamersley's and were generally held up as the thing to aspire to for their downtrodden counterparts in Roxbury, Dorchester, and elsewhere. Brown Brahmins summered in the Hamptons or on the Cape, if they stayed in the U.S. at all, and had homes of historical significance or undeniable luxury. "Brown" designation aside, they were as diverse as they were insulated, with little tolerance for newcomers. Kyle Lawson was still considered the new kid and he'd moved there five years ago.

In her mind, Edy could never be one of them, even as she knew herself to be the epitome of *them*. Hers was the oldest house in Sci-Sci and the second oldest in historic South End, just behind the William Porter place on Washington Ave. The daughter of a celebrated Harvard professor, her lineage included abolitionists, one of the first doctors of color in the city, and two of the earliest professors of color to teach at Harvard—and that was just her father's side.

So, she had the lineage. And Lord knew she had the prestige. But what she didn't have was the stomach for what came with it, the who's who nonsense that meant she had to look the part.

Edy never could figure out how to look the part.

She ventured for the "it" table, not because she belonged on her own merits, but because she went where the boys did. No one challenged that, but the daily glares she earned said they wanted to. Having the right sort of friends made her bearable, or not worth the trouble.

First of the usual suspects to arrive, Edy dropped her lunch on the table and lowered herself onto the attached bench. She dug out a Tupperware dish and plastic utensils. Thick, black hair in a ponytail, high and bushy yet again, wayward wisps fell into her face, threatening her food. Her bowl, near-bursting with the *rogan josh,* a lamb stew, was but the remnant of an evening with Hassan's mother.

Each day, she imagined herself in the midst of a game for little ones, one where they were asked "Which one doesn't fit?"

Hassan's redhead. Hassan's redhead taking a seat across from her. Blouse candy pink and dipped low, it hinted at creamy white skin and attention-seeking cleavage. "Edy, right?"

Edy knew of her, of course, the way country folk knew all their neighbors. Aimee Foss, daughter of fashion designer Michel Foss and his one-time girlfriend Bernadine Roe. A junior who lived not quite on the cusp of Sci-Sci but still in South End.

Edy clenched a hand around her spork and trained her gaze down, on her food.

"Are you really going to sit here?" she said.

The redhead clucked her teeth. "Hmm. I get the impression you wouldn't like that. Why is that, Edy?"

Edy shifted in her seat, unwilling to entertain the burn of unease in her stomach. She didn't trust herself to speak, so she looked for Hassan instead.

"It must be hard, being you," Aimee said. "Being so close to guys like that, investing so much time, only to watch girls like me swoop down and . . .*taste* so easily."

Edy's head snapped up, just in time to see her lip glossed and triumphant smile. It burrowed away in a hustle of teenagers swarming their table. Bright lights illuminated hundred-dollar tees and couture jeans. But one thought ripped through it all. The redhead had been with Hassan.

A finger swooped in from behind and dipped knuckle deep in Edy's food. She turned to see Hassan insert the finger in his mouth.

"Mmm," he said. "Just like Mom used to make."

Edy cleared her throat and willed away the image of him and Aimee together. "Your mom did make it," she said.

"Oh, yeah."

With a tilt of his head, the debutantes who had gathered ushered themselves downstream, moving heartbeat fast to make room. He had come into his own pretty quickly and his own seemed to suit him rather naturally. People moved for him. Lawrence sat down in the new opening first, completely ignoring Aimee, who stayed. Only Hassan shot her an impatient look before opening his mouth, pausing, and letting discomfort swallow his features.

He hadn't noticed her. He hadn't placed her. Which meant what? That there were a thousand redheads getting naked for him?

Edy looked from one to the other, waiting.

"I forgot your name," Hassan said.

Snickers announced the arrival of the twins.

"Aimee," she hissed.

"Aimee," he said. "Can you move?" He jerked his head, indicating that she should slide down like the rest. The redhead jumped up, but instead of marching downstream, she stood over Edy, just as Hassan took her old seat. Edy, who had begun to dig into her *rogan josh*, froze with it inches from her mouth, and looked up.

Aimee must have mistaken her for a mark. "Edy," she said. "Move."

"You're making a scene," Hassan said. "I wouldn't recommend that."

The redhead shot Edy a contemptuous look before sauntering to the opposite end of the table.

"Did you want me to make space for your girlfriend?" Edy asked, switching over to Punjabi so that only Hassan understood.

His mother, who stayed home to care for them both since they were in diapers, had spoken Punjabi at home. Edy learned it right alongside English growing up.

"I don't even know her."

"That's not what she says."

Hassan set down his fork, a single muscle working in his jaw.

"Do we need to talk?"

"Our mouths are moving now, aren't they? Anyway, I'm only commenting on how well high school is going for you."

She forced a smile to her lips and nodded to the *rogan josh*. "Hungry?" she said in English.

Edy fished out a chunk of meat and slipped it in her mouth, pausing to savor it with a few choice moans of appreciation.

"Give me some already."

When Edy looked up and found the redhead and a handful of cheerleaders staring not at him but her, her face turned molten.

It was only with the arrival of Wyatt that she was saved. Sort of.

He stopped at the entrance, eyes sweeping the room. Spotting the line, he power walked over, late for an already short lunch. He grabbed goulash—*not safe*—instead of tacos—*relatively safe*—and crossed over to an empty table toward the back.

Wyatt had the attention of Hassan, the Dyson brothers, and Kyle. It didn't take long before the whole table followed their glares.

"He looks healthier already," Mason said. "Bright sky, clear New England air, brisk mile-long walk in the chill. Really gets the heart pumping."

"Essential for cardiovascular health," Matt chimed in.

41

Edy scowled. "Not funny."

"Neither are you," Hassan said, switching back to his Boston-sharpened Punjabi. He spooned great heaps of her *rogan josh* atop of the filling in his chicken taco. Once done, he slid her Tupperware down to Lawrence, who also took a few spoonfuls, though neatly into one square compartment of his lunch tray.

"I told you not to go over there," Hassan said.*" I told you to wait for Mom. Did you really need to meet him so bad? Was he all you dreamed?"*

Lawrence shot him a curious look, before sliding Edy's food back across the table. She snatched it up and stabbed it with her spork.

"He's a nice guy," Edy said with enough enthusiasm to annoy. *"You'd like him. I sure do."*

Hassan's gaze narrowed to a pinpoint. The muscle in his jaw quivered. Every bad choice he'd ever made could be attributed to that foul temper of his, a temper that meant he'd draw blood first and only maybe mop up the mess thereafter.

"Not everyone's your friend," he said. *"Even if they look it."*

Edy's gaze skated to Chloe, then the cheerleaders, the redhead, and the football players that suddenly couldn't bear to be without him.

"Not the same," Hassan said to her sullen, deadpanning face. "It's not," he added, hesitant though in his insistence.

Five

The new boy blocked the double row of water fountains as he waited in the crowd-swollen hallway. All around him, people swarmed, shoulder to shoulder, person to person, wall to wall without relief. Wyatt slicked back blunted locks from his eyes, only to have them flop back in. When they did, his hand snatched through his hair a second time, scowl as comical as if he meant to tear the hair from his eyes. His expression melted to nothing when Sandra Jacobs passed.

He grabbed her by the arm. Edy started, though Sandra turned on him with expectancy.

Of course, Edy thought. He's a guy, so he'd go for long hair, runway makeup, and an assertive amount of boobs. Even if he had smiled at Edy as if she were buttered sunshine—this girl—Sandra Jacobs—was the trophy worth having.

Words passed between Sandra and the new boy. Hot words, heated words, bitter. Wyatt stabbed a finger in her direction, accusing, and Sandra shook her head vehemently. When he turned to stalk off, it was her that snatched him back. She made a swipe at her face as if to rid it of tears.

"What in the . . .?" Hassan said. He'd come up next to Edy for the sole purpose of staring, and now he looked at her as if hoping she'd explain. She couldn't.

Others slowed and gawked, though that did nothing to temper the performance.

Wyatt stormed off, this time past the grasp of Sandra's arms. She was all running eyeliner and black smears, too much of a mess for class. She started for the girl's bathroom instead. Hassan darted off, abandoning Edy to catch her.

Every set of eyes shifted to them, to Hassan's private whispers for Sandra alone. To him reaching in his backpack for the white towel he kept there—his sweat towel, Edy called it—to him caking it with her clown mask. Edy couldn't hear their words, but she imagined they were intimate. She could picture them lazing about and smiling at each other, lacing their fingers together, doing more when they were alone.

Edy went back to her locker. She had class. Class and ballet and no doubt something else she couldn't remember. She shoved books and notebooks into her backpack in no discernible fashion, with no clue of what they were and whether she needed them. When Edy pulled her book bag on, she strained under the weight of scholarship.

Let them fight over Sandra. Let Hassan and Wyatt and every other boy tear at each other over the obvious beauty. She had a life to get on with.

Head high, gaze on a point decidedly past Hassan, Edy strode in the direction of History, before backtracking at the realization that she had English the next hour.

~~~

Every day after school, Edy sat in on some bore of a meeting. Five days meant five different organizations, each joined at her mother's insistence. On that day—Math Club day—she waded through polynomials for kicks before tearing out, late for ballet, as usual. She'd pay for it

—as usual. Anyway, Edy's ability to juggle all her mother's wants alongside her own made ballet possible.

She had to run. A cut through the 4-H club's composting site, upending a bin, had her back and apologizing and burning more time. Toad, a boy whose real name she could never remember, waved her off in red faced annoyance—facilitating her trip over a spade. *Dang it.* How both a graceful ballerina and an oaf could occupy the same body she'd never know.

In ballet, Edy felt what she never did elsewhere—whole, beautiful and accomplished. While tardiness had earned her the ire of her ballet instructor, Madame Louis, wrath became but a memory the moment she began to dance.

She didn't feel as others did, move as others did, or even allow her heart to beat as another's would, once the music began. Every pore in her bloomed with the promise of movement, and once realized, she transcended all of life's imperfections. She was dandelion dust in the wind, ashes in ocean water. She'd mastered her body and challenged it, challenged it to bend, twist, warp and defy gravity in gracefully daring ways. Edy was the thunder of a hurricane and the weightlessness of yesterday. Dance felt like her destiny.

Until practice ended and reality struck again.

She made it home with time enough to shower before heading over to Hassan's for dinner. Edy stopped at the sight of her mother's Lexus in the drive. A touch to the hood brought her hand away cool. She'd been in grade school the last time her mother made it home before her and food poisoning had been the blame. Edy unlocked the front door and eased in, with the dread of a girl who came home to find her door ajar. Ballet had run over in accordance with her tardiness; it was the way of Madame Louis. She was home later than she should have been and her mom would sling the hammer for it, regardless of blame.

Breath held, Edy eased inside. On turning to close the door behind her, she jumped at the figure on the couch.

Hassan pressed a finger to his lips. "Shh," he said.

Even though he had a key to the place, it seemed wrong for him to lurk in the shadows, unannounced. Still, Edy's attention turned; keen to hear whatever required her silence.

"There's confusion about what did and didn't happen," her mother said from an adjacent room. "No more than that at this point."

"There's more than confusion, Rebecca. There are outright accusations," came a second voice. Edy recognized it as Kyle Lawson's dad, Cam, a long time friend of her mother's. "Doesn't that bother you?"

"Cam, please. How do you find the energy to worry so? I don't give rumors much thought," Edy's mother said.

"I find that hard to believe."

"Do you?" her mother said.

Cam hesitated. "Maybe."

Edy and Hassan exchanged a frown.

"You always did confuse wishful thinking with reality," her mother said.

"Rebecca. We have to know. Our best currency is knowing," said Cam.

"So get the police report and be done with it. Speculation is garbage, as is worry," her mother said.

"Let me do this my way," Cam said. "Let me deal with him."

"Oh be quiet," she snapped. "Witch hunts are so passé. And where's that keen ear of yours? We haven't been alone in this house for at least ten minutes."

Edy and Hassan flung into action, tearing open her backpack and spilling the contents on the couch. Both snatched for a random book and notebook, before spreading out papers on the cushion between them. Edy's mother and Cam stepped into the hallway; just as Edy realized her Latin book sat upside down in Hassan's hand. She snatched it from him, heaved the history book she held at him, and squinted in what she hoped looked like a mimicry of real, serious scholarship.

Out the corner of Edy's eye, she watched her mother's beige heels as they strode down the hall and out the door, never pausing to acknowledge them. Cam did the same.

"What was that about?" Edy said the second they were gone.

"Politics, what else? They're going to burn some sucker alive." Hassan tossed aside his book.

He gave her a once over, gaze snagging for a second as he did.

"What?" Edy looked down at herself. She blushed, before remembering the way he'd rushed to Sandra Jacob said. Heat drained from her face.

"You're late," Hassan said. "Mom cooked your favorite, butter chicken. It's probably cold by now."

He went for the door without looking back. Edy followed, with the taste of his mother's heavy handed spices already on her lips.

~~~

The next day, Edy carried a brown bag lunch of leftovers into the cafeteria. On entering, she spied not just the redhead Aimee at the "it" table, but Sandra Jacobs and Eva Meadows, too. She wasn't in the mood, she realized, and set her eyes on Wyatt Green with the thought. She passed Hassan and the Dysons, in line, and smirked at the weight of their glares. Edy sat down before the lone boy, aware that they had the attention of the room.

Wyatt sat up straighter.

"Remember me?" Edy said.

"Of course," he breathed. He ran a hand down the front of his shirt, another through his tangle of wheat-colored locks and again corrected his posture.

Edy pulled out her lunch, peeled back the lid, and sniffed indulgently. At the sight of Wyatt watching, she extended the container to him.

"I . . .don't know what it is," he said.

"Butter chicken," she said.

He stared. She went on to explain how it was only the most famous Indian dish known to man and the cultural equivalent of a hamburger. "Only tastier," she said and dug in.

When she cautioned a glance up, it was to see Hassan's darkened face, unwavering in his devotion to glaring at them. *Good*, Edy thought. *Feel jaded and set aside.*

Wyatt had asked her something. Something about going to India. She told him about summering there three years in a row, figuring it would answer whatever question he'd had. As she spoke, she made a point of looking at Hassan. He'd started in on his chicken, picking absentmindedly, when the redhead leaned over and said something in his ear.

"Edy?" Wyatt said. He'd spoken her name with the weight of expectation. She racked her memory bank for the last vestiges of conversation. "India" was all she could come up with.

"I go there with his family," Edy inclined her head in Hassan's direction. "But we haven't been in years."

Wyatt's gaze skidded apprehensively to the table of jocks and then back again. The redhead said something and Hassan laughed.

Edy made a point of looking away. "Where do you summer?" she said brightly.

Wyatt's cheeks flooded with color. "We went to the Jersey Shore once. For a week, not a summer." He looked around as if desperate for assistance. "It was my first time at the beach."

Edy broke wide into a grin. Seconds slid home into a minute before it melted from her face.

Stupid. Stupider than stupid.

The image of the battered pickup truck came back to her, the clothes in the CVS bag, the tattered old backpack. He sat before her in a sickly pale polo, rinsed to a listless yellow.

Cruel.

"God. You must hate everyone." Edy remembered making him out to be the hired help, a move no better than the rumors encircling his arrival—that he was scum, a squatter, a sidewalk-sleeping meth addict whose dad was wanted for a convenience store robbery in Hoboken. Okay, so maybe her assumption was a bit better, but all of it stunk of xenophobia and elitism. He was an *other* and a poor other at that, promised obscurity if not outright torment. No doubt, she'd pay some price just for sitting with him.

"Chaterdee," he said simply.

"What?" She'd been shaken from her reverie again.

"It's where I'm from. You wanted to know, didn't you? Where I came from? I'm from Chaterdee. A soot-filled town on the edge of Pawtucket, where steel mills blot out the sun."

He met Edy with a steady, shy smile of his own.

"You're different," he said. "From the other people around here."

She looked up in surprise.

"You didn't hiss when I told you where I'm from."

He took a spork to his roasted chicken, tearing off a bit of flesh before popping it into his mouth.

"I have to admit that Boston's much nicer," Wyatt said. "And I'm liking it more every day." His gaze slid from her face downward, before shooting up as if caught falling asleep.

Edy blushed and dug into her chicken. Somehow, she didn't think he meant his new view of the sun.

~~~

Wyatt walked Edy Phelps home that day. The girl with wide button eyes and the lines of a dancer, the girl so far above anyone her age that she submitted papers on political philosophy and chattered aimlessly about places he hadn't the money to dream of. *That* girl had spent an hour, maybe more, on a roundabout route with Wyatt that only eventually led home. They talked of school and Chaterdee, Boston and dance, and *oh*, did she unravel when the talk turned to dance, companies and schools of thought, productions and most routines. He didn't care, and he absolutely cared. He hadn't even known that both were possible.

Wyatt and Edy parted for the pair of homes facing each other with reluctance. During their walk, she'd gushed about ballet, as though clinging to every thought she'd ever had about every performance until the moment they'd met. Wyatt listened when he could and let his thoughts wander when they did—swept by her voice and the sudden way she touched his shoulder or his arm with a thought. At his last school, he'd been an outcast. An early and gruesome crop of acne on his face and torso made most steer clear, and those who didn't, well, they certainly didn't touch him. And though some of the reddening had cleared, his outbreaks could still be frequent and obnoxious.

When they reached her gate, she was on to something about football and her dad, who had pulled into the drive. Wyatt watched him, dreading the conversation's end. Edy said her goodbye with a touch to his shoulder, promising to share lunch the next day. She then bounded off for her father's black BMW, body light and tight with each step. With a wave of acknowledgment to her father, Wyatt headed home, his own steps bouncing with the truth—that a *girl* had talked to him—a *pretty* girl, perhaps prettier than any he'd ever known. *She* wanted lunch with him. *She* wanted to see him again.

A song came to him, and with it, a pressing need to whistle. He couldn't figure where it might have come from, as he rarely listened to the radio and owned no music. Still, a tune had seized him.

Wyatt bounded up a short set of stairs and dug out the keys to his home. On opening the door, he found the hallway dark. Glass crunched under his Converses. He could hear his mother, Debbie, and his father, Roland, shrieking, same as always. No doubt she was threatening to walk, this time for more than a day or two. No doubt, dad was telling her to, that he didn't give a dam one way or another.

Normally, these confrontations made him want to split his face on the stair rail if not but for a moment of blissful unconsciousness. But not on that day. On *that* day there was a song was in his heart, a lift in his step, and a smile on his lips, placed there by a pretty petal named Edy Phelps. He would say her name twice; it sounded so nice.

Edy Phelps. Edy Phelps.

Wyatt whistled a loud and sassy sound, good as a New Orleans brass band come Mardi Gras. He bounded up the stairs to his bedroom. Once there, he threw back the curtains and smiled at his view of Edy's house. It was a smile so broad and bright it might as well have been a laugh. It should have been a laugh. And then he did it. He laughed. With his mother downstairs screaming that his dad had the prick of a caterpillar, Wyatt laughed. With his father, words slurred, hollering that her horse face kept him stepping out, Wyatt laughed. And as the few possessions they owned shattered and the shouting continued, Wyatt laughed, the song in his heart drowning everything out but him.

~~~

Locked away in a blinding homage to Hello Kitty, Edy pulled up to her desk to do her homework. With her window open and the curtains pulled back, she had a direct view into Hassan's room. As children, they'd scramble over the branches that divided their rooms, slipping from one to the other, undetected. They flashed lights as a means of late night communication before either had been permitted cell phones. When they fought, they made a point of drawing the curtains, glaring through the window panes, making evil faces, or giving each other the finger.

Edy read the assigned chapter on Paleoamericans, made a few notes, and switched over to *To Kill a Mockingbird* for English. Hassan's bedroom light illuminated his room at 6:20, his usual return time from practice. He dropped a duffel bag on the floor and stretched, yanked off his shirt, and let it fall next to the bag.

He'd feel her watching soon and look up. Life tethered them in a way that one could sense the other, know the other's thoughts, and understand without speaking. So, she knew he was ignoring her, even before he strode over and yanked the curtains shut without so much as a nod of acknowledgment in return. *Harami. Bastard.*

Edy yanked out her cell phone and texted him, thumb jamming her screen as if it were his eyes. A single word that she could only hope carried the strength of her annoyance with him.

Really?

She hit send and waited, gnawing at her bottom lip in the process.

One minute. Two minute.

Three.

Edy shoved aside her books, jammed on a pair of Nikes and thundered downstairs. The damp autumn nightfall had her wishing she'd grabbed a jacket, at least. Never mind that, though. Fury would keep her warm.

She used her key to get in, wiped her shoes on the mat, and tore for the stairs.

"Edy?" Hassan's mother called after her. "I'm glad you're here. Come and help me—"

Hassan's was the first room on the left in a house that mirrored her own. Edy tried the knob, found it open, and shoved her way in. Faintly, she registered his mother's complaints at the bottom of the stairs. She said that they were no longer children, that it was improper for Edy to be in his room, that Edy must be mindful of her behavior now that she was becoming a young woman, something else and something else. Not for the first time, his mother's voice had morphed like the adults in a Peanuts cartoon. *Wah wah wah.*

Hassan stepped out the bathroom with a towel around his neck. Saturated, ink black hair clung to him, sweeping his eyes and dripping until he slapped it back. A simple gray tee lay damp, hinting at a painfully well-muscled figure. Edy knew what it took to make a body like that, had watched him transform day by day as he sought it and sculpted through sweat. She swallowed at the thought.

"Edy, come downstairs and help me—" Rani called.

Hassan closed the space between them, wrapped a hand on her arm, and pulled her into his room.

"We'll be down in a sec, mom," he said and closed them in the room.

"So, you're ignoring me?" Edy demanded the second they were alone.

Hassan tossed his towel to the floor. "Maybe, I'm following your lead."

There it was again. The flash of burning fury, the iced mask that had always been others and not hers.

"I did *not* ignore you. I sat elsewhere for lunch."

"I don't care where you sit," Hassan said.

He fell back onto his bed and stretched out, before folding his hands behind his head.

"Really?" Edy said. "So, it's okay if I sit with him tomorrow? And the next day?"

He closed his eyes, mouth thinning with his thoughts. A thunderstorm raged within, a hurricane that he didn't always control. Edy saw that struggle in the lines of his frame, in the inadvertent flex of muscle.

"I don't like him," Hassan said. His eyes flew open with the acknowledgment: green glass spun to brilliance in anger. "Stay away from him because I *don't* like him."

Edy's mouth snapped open in rage, hung there, and then shut on its hinge.

"*Mar sāle*," she hissed in Hindi. Go to hell. "And take your entourage with you."

"Edy—"

In the time it took her to get to the door, he appeared, closing it as she pulled.

"Move."

"Would you at least hear me out?"

"I'll hear you out when you stop locking yourself up in bathrooms with bimbos."

He shut the door and made her face him.

"Okay," he said. "Okay. And does that make your lunches with the new kid go away?"

"What?" Edy cried. "No! Of course not."

"Of course not." His echoed words hung with the weight of accusation. Mouth twisted, he glared at a point above her head. But Edy cared nothing for the anger simmering on that face, gorgeous or otherwise. She boiled with her own rage, and it threatened to overflow, as he stood there, wanting her in his world, all the while making absolutely no room.

Or was that even it? Was it that she needed—no scorched—for a place at his side, and in his future, a place that already stood at full capacity?

Yeah, she did.

The bedroom door flew open with Edy's realization, slamming into her back and launching her into Hassan's arms.

Rani gaped as if they'd been that way the whole time. "Telephone," she hissed and thrust a land line to her son.

"I'm a little busy right now," Hassan said. "We have some things we need to get straight and—"

Rani's orbs doubled in size. "Out of this room," she hissed and grabbed Edy by the forearm. "Go to your house. You'll be taking dinner tonight on your own. I'll bring it to you. And they'll be no backtalk from either of you."

Edy twisted, but found Rani's grip dogmatic, unrelenting. Ushered first into the hall, she made her way downstairs and out the door. Only when the sound of the latch closed firmly behind her did Edy and truth meet.

She'd been thrown out, thrown out of the Pradhan home for the first time in her life. And while she had a key, there seemed no point in using it. Not on that evening, at least.

Six

Edy stood by her locker, hair longer than ever and pulled into a wild cloud of a ponytail. She pulled an algebra text out and another of chemistry before noticing Wyatt just behind her.

"Hey," he breathed.

She smiled. She always had the biggest smile for him.

Two weeks of lunches together had earned them whispers and outright scowls from the oxen she hung out with. Well worth the price of admission, if you asked Wyatt Green.

"Hey, twinkle nose," Edy said. "What's new?"

Twinkle nose. He touched his nose, drew away, and found glitter on his fingertips.

"Art?" she guessed and slammed the locker.

No malice in her voice, no mockery. Was she any other girl at that school, she wouldn't have passed on a prime chance to mock him to stand a little taller by cutting him down. No, Edy Phelps was a different. He'd spent yesterday alone reminiscing about her fingers brushing his arm. Which brought him to this next point.

Wyatt managed a dry swallow. "After school—"

He lost his nerve. It walked off and left him, disgusted by the audacity of the moment. He'd only just met her. He'd never known gall. Better still, how could *he* ever think—

Wyatt shook his head. All morning he'd rehearsed. *Just blurt it.* He might have been a stranger to gall, but he was a quiet friend of humiliation. He had no reason not to welcome it now.

"After school?" Edy prompted.

Her hand rested on a small spiral binder atop a stack of books labeled "Homework Assignments."

"I heard about a place that makes great milkshakes," he said. "I don't know if you want to go. You probably don't want to go. But if you do—"

She rummaged through the pages of her books, engrossed in her searching.

"What's it called?" she said.

"M—Max Brenner's. Heard of it?"

"Of course."

She looked up. Blinked. Wyatt shifted, tongue wagging despite still-pressed lips. His mouth wouldn't seal the deal.

"Meet me here?" Edy offered. "After the last bell? Unless you had another day in mind."

Briefly, Wyatt thought about some of the football players who convened in the hall after school and before the start of practice. While they hadn't come right out and confronted him about the time he spent with Edy, the ones she hung closest to had a habit of bumping him in the corridors, causing him to drop things and, of course, glaring.

"How about out front instead?" he suggested.

She shrugged. "Suit yourself."

~~~

Max Brenner's turned out to be a gluttonous dessert haven, with gooey, guilt-ridden delights like caramel chocolate pizza, ice cream fondues, and banana crepes with dulce de leche. Edy fussed over the endless assortment of items she could possibly order. With each possibility, Wyatt recalculated the bill, subtracting it from the slender fold of cash in his pocket. He'd only lifted enough to pay for drinks. If she ordered something ambitious, he supposed he could always do with water.

When she ordered a peanut butter and chocolate milkshake, he exhaled, grateful to have enough to avoid embarrassment. Wyatt settled on the cookie shake for himself and willed the waiter away before Edy changed her mind.

"Tell me about Chaterdee," she said when her frosty drink arrived.

"It's crap. A factory town where everything, even the elections, are owned by some rich guy who vacations in Tahiti. Everybody's just waiting for them to outsource, anyway. To give 'em the boot and replace 'em with a bunch of Indians."

Ugh. How many ways had he offended in regurgitating his father's crap? *She* vacationed in Tahiti and only failed to be Indian through accident of birth.

"I'm sorry. I—"

"It's okay," she said and took a sip of her drink so deep that he knew it wasn't okay.

"I was thoughtless," he tried again. "I didn't mean to sound so . . ."

She held up a hand. "Really. It's a predictable feeling, if you think about it. Daddy says that capitalism is born of the internal struggle between classes, and that the bourgeoisie, if left to their own devices, would always leave the working class oppressed. Ali—that's Hassan's dad—thinks that's a little reminiscent of Marxism, you know, with the whole 'dictating the bourgeoisie' thing, but," she shrugged. "Daddy's not Marxist or anything."

Wyatt blinked, grasped at the only word in that speech that hadn't shot over his sense of understanding.

"Ali?"

"I just told you. *Hassan's* father."

The jock. He came up every day.

"Let's talk about you," he said.

She raised a brow. "What about me?"

"I don't know," Wyatt said. "Tell me anything. Tell me what you love most."

She stared back at him with those button-wide eyes, huge, thoughtful, weighted in consideration. Wrestling with things he hadn't the courage to ask about. *Please not the jock. Please.*

"Dancing," she said and leaned forward. "Want to know a secret?"

"Of course."

"My mother hates ballet."

She giggled. If her laughs had texture, he imagined them light and fluffy, like fresh spun cotton candy.

"She's the district attorney," Edy explained. "With aspirations for a senate seat. My grandmother, her mother, was a circuit court judge once, while my mother's grandmother was a women's rights activist. I won't get into daddy's side. Let's just say, he wasn't even the first to teach at Harvard." Edy sat back with a sigh. "The way my parents figure it, I can be either president or a Nobel Prize winning scientist. Anything else is a step back for our good name."

Edy stared down at the thick froth of liquid that took up a third of her oversized beverage. She'd attempted humor, even while giving him everything: who she was, who she was expected to be, how she never hoped to measure up. She'd given him the very thing he'd needed: the secret of her heart. But it felt heavy, off balance and demanding, as if waiting for a sacrifice from him—for the thing that made them equal once again.

"My dad's an alcoholic," Wyatt blurted. "I can't remember what he looks like sober anymore."

Edy looked up, face pinched, eyes glistening. "I'm stupid," she said and surprised him by slamming a fist on the table. "God. I can't even get decency, right. Here I am talking about parental pressure when you're dealing with—"

"Don't," he said, because their relationship couldn't be built on her sympathy. He wouldn't be her pet. So, her apology meant nothing to him. What interested Wyatt, what roped him in, was her passion, her sincerity. She wanted to be good to him. It was more than he'd seen in a long time.

Not since his Lottie. He shoved that from his mind.

"Tell me about your mom," Edy said.

Wyatt shook his head free of the clutter. He told himself that these questions were necessities, born of honest curiosity, and that they wouldn't be used as an excuse to ditch him in a moment.

He said that, though he couldn't make himself believe it.

"Hopped up on meds," Wyatt said. "My mom depends on them to get by."

There, he'd said it, and she hadn't run yet.

Edy looked at him, brown eyes softer than he'd known any could be. He pushed back at the thing that swelled up in him, admonishing it as too soon. Intensity flared swift and violent, bold and blinding as lightning from a summer storm. Edy reached across the table and touched his hand, fingers light atop his, more than he could stand. Wyatt strangled an exhale, hesitated, and then laced his fingers with hers.

Never had he felt anything so good.

~~~

Edy lay awake that night listening to her own breathing. Despite the blankets, her body laid cold, prisoner to a chill within.

They weren't fighting exactly, she and Hassan, but they weren't right, either. All rigidness and tight-lipped looks. All under handed comments and back door scowls. It weighed on her, every moment of every day, in classes and across tables, dragging her down like a ball and chain. Far from being alarmed, their parents found their spat amusing, using it as an excuse to pinch their cheeks and recall old fights over dumb things. But she wasn't theirs to laugh at. She wasn't there to be mocked. Some part of her, some bubbling bastion deep, boiled up in pain—real pain. New feelings aside, Hassan was her closest friend, oldest friend, and his ability to brush her off wouldn't heal.

It wasn't fair. He wasn't fair. To spend so much time with people who couldn't have been bothered with his name before one stupid touchdown. Then to choose those people over her. Damn him to hell.

A predictable lump rose in her throat and Edy shoved it down with angry swallows. Her cell went off with a message. She dove for it, saw Wyatt's name, and slung her phone aside in self disgust.

"I won't ask what the phone did to deserve that." Hassan. Hassan at her window.

Edy scowled. Not that he seemed to notice, judging by the way he climbed in.

Her gaze skated over him. Black hooded sweatshirt and rumpled jeans. He'd pulled on these clothes to come over. To see her.

"Why are you even here?" Edy said.

A flicker of disapproval wrinkled his features. He didn't like the question.

Good.

"I want to be here," he said softly. "Can that be enough? At least for tonight?"

She should have said 'no.' She should have told him to call the redhead, or his promised bride, or at the very least to get out her room. But her heart would have reached up and strangled the throat that delivered those words.

Edy nodded, slow. No more needed to be said. She shifted in bed to make room for him. Hassan locked her door, dropped his sweatshirt on the floor, and slipped under the covers next to her.

Their bodies knew each other this way. Even as little ones, they'd curl together in a playpen, napping. Later, older, they'd nod watching cartoons on the couch, or beside his mother in bed. When Edy started in with her monster nightmares in elementary school, Hassan scaled their tree to be with her, even though the shadows sometimes scared him, too. Together they'd sleep with the lights out, because they agreed they needed to face their fears . . . just not alone.

Hassan pulled her in so that her head rested on his chest. He smelled clean, pure, different. Edy pulled back and sniffed.

The finger winding in her hair froze. "What?" he said.

Citrus. Leather. Jasmine?

"You're wearing cologne!" she cried.

He stiffened.

"It's my natural scent," he said, coyness in his voice.

She liked it. It and the prickly feeling she felt at his jaw. Another thought rushed in, flooding her with ice.

"Are you wearing cologne because—"

"You always—," he clamped down on whatever she always did. "Sleep, okay? For a few hours, at least."

She hadn't been sleeping so hot, but he couldn't know that. Right?

Hassan contorted so that he reached the lamp on the nightstand, his arm still around her.

Steady, even breathing met her alongside the rise and fall of his chest. The arm that held her grew heavy, then—

"Do you like him?" Hassan said.

Edy waded in confusion, attempting to extricate a "him" from her mind. She didn't want to talk about "hims;" she wanted to bury her face in the crook of

Hassan's neck and drown in his embrace. She didn't know any other hims.

"Edy? The twins think you like him. Lawrence doesn't though."

The boy she wanted lay in bed beside her, lean and hard bodied, stripped down to his boxers, content to spend their time talking about the next guy.

"Never mind," Hassan said.

You think?

But he did mind, judging by the hard, guarded grip he held her in. Neither of them could sleep like that, but Edy said nothing.

He'd been trained for this, she told herself, this fierce protectiveness, that wasn't just his but the Dyson brothers' too.

Like siblings, was what she told herself as his grip loosened. Family, she insisted to her thudding heart. But she was aware of him in a way she never had been before and beat back the heat that came with that knowledge.

"I'm still me," he whispered in her ear, curling awareness through her in sharp tendrils. "And we're still us. Right?"

Edy nodded and felt his lips brush her ear. It was the closest she'd ever felt to a boy, and yet identical to so many of their moments. If only she could convince her stomach.

He exhaled. Only then did Edy realize he'd been waiting on her answer.

"I haven't done anything," he whispered as if the walls might hear.

But she'd seen him, seen him go upstairs with Aimee. She'd seen their fingers laced, too.

Hassan meant it though. Lies didn't pass between them. And he was obviously still waiting on his answer about Wyatt.

"He's nice." Edy said. "But Wyatt's a friend. Same as a girl would be."

"Mhm," he said and pulled her in.

They'd snuggled up body to body with her face in the crook of his neck. She drew close, lured by his scent and floating on some bare petal of sweetness, gliding until her lips brushed his neck.

Until her lips brushed his neck. Oh God. She'd kissed him. Edy drew back in eye gaping, mouth gaping, nostril gaping horror, breath held and waiting for the fallout. What had she been thinking?

Seconds later, she heard the snores.

Relief disguised itself as sorrow, and briefly, she thought about waking him. But for what? To tell him that she'd kissed him and he'd been too asleep to notice? Those words would never leave her mouth. Better to take heaven's gift of a narrow escape and run with it.

Edy adjusted to face him better in the dark. She traced the lines of his face and the shape of his mouth with her gaze. He'd slipped into stunning overnight, sifting and shifting so that old features were only hinted at, memories of times past.

This would never be easy for her. Not so long as her best friend took on beauty in effortless strides, or drowned in talent and a willing pool of girls. They'd grow older and further apart as time and tradition weighed in heavy, as the truth of him never being meant for her found its way to them both at last. And like always, parts of her withered at the idea of relinquishing him eventually.

Edy woke with a draft cooling her side. She opened her eyes to the sight of Hassan pulling on last night's crumpled clothes.

"See you in five." He bolted for the window, doubled back to plant a smack on her forehead, and escaped the usual way.

Edy's bedroom door rattled.

"Edith Phelps! You unlock this door," her mother shrieked. "The Dyson boys have been honking for you—"

Honking for her? Edy shot a look at her bedside clock and scrambled to her feet. She should have been halfway to school already.

"Eight o'clock," Mason said and cursed under his breath. "Any reason both of you are late as hell?"

From the driver's side seat, he glared first at Hassan, then Edy, the second she slammed the car door closed behind her.

"Just drive," Hassan said and settled in.

As Mason took him up on his advice, Edy gave Hassan's appearance a once over. A black South End tee with noticeable wrinkles. Yesterday's jeans. No time for a shower, she knew. Judging by the way he kept running a hand through his hair, no time for a comb either.

Edy looked up to see Chloe's thinly veiled look of distress directed at her. So, skinny jeans and a thermal weren't all the rage. Her appearance was still neat, clean and wrinkle free. What more could be asked of her?

"Are you done staring?" Edy demanded.

Chloe jumped, then blinked a few times for good measure. "Your hair," she said from her seat in Lawrence's lap.

What a snob. Edy's hair was no different than any other day. A simple ponytail had always been good enough for her.

Chloe fished out a brush from an oversized Marc Jacobs bag. She reached over and yanked out the office rubber band that held Edy's hair together and let it fall to the floor with a look of disgust.

She gave Edy's hair a thorough brushing, the sort she only received when Rani took to it. With Chloe working frantically, Edy's head bobbed and jerked with every knot and tangle. The brush just kept snagging.

"You're doing that on purpose," Edy said.

"I'm not. I'm trying to hurry. It's hard, with you never doing much to comb your hair."

"Well, stop and put my rubber band back."

"No. It's grotesque. And anyway it's broken."

What the hell was she supposed to do without a rubber band? She had a mountain's worth of unruly coils cascading to her shoulders. Should she ever straighten it, it would likely fall to her back.

"I'll figure out something," Chloe said and rummaged in her bag again.

Edy cautioned a look up to find Hassan watching them with open amusement. Lawrence, as always, looked disgruntled.

"I've got a headband in here," Chloe said. She held up a lacey one affixed with a comb. "I could twist some of your hair into it and leave the rest hanging in the back."

"Fine. Whatever. Just . . .get it over with." Already, she'd resigned herself to Chloe's ministrations.

The girl grinned. "It's like you spent two minutes getting ready this morning. You and Has—"

Chloe froze, brush in the air.

"What?" Edy said.

The other girl's gaze traveled to Hassan, where it skated over his appearance before turning back to Edy.

"Nothing," Chloe said. Done with Edy's hair, she tucked the brush away fast.

The gang rode the rest of the way to school in uncomfortable silence.

"Dyson. Dyson. Dyson. Pradhan. Phelps. Castillo."

Principal Rhinecorn fired off names like bullets from a shotgun, his finger punctuating each hit. A roll call, Edy realized, with a slim dark kid by his side jotting them down greedily.

They froze just past the front entrance of the school; the doors hadn't even managed to close behind them. Rhinecorn, who had more middle than height, strode left, then right, with an arm tucked at the small of his back. Deliberating was what his to and fro told them. Posturing was what they knew. He stopped before Matt.

"Detention," he said, head tilted as if he meant to plant a kiss.

Matt's face screwed into a pucker.

Rhinecorn moved to Mason.

"Detention," he repeated.

Mason flinched at the word.

He moved to Lawrence, then Hassan, Edy and Chloe. Each one received the word in a puff of putrid air. Detention for two days was what each of them received.

~~~

Edy caught only the tail end of the attendance call before being shuffled on to her first class. She stopped at a slender set of long steel lockers and keyed in her combination quick. Chloe came up beside her.

"Yeah?" Edy said with looking. She slung her Chemistry book on the top shelf, grabbed a gray notebook from there, shoved it in her backpack and zipped up the bag.

"I need to ask you something," she said. "So, please. Don't take my head off."

The image of Chloe looking from Edy to Hassan returned. Edy stilled, too aware of her own breathing.

"Ask," Edy said. "Otherwise, I need to get to class."

Chloe nodded and a sweep of dark curls tumbled into her face. She tucked them back with manicured fingers.

"You," she said. "Don't have anything with Hassan, do you?"

A sound leapt from Edy's throat. A choked, startled something that she stuffed back into the hell it abandoned. She opened her mouth, found it too dry, and turned back to her locker for cover.

"Why would you ask something so silly?" she said and concentrated on deep even breaths.

"It's only . . . " Chloe's voice drifted alongside her gaze. Edy followed it to a pack of girls. Aimee the redhead, Sandra Jacobs and Eva Meadows. Sandra lifted a hand and waved, before the three erupted in giggles.

A match lit under Edy, engulfing her in an unreasonable fury.

She was there for *them*. She was one of them. No matter how many days they rode to school together, Chloe Castillo was one of them. Edy wouldn't forget it again. Not ever.

She ripped Chloe's headband from her hair, heard the audible tear, and tossed the hairpiece to the floor. It in were thin strands of dark locks.

"Learn your place," Edy said. "You're Lawrence's skank; not one of us. We don't have to humor you when you talk."

Edy slammed her locker and strode off, pushing past Chloe on her way to class.

~~~

At lunch, Edy took her seat with Wyatt, gaze boring into the three girls first to arrive at the "it" table. Aimee, Sandra and Eva. They sat huddled together with Caesar salad on each plate, talking without the slightest flicker of hunger. When Sandra looked up and saw her, she gave a little wave of fingers meant to annoy. Aimee followed it by puckering up her lips. That's right, Edy remembered, she'd been eager to brag about tasting Hassan. Maybe she'd be interested in a fork buried right through those lips. Edy sighed. So much for pacifism.

Hassan, Lawrence and Kyle arrived as a set, went for the lunch line, came away with double helpings and sat with the girls. All three went erect at the sight of their cattle, with Sandra going so far as to tease her curls with fingers.

"I called you last night," Wyatt said. "I was concerned when you didn't respond."

Edy blinked. Tried to think of something to say. "I wasn't available," seemed snarky, yet it was all she could come up with. She turned to her food. Nothing special that day, just twice warmed butter chicken, leftovers because of Rani's headache the night before.

"I have a class with him," Wyatt said.

Edy looked up. "Who?"

"Him," he nodded in the direction behind Edy.

She turned to see Hassan approaching with his tray. Back at the "it" table, Lawrence, Kyle and the twins gathered their things.

A mass exodus, Edy realized with a twist of a smile. A mass exodus for her, she wanted to tell the queens of primping.

Except, not quite.

The twins dropped down on either side of Edy, while Hassan and Lawrence sat down to bookend Wyatt.

"Edy," Hassan said without looking at her. "Could you excuse us for a second?"

She half expected a camera crew to appear and taunt her with jeers. "I will not," was what she said.

The twins sighed as if exhaling from a single pair of lungs. No doubt, they'd elected Hassan to deliver this idea that she should get lost.

"You move," Mason said in her ear. "Or this gets real embarrassing for your boyfriend. You know, with us dragging him to privacy and all."

"Oh, for God's sake!" Edy snatched her lunch bag and stood, scanning a still life of what should have been a bustling cafeteria. Every pair of eyes watched, thirsty for drama and banking on it.

Then Edy realized it. The one place open, the one place she could sit was the "it" table. She dropped down next to Chloe, never bothering to look up.

"Edy—" Chloe said.

"Please," Edy said. "This day has already exhausted me, and there's still detention to look forward to."

And that she'd slept almost none the night before.

~~~

Across the aisle, at the table Edy used to occupy, Wyatt looked from one Dyson brother to the next, before settling on Hassan. An irrational swell of claustrophobia threatened to swallow Wyatt.

"Where'd you come from?" Hassan said.

Wyatt dropped his gaze. He knew boys like this, guys with easy looks and hulking muscles, who took failure as a personal challenge. His failure to answer would be seen as motivation to get an answer. Wyatt wasn't keen on motivating them.

"Rhode Island," Wyatt said. "Chaterdee, Rhode Island. You probably never heard of it."

"Why'd you come here?" Hassan said.

Not why he'd moved, but why Wyatt had come there specifically. A subtle but powerful difference that had Wyatt giving Hassan a closer look. He'd heard of him, of course, and not just because Edy led up his fan club. Football titan extraordinaire, drool extractor of girls, and smart enough to manage an advanced placement class or three.

"My dad wanted to move here. That's all," Wyatt said. He didn't look up to see if the answer took.

"And that scene with Sandra? What was that about?" Matt said.

Wyatt shrugged, feeling like a turtle shoved into its shell. "Nothing. Just a misunderstanding."

"I don't like you," Hassan said. "And I damned sure don't like the way you look at Edy." He looked him over, jaw tightened with thinly veiled contempt. "If you think this is over, you've got another thing coming."

It occurred to Wyatt that while the twins were older, bigger, and presumably the alphas of their group, Hassan stood at the head of this expedition.

Hassan was the one to watch.

~~~

Detention ran long for Edy and Chloe and short for the boys, who had the excuse of practice for a winning team to get them out. By the time Edy had been freed, ballet practice had begun and there was no way she could put a respectable face to that sort of tardiness. She decided to walk home. Why Chloe joined her in those stupid heels, Edy would never understand.

Except, understanding came with the next breath.

It used to happen all the time in middle school. Girls cozying up in the hopes of catching an eye from one of the boys—Matt, Mason, Hassan, Lawrence. Sweet smiles and lukewarm compliments, all made as they looked elsewhere. Just as Edy got ready to tell her she wouldn't be used, Wyatt came tearing out of the school, closing the half block they'd crossed quick.

Cold winds slapped his cheeks red and left his blond hair flapping in the wind.

"I've been looking for you," he said.

Edy raised a brow. "Since school let out?" She shot a look at Chloe. Her face stayed smooth as marble.

"Yeah, well, you didn't answer your cell."

Edy started off again. "No phones in detention."

"Ah," Wyatt said and fell in step.

The three headed for the end of the street, with Chloe's heels as sound and sure as their steps.

Edy looked at her. "How are you doing that?" She nodded toward her feet.

Chloe shrugged. "I could show you sometime."

"I'd rather you didn't," Edy said.

Who said she needed heels and makeup and all that other silly stuff? Once a year she pressed into it, pressed into because it made her father happy. Even if it felt absurd.

"I think Edy looks great the way she is. She doesn't have to try as hard as the rest of you," Wyatt said.

Chloe shot him an acidic look.

"And I thought the boys would've straightened you out about that," she said.

Edy jumped in. "About what?"

Chloe picked up selective hearing.

"About what?" Edy pressed and put a hand on Wyatt's arm.

She thought she saw him flinch.

"Nothing. It's just your—whatever they are—set a few boundaries." Wyatt smirked. "For some reason, they don't seem too impressed with me."

Edy snorted. If those standards worked both ways, then the boys find themselves in scant company indeed.

"You really should watch it, Edy," Chloe said. "You'll have people thinking you'd never be friends with someone like me when we both know better."

Edy dropped Wyatt's arm, which she didn't realize she'd still been holding, and forged ahead of the pack. If that dimwitted cow wanted to bring up the past, she could do it to him. As far as she was concerned, they had never been friends, they had only been childhood playmates for a spell, and then Chloe had decided in the sixth grade that pretty girls should unite, or whatever. She promptly forgot Edy. And Edy forgot her, end of story.

So Edy was content to leave their story right there.

Seven

Two weeks past their ice cream dinner at Max Brenner's and four since depositing underwear on Edy's feet, Wyatt had become Edy's faithful escort to six-days-a-week practice sessions. Each night, he faded to the back, bewitched by every bend and bow, every leap and private smile she fed him.

Enraptured. Inescapably so.

Her friends could do nothing about it. These moments were his alone. With them perpetually at practice, they could never intervene, never intercept. Ballet was Wyatt's to have.

He sat on a pale pink bench at the back of the studio and extended fingers across the thin leather cushion. A wisp of white ran from knuckle to wrist and back again, old scarring from waking his mother prematurely from a night terror. On the opposite side, a valley of furious pink ran parallel to his palm's life line, remnants of another mother-father fight, also rendered unknowingly. He ceased to exist when they fought, which meant mostly that he ceased to exist.

Half a dozen dancers, all female, extended onto a barre before him, bodies lithe, supple, stretching without hesitation. Each was thin and serious-looking, in leotards of black or white, hair pulled into prim buns, emphasizing an assortment of tight mouths. Only Edy varied from the scheme, hair burgeoning like a fountain, skin warm—rich brown near pale pink, mouth full, pouty, playfully coy.

Once, as a boy, Wyatt saw an ebony butterfly at the place where the waters of Bishop Cove met Swan Point Cemetery. It was the day of his grandmother's funeral, his mother's mother, and as far as he had been concerned, they couldn't put her in the dirt fast enough. Wyatt had stood, wedged between a theatrical red-eyed mother and a father still reeking of last night's whiskey, when the butterfly fluttered upwards before him, drawing his attention with its beauty, singularity, and mystique. Gaze pinned, Wyatt had followed, hypnotically at first, frantically next, sliding on mud, gripping at scrub, never daring to look away. Never had he seen the flutter of black silk and never had he seen a butterfly in winter. When Wyatt had reached it, his hands and pants were caked in filth. He'd extended a hand, brushed it, and gasped in horror, remembering that butterflies were supposed to die if touched. To hurt a thing so beautiful had to earn God's wrath. It had stuttered through the air, dropping once, twice, and then soaring for the heavens.

Wyatt's dad had snatched him from the water's edge and smacked him upside the head, asking if he meant to ruin the old lady's sendoff. Later, in secret, his father admitted to wishing he'd gotten up the nerve to do something, at the very least write an "F— you" on the casket and fertilize the soil with his waste.

The black butterfly's image stayed with Wyatt. When he mentioned it to his father, he called it a moth. His mother hadn't even seen it. No matter, Wyatt knew better than them both. He always knew better than them both.

~~~

The sun had long since set when Edy and Wyatt stepped out of the ballet studio. A chill seized the air, sawing to the bone as they walked. She zipped her goose parka up and yanked the fur-lined hood to her brow before giving Wyatt a grieved look. His polyester-lined trench coat stood as a pitiful first and last defense against an arctic New England winter well underway.

"You know, we're still considered children," Edy hissed. "If I told my mom—"

"Don't."

They fell into an awkward silence after a now familiar conversation.

He hated for her to see him like that, cold, and needing something basic. It made him seem weak, piteous, not a thing to be desired. He decided to redirect.

"You were beautiful today," Wyatt said. "And you always stand out. They're nowhere near your caliber."

Edy snorted. "That's because I belong in advanced classes. Mom's still warming to the idea. Rani's pressing it, so it should happen any day now."

Rani Pradhan. The jock's mother. It seemed she came up nearly as much as Hassan. The thought gave him another.

"You speak Hindi?"

"And Punjabi."

He imagined the hours she must've spent in the Pradhan household to learn their languages. "It must've taken forever for him to teach you."

Edy spasmed. "For starters, my Hindi's better than Hassan's. The first word I ever said was *dada* and the second was *duppar*. Hassan had two dozen English words before he even gave another language a try. An omen, Rani says."

Duppar. For some reason, he suspected he wouldn't like the meaning, but had to ask anyway.

"Cake," Edy said.

Cake. As in what Hassan called her.

"You always talk as if the two of you live together," Wyatt said. He heard the envy in his voice and buried it.

Edy shrugged it off.

"So . . . he's like a brother then?" Wyatt tried again.

She paused. Considered. "No. Not really."

Wyatt glanced at the Phelps home, a towering lemon-colored dollhouse, accentuated with hints of pearl. He scowled when the front door opened.

Hassan. That guy again. The guy who kept busy enough for his lifelong friend to feel slighted, but nonetheless had a knack for finding her in Wyatt's company anyway.

"I speak English, Punjabi, and Hindi," Edy said. "And all of them better than *him*."

She nodded toward the sturdy ninth grader emerging from her home, a guy who should've been promoted to the tenth off size alone. When their gazes met, Wyatt offered something of a disarming smile. It wasn't returned.

"No argument from me," Hassan said and pressed a kiss to her forehead. He'd wrapped a hand around her forearm to do it, and pressed lips to a place near her temple. Wyatt wondered what he was thinking, what he was feeling, and whether he knew that Wyatt envied him more in that moment than in any single one on the field.

He kept his lips there too long. But if anyone seemed to notice, no one cared.

Except Wyatt.

"How goes it, Slim?" Hassan said when he parted from her.

"What?" Wyatt blinked.

"He asked how you were doing," Edy said.

"Oh. Fine. Just returning from ballet with Edy."

Hassan raised a brow. "Yeah? Sit in often?"

That wasn't the question, of course. There was a conversation within a conversation here that Edy wouldn't be able to sense.

"I do actually," Wyatt said. "Why? Did you?"

Nothing.

But then he saw it: a ripple beneath otherwise calm waters. A flicker of menace dissolved in an instant.

"Let's go, Edy. I've got three hours before I hit the gym with the Dysons. That's enough for a movie."

Hassan placed an arm around Edy's shoulders and steered her toward the house. Wyatt couldn't help but notice the easy way she turned for his touch.

But then she stopped.

"I'll give you a call later on, Wyatt. We can do homework later or something," Edy said.

Hassan stopped, every muscle in his back and arms rendered taunt as a bowstring. When they started off again, Wyatt couldn't keep the grin from his face.

~~~

Hassan slipped onto the back porch of the Phelps' house just in time to see Edy kneel, a bowl of milk in one hand, two open cans of tuna in the other. They were perched on the cusp of November, with the vibrant shimmers of autumn already having dwindled to a listless frozen winter. Edy bunched the fabric of a wool coat together to shield herself from the brisk breeze. Just as she made it to the porch, a gray shorthair cat curled out from under the stairs and bounded up to meet her. A mangy black cat followed on its heels, and after that, two more, both striped steel and white. The last of the bunch had a back paw out of sync and nursed it on a tentative climb up, the last in a procession of strays.

Edy went for the hurt one first, scooping him into her arms. She plucked a choice chunk of white tuna and held it under the cat's nose. Tiny teeth tore the chunk in two before it disappeared from sight altogether.

When he was done, Edy dug out another, larger piece, and carried him over to the milk.

For their entire lives, Edy's mother had been screaming about the strays. Once, she'd threatened to drown them. Hassan knew, not because he'd been there, but because Edy had run to him, crying and threatening to run away. He'd been ready to run with her then. He'd run with her now.

"Ready for ballet?" Hassan said, trying to unhinge the old memory with a shake of his head.

"You're here to walk me?" Edy sounded surprised.

"As soon as you're ready," Hassan said. He shifted, suddenly hyper-aware of his body's breath, movements, and proximity to her. Seeing her with the strays, remembering her coming to him like that . . . He cleared his throat and looked away. "Do you need another minute with the cats or something?"

"I'm ready," she said. "It's just . . .Wyatt's agreed to walk me." She shot a look at her house, *past* her house.

Wyatt.

Hassan couldn't help but wonder what else he had offered to do. "I'm here now," he said. "So, there's really no need."

Edy dropped her gaze. She returned to her cats, picking up an empty can of albacore and running a finger along the inside before offering her findings to a weak cat that licked from her finger.

"It's alright," Edy said. "He likes it. He enjoys walking me and he enjoys sitting in on the lessons."

"For two and a half hours?" Hassan said, deadpan.

"Yes!"

"Yeah, right," he snapped.

She stood. Gentleness washed away as her jaw set and hands clenched, giving her a ferociousness that likened her to her mother.

"Is it really so hard? To imagine someone with me when it isn't their duty?"

"Edy—"

He took a step forward and the cats scattered. They knew only her, trusted only her.

"Listen to me. Listen good. He's after something. And if he gets it, I'll snap off his—"

"Hassan."

Apparently it wasn't the right thing to say, as Edy's face turned like the clouds on thunder's approach. "Go. Away. Find someone else to babysit," she said.

She started for the house. Hassan took after. Edy wasn't listening. She wasn't even trying to listen. Instead, she wanted to scramble everything he said.

Well, he'd make her listen. "Edy—"

She whirled on him, eyes wide, nostrils flared. "Let me guess. He's using me. Because no one could actually *want* me, right? I'm not some redhead with humongous boobs and kissable lips!"

"Edy," Hassan said. "Would you stop that, please? You don't know . . . "

But the truth was, *he* didn't know. He didn't know what he was feeling or what his next words would be.

"Forget it," she said, face suddenly slacked with fatigue. "It's nothing. I just—" She turned away from him, "you should leave me alone right now."

Hassan stared at her back, rigid with resolve. And yet . . . he had this overwhelming urge to say some--thing, do something, to connect with her so that the ice and the freeze evaporated between them.

"Cake—"

She slipped into the house, silent; no longer interested in anything he had to say.

~~~

Wyatt crossed the street to the Phelps' house at the exact moment that Hassan exploded from the front door. Hassan stalked down Edy's walkway, burst through the fence, and made it halfway down the sidewalk when he stopped, taking note of Wyatt.

She chose me, Wyatt reminded himself. *Hassan was there to walk her, but she chose me.*

Be steady. Be steady, despite Hassan's caustic glare. No ass kicking will actually commence.

The front door flung open again, and Edy stormed out, stopping to kick it closed behind her. She slung a backpack on and threw up her hood before charging from the yard onward, in the direction of practice. Without Wyatt.

So much for victories.

He took off at a trot to catch her. "Hey, wait! Did you forget about me?"

He didn't see how she could, when he took so much care to ensure she didn't: lunch every day, walks home from school and to practice, text messages, phone calls, emails. Wyatt not only had Edy's schedule memorized but knew every nook and cranny of it that he could exploit.

She shot him an impatient look.

"I have to get to practice, okay? So, if you're not ready to go—"

She glanced down at his hooded sweatshirt, no doubt looking for a coat he didn't own.

"I was standing right here, ready," Wyatt said. "Here before you."

Hassan called out to her from his place on the sidewalk. Wyatt hesitated.

"Edy," Wyatt said. "You don't have time to—"

She headed back.

Wyatt backtracked, too, staying just close enough to be in hearing range but just out of arm's reach. Since the moment he had taken to being Edy's constant companion, Hassan's brooding glares had registered as adequate warning. Wyatt treaded near him with care.

Edy went to Hassan, who stood with hands burrowed in his pockets, eyes weary and thoughtful.

He pulled her into his arms.

Long seconds passed, maybe even a minute, where he held her. Only held her. His chin brushed against her forehead—maybe even his lips, before he murmured something, too soft for Wyatt's ears. When they parted again, their hands were the last to separate. Edy turned back to Wyatt, eyes brimming with the threat of tears.

"What?" he whispered the second she stood close enough. "What's happened?"

Wyatt verified that Hassan was out of hearing range before speaking his next words. While he had no means to punish Hassan for any form of maltreatment, it seemed that implying he could or would, would only help his cause.

"Tell me what he said," Wyatt insisted. "Now."

She looked up with eyes way too beautiful, brimming with intensity, more alive than ever.

"He asked me if I still knew he'd run away with me," Edy whispered. "That he'd take it, if that were ever an option."

She choked out a hiccupping laugh, wiped her face on her sleeve, and took off, leaving Wyatt to look from one of them to the other, desperate to understand a message never meant for him.

~~~

Wyatt supposed that coming to South End qualified as a raw deal. After all, he'd been jettisoned over the course of a week from the known to the unknown, and the unknown had been about as receptive of him as the bars in Charterdee were of his dad. When the pressing need came for Wyatt and his family to get out of town, South End became their first and only option. But it wasn't the roll of the die it appeared to be. Wyatt's mom, who had once been as beautiful as her one-time supermodel sister, called on that sister to bail them from yet another nightmare. She did so with a caveat, as everything came from Cecily Jacobs with a tangle of strings attached. Wyatt's aunt, who lived in Milan, wanted property in Sci-Sci, though real estate was rare there. One house sat on the market and it had done so for close to a decade. Since Wyatt's dad was something of a handyman, Cecily agreed to buy the property and rent it out to them at a significant discount, should the Greens fix it up while there. While no one liked to be indebted to Cecily for anything, it was a solution at a time when no others appeared.

Not every face was unfamiliar to Wyatt at South End High. After all, his mother's roots came back there, even if her downtrodden state didn't show it. Still, those were his mother's memories, not his own, and at a time when he could only grin and bear conditions he'd brought on, Wyatt looked forward with breath-stealing trepidation to his new start. How could he not? He spent every free moment thinking of the girl he'd met on his first day. He anticipated every brush with her in the hall, only to replay it in his mind, like a game changer at the Super Bowl. The walks home, the ballet, he longed for the days when he could do more than watch her, when he could reach out and hold her, when his lips could demand hers, when she trembled for his touch. It was all he thought about, every day, without end.

Wyatt pushed through the press of a bustling hall at lunchtime, eyes keen in their search for Edy. They met at the space between his locker and hers, every day since the first meal they'd shared. Three minutes from math to the meeting place for her, fifteen seconds from world history there for him.

But he was only a little late that day, held up by a bumbling and hulking black guy in a football jersey who had a ton of questions and no clue how to get out the way. An awkward shift left and an awkward shift right and finally Wyatt resigned himself to explaining what they'd just been tested on. What was the point, he wondered. But the boy said he'd wanted to know for future reference.

Wyatt made it to the place where the lockers met the fountains at the exact same moment that he spotted Hassan. Hassan draped an arm around Edy and wheeled her in the direction of the cafeteria. She tossed a look back only to have their field of vision split by two copies of the same person.

Four hands seized Wyatt by the shirt and pitched him headfirst into a pile of people. Everyone scattered, shrugging away from his outstretched hands, backs at the wall in an instant. The crowd's density saved him for a second, keeping him from a fall before hands pawed him again. Matthew and Mason, Mason and Matthew, Wyatt couldn't tell one from the other. No matter, both held him, gripping him by the shirt, wrenching it up to his throat and exposing his back to the masses.

They laughed, expectation painting everyone's faces.

"Bathroom," one twin said and they hurled Wyatt toward it. The first paused to open the door, the second to fling him in. "You've got two minutes to convince us you're not trying to get your pogo stick in Edy."

"What? No!" Wyatt didn't even know which twin had spoken. Mouth dry, throat closed, he looked from one to the other, pulse shallow, breath absent.

Lawrence slipped in, closed the door behind him, and leaned against it. One of his older brothers took a seat on the sink's ledge; the other hovered over Wyatt.

"Jesus," Wyatt said, cheeks flushed with the shame of their words. "I just got to this school. I just met her."

"Wrong answer," Lawrence said from his place at the door.

Wyatt glanced at him, then back at the twins. God, did his stomach burn. Acid simmered in his gut like a cauldron, bubbling straight up to his throat. He needed a defense. Yet, one wouldn't come.

"Losing time," the twin on the sink warned.

"We're friends," Wyatt said. "Please."

The bathroom door jarred. Lawrence barreled into it, stilling whoever had been on the other side.

Wyatt stiffened. "We eat lunch together," he blurted. "And walk home. We talk on the phone sometimes. But that's all. I swear."

"Sounds like a man expecting something to me," said the sink twin.

"Just punch him," said the other.

"No! Please. We're not *doing* anything," Wyatt cried. "We just hang. Come along and see if you want."

Sink twin rose; smile broad when he clapped Wyatt on the shoulder.

"Now that's more like it," he said. "Start inviting us. Or find something better to do."

That afternoon Edy texted him in study hall, asking what happened at lunch. It was then that Wyatt saw the black guy who'd blocked his exit from class before the Dyson twin run in. This time, he could recall the boy's name. Kyle Lawson. One of Hassan's boys.

How had he forgotten?

Wyatt turned back to his phone, all the while considering. He thought of Edy's eyes, sweet, brown, enchanting. He thought of her mouth, full, lush, and tempting. He thought of her touch and wanted it, in his hand, on his skin. He thought of Kyle, looked over, and thought again.

Wyatt deleted the text message, concentrated on facing front, and avoided Edy's questioning stare.

~~~

Days passed. Edy with Wyatt, Edy with Wyatt, EdywithWyatt. Hassan knew because people were so eager to tell him.

But why did it bother him so?

Hassan ventured over to his bedroom drawer and pulled out a weathered, well creased world map. Blue markings delineated every place he and Edy had been by land, sea, or air in every time zone on earth. Copenhagen. Cape Town. Cairo. Kolkata. Bangkok. His parents' hometowns of Delhi and Chandigarh. Back when their fathers fled the city limits at the slightest promise of research, Hassan and Edy hadn't been far behind, wide-eyed, pitiful, and determined to go. They'd get lost in cities others saved pennies to go to. As a boy, Hassan swore that he and Edy would turn his battered map blue, visiting every place that man inhabited and maybe one or two places that man didn't.

He hadn't counted on growing up.

Hassan folded the map away without looking at it and ventured to the window. Edy's window faced back, eclipsed in darkness, swallowed in the still of the night.

He wasn't jealous.

He absolutely wasn't jealous.

Hassan shut his eyes and pressed the flat of his forehead hard against iced and unforgiving glass. *Redirect.* Redirect to a big play, to the adoration of all those girls, to tossing the pigskin with Nathan. Edy. Edy and Wyatt. *Edy.*

Damnit.

Hassan lifted his head. He imagined Edy calling her new friend on a night she couldn't sleep, a night like this one. She wouldn't know that Hassan stood there, watching, willing to come if only she'd call.

He imagined Edy wanting Wyatt for company after some fitful sleep, welcoming him as if *he* were Hassan. And Wyatt, Wyatt skulking across the yard and up their tree before yanking open her bedroom window. And Hassan knew what he would do, what he would do when the doors were shut and the windows were shut, and only the two of them were alone.

The corners of his mouth snatched down and hands clenched into merciless fists.

Wyatt would slip into her bedroom and lace his fingers with hers. He'd draw her in close, hand at the little dip above her backside. But would she tilt for him and welcome him? Would she want him? Because that was the question, wasn't it?

Hassan turned from the window with a groan.

Wyatt would kiss, touch her, and would slip underneath Hassan's window to do it.

Never.

Hassan pulled on jeans over pajama pants, slipped into a hooded sweatshirt and crept downstairs, careful to avoid the creaking third stair. Once out, he ventured to the edge of the yard and became the silhouette facing Edy's house.

What did he hope to see? Or learn?

He squinted at her window. Frost slicked the tree he'd need to climb to get in, though it was a feat he'd accomplished before. Carefulness and a steady hand would bring him to her.

But then what?

Once, invitations had been unnecessary, and he could have yanked her window open at any hour of any day and she'd have been there for him, for whatever he needed.

Wyatt had changed that.

Except he hadn't. And he had.

Hassan's wanting to protect Edy had begun like all things good: pure and unsullied with the mark of selfishness.

But then it changed, warping from the inside out till the nasty workings of its interior revealed their true selves.

Rain began to fall. It pelted in freezing needles, demanding his attention. What was happening to him? What was happening to them?

The answers he sought were right there, beneath his nose, if only he could focus.

He didn't want Edy with Wyatt Green. It ate at every good thing in him, till only the nastiness remained.

He wanted to call her name, if only to know that she'd still answer, that she still felt the connection that always drew them near.

He wanted to tell her about how little he trusted Wyatt and how it blistered to be replaced. Those feelings had him standing beneath her window in the rain at night. He imagined himself gaining courage, scaling the tree and telling her the truth, whatever that meant.

No.

Don't even think.

Sports kept him disciplined and discipline was a gift.

He redirected and considered the options.

He didn't want Edy with Wyatt. There were ways to address that. As for everything else . . . he wondered how much things had truly changed.

They still saw each other every day at school and for dinner most nights. They still whispered across the dinner table and had covert conversations with their eyes at school, around their parents, everywhere. And she still visited him on the sidelines after every game, albeit with the pale one in tow. Each time Hassan saw him, he had an irrepressible urge to bury him under the earth, take Edy by the hand, and . . .

He envied Wyatt. Not for the time he spent with her, but for the unhindered way he looked at her. As if loving her were the most natural thing in the world.

Hassan's head began to throb.

Girls called him. All the time. Girls who liked the idea of a guy who could strong-arm on the field, who could take an everything or nothing moment and come out victorious every single time. He thought of the redhead whose name he couldn't recall. He thought of other girls, too.

The week after her, some strange girl had sauntered up to his locker and planted her mouth on his, right in front of the guys. At a party the following weekend, an older girl with beer-laced breath had pinned him to a wall and asked why he hadn't taken advantage of her yet. He'd stared, at a loss for comebacks that usually came easy. At another party, one where he'd rushed too many beers, the blonde cheerleader Sandra Jacobs had offered to dance with him, only to grind so rough and rugged his hard-on sprung like a jack-in-the-box. A whisper in his ear said she wanted to go upstairs and liberate him. She had been easier to get rid of. Another week and another party brought a girl named Adelita, also keen on freeing the rod. The easies came faster than he could count, faces a blur, with temptation lasting the length of a lit match before revulsion settled deep.

He would make himself enjoy them. Girls who wanted to kiss and touch and make him their first, all because of what he did on the field.

He tried to imagine wanting to talk, to open up, to share the strangeness of this new life with one of them. He tried to imagine his moments of weakness before games: the vomiting, the trembling, the uncertainty. He couldn't do it.

Hassan pictured a girl among them that could switch from English to Hindi and Hindi to Punjabi on a whim. They would leap from the technicalities of football to the jumbled thoughts that waded in his head: on politics, religion, philosophy, or what it meant to be American and the child of immigrants. He tried to imagine a girl not laughing when he pondered the likelihood of reincarnation and figured out how to link even that to football. Then he tried to imagine her not being Edy.

It wasn't the first time he'd had the thought, only the first time it weighed so heavy, and shoved so insistent. Still, he rejected it, buried it, and managed a laughed for being absurd.

Girls called him all the time. Tall ones, short ones, smart ones, dumb ones—a lot of girls who weren't Edy. It was time he called them back.

It was time Hassan proved to himself what his parents insisted all along: that there was someone out there for him. Someone other than Edy Phelps.

Eight

Winter ripped in harsh. Stark, snow blinding, arctic glacial days bled to mind numbing nights, resolute in unyielding bleakness. Even the thin, scattered clouds seemed iced, a mirror of the permafrost blanketing the city. Keeping warm became a perpetual task of diligence, with thickly layered clothes, puffy coats, hats, scarves, mittens and lumberjack boots the only things keeping Edy alive.

Thanksgiving loomed, and along with it, her birthday. Early Monday morning, the Phelps' phone shrieked. At a wink past six, Edy stumbled from bathroom to hall, grasping for bearings as no one but her seemed able to hear it. Slippered feet dragging, fist rubbing her eye, she got to the call, mumbled a hello, and received word that the secretary of state would be put on the line.

She tore out for her father, yelling for him as she went. Seconds later, she stood in the doorway of her parents' bedroom with her father's back to her as he picked up the phone in his room. Her mother, ill content to sit on the edge of the bed, paced before Edy's father, arms crossed, body rigid with the tenseness of the moment.

They could turn on the television, Edy supposed. No doubt, whatever had roused the secretary of state herself would be cause for snippets of burning things, bold flashing headlines, and grasping reporters speculating and retracting in the same breath. Mother and daughter exchanged a look of trepidation. They could go downstairs, or, they could wait for the real news, right there, in their very own home. This was what it meant to be a Phelps, right here in the flesh.

The conversation dragged on without leaving much to piece together. Lots of nods and simple affirmations, confirmation that he could leave immediately. The federal government seeking her father's counsel wasn't new; he'd advised on the pitfalls of nation-building in Iraq and Afghanistan, on the intersection of human resource deficiencies and human rights in the Middle East, and most recently, as a special adviser at a U.N. conference on least developed countries.

But none of those calls had come at six a.m.

Edy's mother must have had the same thought, as she began pulling suits from the closet, shoes from the rack, ties from the drawer, and barking at Edy to help lend a hand. Though she had no idea what to do, Edy stepped forward; never brave enough to question her mother's direct instruction.

Husband and wife communicated through brief glimpses and slight turns of the head, enough for her to know when a shirt or pair of shoes was undesirable. She tossed things to Edy, who folded them neatly, only to have her mother fuss and refold them. Edy's fingers fumbled with the truth of what her mother's shaking hands meant: that they were ushering her father toward someplace even she wasn't certain about.

Finally, the call ended.

"Egypt," he said. "There's complete and utter chaos. Again. People have taken to the streets, rioting and immolating themselves in a violent rebellion of government."

"So?" Edy blurted.

She didn't mean "so" as in "so what if people are dying." She meant "so, what can her father do?"

"Their democracy is decomposing. As a scholar, I'm obligated to discover why and aid my government whenever called."

That. That endless need to be a Phelps. As if anyone knew what *that* meant.

"I've seen those places on TV," Edy said. "When order breaks down, they fix it by shooting everyone."

"Edith," her father said. "That's a tad overwrought."

Only a tad? Well, good.

He'd been to dangerous places before, but after conditions settled and once troops were brought in— certainly not before breaking news could make sense of what had happened.

"You can't go," Edy said, in a groping childish grasp at control. "My birthday's coming up. You can't miss that."

It was weak, she knew. And he could go; he would go. Just as he'd gone to Libya, Yemen, Syria, and Iraq. Just as he'd traversed much of South and Central America, and a handful of the worst places in Africa. He would go and be thrilled by the prospect of going.

Edy's mother groaned. "Must you always audition for Hollywood, child? Your father's going. It's the opportunity we've been waiting for. So, shut up and be grateful," she said.

"Rebecca," her father warned, voice distant.

"Don't 'Rebecca' me! The girl is impossible. Spoiled beyond my capacity for tolerance. 'It's my birthday' she said. Of all the asinine, contrite—" Her mother looked around, as if the walls or ceiling might calm her. When they didn't, she turned back on Edy. "The secretary of state just called your house. Can you understand that? You don't shirk opportunity when it comes. Especially when fear is your rationale."

Edy's father cleared his throat.

"When your country calls, you come," he corrected.

"But it's not safe," Edy blurted. "You shouldn't have to go if it's not safe. They might—"

"Stop it," her mother snapped. "Stop the manipulative hysterics. You're fine and well when he hauls you and Hassan off with him, no matter how questionable the destination, but now that he's going without you, it's a show. But if you're going to perform, why not get serious? Fall to the floor. Kick. Scream. Go on being an insufferable brat."

"That's enough, Rebecca," Edy's father said. "She's only concerned."

She looked from husband to Edy, husband to Edy, face lined with distaste. Still, Edy's father hadn't moved. He sat rooted in contemplation.

"Concerned," her mother said, as if the word were bird droppings in her mouth. "For who is the question."

Edy lifted her head. "I don't know what you mean."

Her mother stepped forward. "You *know* he'll be fine. And you *know* your only concern is Daddy being absent for your birthday," she said. "But you needn't worry about what extravagant thing he'll come up with this year. We all know how you crave male attention."

Edy heated through to her bones. Were they even talking about the same thing? No amount of courage could make her ask. It was true; she had felt some disappointment at the thought of her father not being there for her birthday. But it simmered low. Had it been wrong for her to feel it at all?

"I'll be home soon," her father said. "And I'll call often. In the meantime, you'll enjoy your birthday party at the Dysons' just as you always do."

He believed her mother. He believed Edy's fears were little more than a child's worries about Daddy not being there to spoil her.

Murder. Resistance. Islamofacism. Journeying to Egypt sounded about as safe as turning donuts on the interstate. And yet she couldn't deny the ravenous way her father set about preparing, as if the sole purpose for which God had created him lay just outside, a plane ride away.

Edy pushed thoughts of discord and danger from her mind as she showered and pulled on clothes that might or might not have been ironed. She brushed her hair up and secured it with an office rubber band before shooting a single, furtive look out the window. They would be there for her father soon. The unmarked sedan, the men in suits, ready to transport him by private flight to another world.

She decided to focus on breakfast. Chewing was something to do; something to concentrate on, if she did it carefully, methodically. So, Edy shoved random books in her bag, sucked in a shuddering breath, and thundered downstairs into the hall. Voices in the study stopped her. Her father's. Ali's.

"I would love to accompany you," Ali said. "In an unofficial capacity, of course. After all, the opportunity for observation and research is enormous. But it's far too precarious a situation for both of us to venture into. That's our agreement and I aim to honor."

"Listen. In the event something went awry—"

"You needn't ask," Ali said. "She's my daughter. Hassan's your son. Hasn't it always been so?"

"I know. But—"

"Heard enough, yet?" Hassan said.

Edy whirled at the sound of his voice.

"Don't make it harder on yourself," he said. "Nathan's gotta go. Plain as that." He reached past her and slipped the office door closed, eyes never leaving her face.

How could she explain a fear to him that was both rational and irrational? That she could lose her father, the only person that had ever been hers entirely, unconditionally? That there was no way to *not* make that hard on herself?

"Let's go," Hassan said.

Surprised by the dampness of her face, Edy wiped it with the back of her hand.

"But I haven't had breakfast yet," she said.

"We'll get it on the way."

He took her by the hand, led her out the door.

"On the way?"

"To school. We'll be a little late, that's all."

Twenty minutes later they grabbed a corner table at Ted's Diner and ordered waffles, hash browns, coffee, and kept heads low in the event of nosy neighbors. There were always nosy neighbors. How much time passed in silence, Edy couldn't say.

"He'll come back," Hassan said into his coffee. "He'll come back because we need him."

When he found her staring, Hassan chucked a bit of potato at her nose.

Edy responded with a boiled egg to the eye.

He could have blocked it, she knew, but apparently he'd found the idea of being attacked with an egg too amusing to pass on. When she followed the egg with a strawberry, he swatted it, eyes still on her.

"You don't want to rumble with me, Edy. You must realize you're outgunned."

He gestured to all the food before him, twice as much as what she'd ordered.

Edy snorted on a laugh. "Rhinecorn would spazz if we showed up late and filthy."

Hassan shrugged. "Maybe we won't go today. Maybe we'll just . . . slip back in the house once all is clear."

Edy stared at him. This wasn't funny anymore.

"Breathe," Hassan said. "I'm kidding. We'll only miss a few periods."

"We'll get in trouble," Edy said. "Detention, again for starters."

"Yeah?"

"And your whole team will have to run laps."

"Yeah."

"So why are you doing this?"

Hassan shrugged, gaze on a still full cup of coffee. "It bothers me to see you upset. That's all."

He reached over and pinched her nose, earning her smile despite her best efforts.

They did indeed earn detention, having arrived at school one period before lunch. In class and after, she felt the stares of the masses and bet they all knew that she'd missed half the day, that she had no excuse, and that she'd arrived with Hassan—both with food on their clothes.

Hassan, to his credit, found the whole thing hilarious. The smile faded, however, when he pulled her to join him in the cafeteria and she insisted on waiting in the hall for Wyatt, instead. After ten minutes in the corridor at their trusted meeting place, Edy entered the cafeteria and spotted Wyatt at their table, shoulders hunched, shoveling food into his mouth as if bent on first place in a race. Hassan sat a little ways off at his usual table, eating at a leisurely pace.

He'd let her wait, like an idiot. It wouldn't have taken much for him to stick his head out and tell her to come and join them.

Then again, it was Wyatt who'd blown her off without saying why.

For three days he'd been too busy to talk in the halls, always en route to someplace else. For two days he'd been MIA at lunch.

Edy powered for him, brown bag lunch swinging. Wyatt looked up, registered her, scanned the room, and grabbed his lunch tray. He headed straight for the "it" table. Matthew and Mason made room.

Edy stopped, waited, and watched the boys resume eating. Only when her arms began to ache did she realize she still stood there.

"Hey, Cake," Hassan said as she dropped into a seat.

Matt tugged her ponytail in greeting. Mason managed some sort of food spewing greeting around a mouthful of taco while Wyatt only waved. Edy raised an eyebrow.

"Did we have a fight and you forgot to tell me, Wyatt?" she asked.

Wyatt studied his chili.

"Leave him alone," Matt said. "He's enjoying the food and hanging with the boys, you know."

She turned on Wyatt. "What did they do to you? Tell me and I'll fix it."

Red blotched Wyatt's face. His gaze darted from each boy back to Edy. "What makes you think anyone did something to me? Or that anyone could? I'm my own man."

"Slow down, Slim," Hassan said.

"I'm sitting here because I want to," Wyatt said. He swallowed. "Because I do what I want."

A pair of blondes at the table snickered. Wyatt shifted his gaze to Matt.

"Isn't that right?" he said.

Matt's spoon hung in midair, halfway to the chili.

Edy raised a brow. "In that case, my birthday's coming up," she said, gaze even with Wyatt's. "And I always have a party. Want to be my date?"

"No," Hassan blurted.

Lawrence choked on his chili. Hassan burrowed a demonic glare into Wyatt, even as Wyatt stole furtive glances at the twins. After a thick swath of silence, Mason cursed, then gave him an indiscernible nod.

"Well, I guess that means 'yes,'" Edy announced. "So I'll see you if your captors permit it."

She looked from one boy to the next, conflicted. Not for the first time, an avalanche of contrary emotions yanked at once. She hated their swarming, and hated their insistence on meddling. She wanted to show them that she could thwart all their plans. Edy could think of no better way, than going out with Wyatt. Yeah, she didn't *like him* like him but it made her point. If only it didn't kind of grate her teeth.

Edy stormed from the table, lunch uneaten, eager to get away from it all.

They were always micromanaging her, always hovering, with their overcharged masculinity and patriarchal fixations. She could rule her own mind and her own body, as good, if not better than one of them. Weren't they the ones always in trouble? Drinking at parties, sleeping with girls, driving like maniacs with the devil on their heels? Edy had always been the responsible one, the obedient one, the sensible voice, and never did more than simmer, not even when wronged. At least that's how she used to be. She didn't know what was happening to her just now.

Anger seized her so much; she needed to rage right then. She could claw the paint from the walls and shriek at the ceiling that she-had-her-own-mind. Only, who would hear; who would care? So, Edy didn't scream. She never did. Instead, she went to her locker to get the books for her next class, head low. A lucky break had her turning up a Tylenol sample on her top shelf. She didn't know how they'd be for stomach aches, but something had to help the grating, churning, roller derby underway in her abdomen.

By fifth period, whispers drifted through the halls. By sixth, they'd been replaced by open gaping, wide eyed staring: the equivalent of shouts at their high school. Word was that she'd thrown herself at the new boy and even he had rejected her. Just like the Dysons. Just like Hassan. But just as quickly as the rumors appeared, they disappeared, crushed behind some unseen force.

Protection. That was what her boys gave her. Whether Edy wanted it or not.

Nine

Six days since her daddy left. A few more till Thanksgiving. Edy's eyes flew open, and the scent of ocean water receded with each waking moment.

She turned fifteen today.

Fifteen and without a period, though the impertinent thumbtacks she passed off as breasts hurt like hell. She supposed that counted for something.

She'd spent the last three days in detention. Skipping the first three periods of class with Hassan had earned her an afternoon for each hour of tardiness. When compared to Hassan's punishment of running drills until nightfall, Edy felt like she should have been able to muster more outrage. She hadn't.

Her gaze slid over to the window facing his room. A shot of blue through the fogged pane caught her eye. She went over and used the sleeve of her pajama top to wipe a path for her vision. It was just as Sandra Jacobs scrambled out and made an unceremonious dump to the ground. Hassan's head followed her exit, and he watched her descend, waiting to ensure her safety.

Had she been there all night? Had she kissed him in the dark and slept on his favorite Patriots sheets? Had he held her as he held Edy, with her cheek to his heart as they slept? His sheets, his bedroom, his body, it would all smell of that cloying fragrance she wore. He'd come to Edy like that; he'd come to Edy *on her birthday*, smelling like the girl she hated most.

Hassan's head snapped up and their eyes locked.

Edy jerked away from the window.

"Good morning, my *sanam*! I see you're up early!"

Edy's bedroom door flew open and Hassan's father marched in. She whirled to face him, heart thumping, back pinned to block his view. Ali Pradhan, formidable girth that he was, stood in her doorway, dressed in the simple white button-up and slacks that he preferred for most everything. He held a clear Dixie cup of blueberry *lassi* out in one hand, Edy's favorite drink.

"Have you seen your dress yet?" he asked.

The dress. The birthday dress. Edy's gaze slid over to the swath of tangerine fabric draping the backside of her door.

"I know your father usually takes the honor," Ali said. "But I couldn't help myself. All things considered, of course." His eyes darted from Edy to the fabric in beaming certainty.

Edy lifted it from the door for a careful inspection. Blinding tangerine in winter. Puffed long sleeves. High waisted. Ankle length. Gleaming gold trinkets attached, seemingly at random. Madness could be bought, it turned out.

Every year for her birthday, Edy's father bought her a dress. When she was little, they were coupled with tiaras and pin curls. Growing up, the years were measured in fabric, marked in lace, noted with pearls. But the dresses never changed. Hoop skirts and tea-length numbers, unabashed in width, nauseating in sweetness, ruffles innumerable, with Rani standing by, resident stylist, ready to place a fountain of ribbons in Edy's hair. More than once, Edy wished them longer, so that she might tie one around her neck and jump.

"*I* had this one made," Ali announced, chest puffed. "The fabric? Imported from Mumbai. The design and sewing? Done to my specifications by a very exclusive shop. No one can boast a dress like this." He waved both hands. "For you, my *sanam,* only one of a kind will do."

Her eyes watered. This should have been the year she refused the dresses and scorned the smothering patriarchy that dictated what she wore on her most special of days. After all, she'd be sixteen next year—too old for frosting and tinsel and grownups at her parties. Truth told, she already was. But even as she thought all that, her hands reached for the garment. This was Ali. He'd read to her on countless nights and pushed her too high on swings, catching her when she leapt off as she always, always did. Of course, she'd wear it for him.

Her mother had been wrong about one thing though. Not since she bounced on her father's knee had she worried about the scope and grandeur of her birthday parties. Instead, the mandatory frills made her cringe the way watching the boys tag-team wrestle sometimes could. Getting propped up in lace so that all her parents' friends could drink imported beer and pinch her cheeks wasn't exactly tickles and giggles. Were Hassan or the twins celebrating a birthday, it would have been cause for a nighttime extravaganza filled with sweat-laden dancing, underage drinking, and fornicating teens. No, she'd get to spend her day with up and coming politicians, middle-aged power women, and men desperate to slip away for the Notre Dame Boston College game.

"I'll try it on for you," Edy offered.

She draped the dress over an arm, took a sip of the *lassi* she knew to be for her, offered what she hoped to be a reassuring smile, and took both the drink and the tapestry of horror with her to the bathroom.

Once there, Edy wrestled with zippers and cursed over buttons before slipping the rustle of crinoline over her head. She fastened the eyehooks as best she could and inhaled. Who knew? Maybe when she looked, a stunning and grandiose princess would stare back at her, as glamorous and swoon-worthy as the girls who caught Hassan's eye, and who apparently spent nights with him.

Edy turned to face the full-length mirror draped over the door.

What stared back at her was preposterous. A grotesque burlesque of absurdities in fashion. A high-throated Victorian neckline, Regency sleeves, and an empire waist. Fabric that would have been beautiful as a sari looked garish as a gown. Her eyes began to water. She looked *ugly.* Like, hysterically ugly. Her only consolation was that she needn't worry about any friends seeing her, as she had none to begin with. As usual, the boys would never breathe a word of what went on in their world, while any other kid who happened to be there wouldn't dare risk their reputation by admitting to it.

Sandra Jacobs would never look like this.

Edy stilled the quiver within with a deep breath, grabbed her *lassi,* and stepped out into the hall. A deep drink followed another, during which she reminded herself that there were things more important than looks, that to worry about looks over feelings was to be as shallow as the runway girls of South End High. Never mind that you look like a fool, she told herself. Never mind that the boy you're in love with thinks of you as a sister. Never mind that not even in your dumbest daydreams could you look half as perfect as the perfection he wanted.

The *lassi* found her mouth again and she drank as she walked. Ali had always adored her and she him. If Edy couldn't do this small, distasteful thing for him, then she wasn't much of a—

The cup flattened in her face, crunching and splashing blueberry from nose to waist and wall to wall.

"Oh crap!" Hassan cried. He reached with both hands for her, then withdrew, before whirling in place as if something would appear to aid him. His hands flailed. "Jeez, Edy. I'm sorry. I just—" He flinched at her dress. "Oh, man."

Ali stepped into the hall. He looked from Hassan's cringe to Edy's wide-eyed one and registered the dress only last.

"Hassan," he said.

"It just happened," Hassan said. "The second I hit the corner we collided."

"But you are reckless, always reckless! Running around as if all of Boston is a football field. You could have hurt her."

Ali softened the second he turned to Edy. "I'm afraid there's nothing that can be done for the dress, my dear. Bring it to my wife later. Perhaps she can salvage it. And in the meantime, you'll have to find something in your mother's closet to wear."

He shot his son a final scathing look and barreled downstairs in a huff.

"Edy—" Hassan said.

"Thanks for the save. The dress was atrocious."

She started back for her room.

"Edy, wait. About what you saw—"

She ducked in her room.

When Hassan's mouth opened, she slammed the door on his answer and locked him out. What could he say to assuage the raw and pulsating wound of her heart? He couldn't know the way she ached for him or how he stabbed her anew every single day. What apology could fix that? What could he possibly say? That he was sorry she wasn't more attractive? Sorry he didn't want her?

Edy leaned against the door, soaked in blueberry yogurt. She let the tears fall on her fifteenth birthday.

An eternity passed.

"Edy," Hassan said. "Open the door. Please. You're killing me."

Had he really just sat there and listened to her cry?

It didn't matter. In the larger scheme of things, it didn't matter what he did or whom he did it with. A chasm divided them, deepening and widening every single day. She could accept that. She would have to.

Edy stood up straight. She wiped her tears with the hem of her gown and only succeeded in smearing blueberry across her face. A hiccup-laugh tore from her, making her choke in the throes of it. She was positively a mess. And it was all because of Hassan Pradhan.

~~~

Edy's morning was filled with hidden gifts as part of another, much more tolerable tradition. Among her stumbled-upon presents were Nike ballet slippers from Ali, a *salwar kameez,* or a pink, Punjabi-style pantsuit, an earring and bracelet set from Hassan with dangling, silhouetted ballerinas on both, and a monogrammed organizer from her mother. The last, of course, hadn't been hidden at all. It sat in plain view of breakfast alongside a note that read:

Business at the office.
See you at the party.
-Mom

Edy had no idea why she stared at the note so long. Or why she compared it with the three-page, rose-scented letter from Rani, stuffed inside the folds of her gift. Simple things were in the writings from Hassan's mom, reminisces about the first time she'd pressed Edy's hair, the first time she'd seen her dance ballet. She reminded Edy of a trip to Mumbai, where they'd sat through three showings of Kaho *Naa . . . Pyaar Hai* on the night of its debut. She fussed over how fast Edy had grown, how old she'd become, and called her "her beauty," promising that she was already the thing she wanted to be: beautiful. As was always the case, when comparing Hassan's mom with her own, Edy found there was no comparison at all.

At a stone's throw past five, Edy met Wyatt in the middle of the street. She wore a simple, long-sleeved black sheath dress from her mother's closet—simple except for the hint of skin exposed at the crocheted abdomen. She'd partnered it with low heels—the only kind she could maneuver, and the flaring, dramatic Michael Kors jacket that her mother loved. Edy gave herself thirty seconds of scrutiny before stepping out of the door. As she walked, she told herself that the designer clothes were just a byproduct of shopping in her mother's closet; she had no special preference for them. Likewise, the burst of confidence she felt while wearing them had absolutely nothing to do with egotism, even if Wyatt did look at her that way.

"What?" Edy said.

"Nothing." Wyatt continued to stare. "Just . . .wow. That's all."

Edy touched her hair, pressed and swept up into pin curls by Rani, and took her hand away at the thought that it was something the "it" girls would do.

"The dress is a little big," Edy said. "Mom fills it out much better."

Her cheeks heated on reflection. Why had she chosen those words?

Edy glanced down the street, toward the Dyson house, hoping to distract him from her invitation to see how well she did or didn't fill out her mother's dress.

"Let's just go," she said and started off, leaving Wyatt to follow.

"You look incredible," Wyatt said. "I'm gonna pay hell for showing up with you."

Edy paid him a look, stride picking up as iced, eye watering wind cut through her ensemble.

"So, you admit it now," she said, touching her hair again. "Before you were all Don Corleone on me. Now you sound like Freddy."

Wyatt blinked. "Who's Freddy?"

Edy stopped. Took him in. Started again. "Hassan would have got that. Or Lawrence and the twins. Anyway, it's a *Godfather* reference. Me and the boys have seen it a lot."

Wyatt fell instep alongside her. "Is Hassan bringing a date, too?"

She could have kicked his ass for that. Such an innocent question. Yet, it brought a flood of emotion and the image of Sandra Jacobs tumbling out his window and down *their* tree, god damn her. Edy braced herself, fists clenched, nails digging, before flashing Wyatt her politician's smile. Having a politician for a mother was worth something after all.

"I doubt he'll bring a date," she managed. "It's really a casual sort of thing."

"Yet, you have one," Wyatt said. "You asked me."

"Changing the conversation now," Edy said.

They continued to walk.

"So, this party is something you do every year?" Wyatt asked.

"Yeah."

"Since you were a baby?"

"I guess."

Edy inspected her wrist. Not all the dancers on her bracelet from Hassan were exactly the same. Some were mid-pirouette, others mid-leap. She liked the leaping ones best.

"So, the Dysons have been throwing you a birthday party since you were born?"

"No. Just as long as I can remember."

She found a dancer doing a handstand in a tutu and squinted at it.

"They're pretty popular guys. Hassan, too."

They halted at a stop sign and waited for a cherry Bentley to breeze by. The driver sounded two lyrical honks for Edy before running the intersection altogether. She waved in response.

"You *know* that guy?"

"Yeah." Edy started off across the street, dress fluttering in the wind. She punched a bit of skyward fabric in impatience and touched up her curls again. "He's Brock Maddow, an old teammate of Lawrence's dad when he played for the Raiders."

"His car is incredible."

"It should be. He's rich."

A mint green Audi and black Jag followed Brock in quick succession. Like him, both honked. Edy waved.

"Jeez, Edy. It's like a car show with—"

"Look." She whirled on him so suddenly they almost collided in the street. "If you're going to be doing that all afternoon, you might as well go home now."

"Doing what?"

"Acting green. Like the sky above and the ground below impresses you."

Wyatt's mouth worked as his cheeks flushed irretrievably. "I'm sorry. I didn't mean to embarrass you. I—I'm sorry."

Edy cringed. Had she really yelled at him? Chastised her friend for lacking the privilege she took for granted? Her insides turned gray and putrid with the thought. She sucked. And that was all.

"I'll behave," Wyatt continued. "You'll see. I can act like I'm one of you guys. Although the clothes aren't likely to fool anybody." He opened his trench coat to reveal a wash-worn, peach polo, straight-legged jeans, and thick, white sneakers. But instead of him blushing at the ensemble, Edy did.

Shame. Shame like a canyon, swallowing her whole.

Edy turned away. When the wind battered her eyes, drawing tears in her punishment, she accepted it readily enough. "Promise me you won't do that again," she said.

"Do what?"

"*Contort* yourself into whatever you think'll please me. You're good enough as you are. Whoever doesn't think so can suck it."

Wyatt howled with laughter. "Suck what, Edy?" he said as they started off again.

She stole a look. "*You* know."

"But I want you to say it. I *dare* you to say it."

Edy laughed. "Leave me alone. I can't. You know I can't." She looped an arm through his as if it were a consolation prize.

He accepted it with a broad mouthed smile.

~~~

The Bentley and Audi were just primers for the Dyson house, and Wyatt's eyes threatened to leave his skull at the sight of it. A three-story corner lot that swallowed most of the street, it was newest of the homes in their neighborhood and by far the most opulent.

Shimmering gold in its rush skyward and flanked by sweeping porches, its boastful bay windows jutted elegance, its trimmings exquisiteness, as gables and spires and marks of another time blotted out the sun. People at South End High only faked this kind of wealth, the sort that came from multi-million dollar NFL contracts, piles of endorsements, and an ultra-successful franchise. Still, the Dysons were indifferent to it all. Only outsiders really cared about their net worth. Outsiders and Edy's mom, of course.

Edy led the way up a sweep of gold steps to a double pair of walnut doors. They were stopped at the entrance by two boys in jackets that read "Dyson Gyms."

"Names," one blurted as he scrutinized a list.

Edy snorted. "Same as last year, Evan. Same as every year."

He didn't bother to look up from the clipboard.

"I don't care if I know you. I still need you to say it."

"Mother Teresa and Pope John Paul. Now move." She shoved between the two.

But Wyatt stayed behind. The boys looked from her to him.

"You better not try that, too," Evan warned.

They were big boys, defensive football players who were among the best in state. As part of a program the Dyson boys' dad, Steve, ran, they received free memberships at his gym, plus mentoring. Needless to say, they were loyal to him.

"Move," Edy said and folded her arms. "Or I'll say that the two of you touched me."

They parted wide for Wyatt. He looked at one, then the other, before following Edy in silence. But he stopped at the foyer. Creamy marble flooring, ivory walls were trimmed in gold. Spiral stairs on the left and right ventured upward to vaulted ceilings and beyond.

"Ballroom's in the east wing," Edy explained and veered in the direction of pulsing hip hop music.

"Ballroom?" Wyatt mumbled and touched his polo.

"Yeah," Edy said. "This way."

She could lead him in the dead of the night, blinded. How many times had she run down those same gilded halls? In patent leather Mary Janes, in rubber-soled jellies, barefoot and wet from the pool? There were nicks in the house, little things that the grownup eye would never see. Marks of five childhoods spent there. A miniscule drawing of soldiers in the corner of an alcove—one for each Dyson boy plus Hassan. A hole at the baseboard that separated Matt's room from Mason's —remnants of a failed effort to facilitate communication through the walls. Names carved on the belly of the south side porch—each of theirs and Edy.

It had always been that way. Each Dyson boy, Hassan, and Edy.

But "been" was a past tense word.

She shoved open the doors to the ballroom and a roar of greeting met them.

The boys, over near the food, noticed her in an instant. Tessa Dyson, clan mom, already made her way over. Other guests, probably after a faint tug of memory reminded them that they were there for Edy, managed to speak, too. Edy offered them a half hearted wave.

Pink and turquoise balloons drifted toward the ceiling, accented by the lilies at every table, centerpieces all around. Steve Dyson stood at one end, fussing at a massive wood-burning fireplace and grill. Broad-shouldered and powerfully muscled, he handed a rack of meat to Lawrence and waved him away. An elaborate spread of food lay out to one side, towering stacks of delicacies and deserts, rows of deliciousness. At the center of the display stood a three-tier birthday cake, high enough for Edy to count the candles from where she stood.

"Look at you," Tessa said and wrapped arms around Edy. "So grown up and pretty." Lower and in Edy's ear, she added. "Did you and Hassan fight? He's been here since breakfast, doing the work of three men."

As Tessa pulled away, Edy shook her head slow, discreet. Tessa Dyson pursed her lips in a show of disbelief, before returning for a second embrace.

"Fine," she said. "Be secretive. Oh, and F.Y.I., I've already heard an earful about your date."

She pulled away to face Wyatt.

"Pleased to meet you," Tessa said, and turned a pageant smile on him.

Wyatt looked as if his mouth had filled with dust. Tessa Dyson, the one-time head cheerleader and former University of Georgia homecoming queen, had no doubt stolen his ability to speak. Not that it surprised

Edy. As a little girl, it was her glamour that Edy had tried—and failed—to emulate. Now an aerobics instructor, the mother of the rambunctious Dyson brood had to be every bit as tight and firm as her years in college, belying the natural births she'd endured for all four of her children: the twins, Lawrence, and her youngest, Vanessa, that kept indoors mostly.

Edy exchanged introductions and excused herself to make the rounds.

"How'd I do?" Wyatt said.

She took in his shaky exhale and smiled.

"Great," Edy said. "Don't change a thing." She bopped a finger off his nose and earned herself a grin.

"Let's make the rounds," Edy announced. "I'll introduce you to people you'd foam over if you only cared about sports 30 years ago."

Already, scores of people milled about, some with wine in hand, others with beer or soda. They steered far and away from a gaping Hassan, Lawrence, and the twins, who stood by the food, unimpressive in a pack of men who were equally big and bigger.

They passed the only two other teens seemingly mandated to be in attendance: Jessica Wilson, an upperclassman who hadn't spoken a word to Edy in five years, and Alyssa Curtis, a cheerleader whose dark eyes scorched a perpetual threat in the general direction of the twins. Both had an unceasing habit of attaching themselves to Matt and Mason. And for what? To bawl in the girls' bathroom? To curse and claw the next catch wrenched out from underneath them? Still, they rode the rollercoaster of madness with those boys on again and off again endlessly, ever enthusiastic for the next thrill.

Some girls, it seemed, never found the exit.

Edy's gaze fell on her mother, clustered in a group of half a dozen that included Kyle Lawson's father Cam, a bruiser of a politician who had fielded accusations of questionable campaign contributions in the past. While Edy only knew his kindness, she also knew he'd once sucker-punched a reporter seeking clarification on how his wife had died. But Cam was nothing if not the people's champ—a holdover from days of glory in Boston College football. And since the people loved Cam Lawson, then Edy's mother loved him even more. In fact, if she were human enough to have something as normal as a best friend, Cam Lawson would've been it.

Remembering Wyatt at her side, Edy took him around to meet the washed-up athletes, aspiring politicians, deans, scholars, and powerhouse attorneys that made up the crowd. She accepted the hugs and dollar bills pressed into her palm, the biggest of both coming from Cam.

"Finished your parade route?" Matt said when Edy and Wyatt ran out of people to greet, having finally circled around to them. He embraced her before passing her on to his duplicate.

"This is the last year we do this, right?" Mason said.

Edy frowned. By "do this," she assumed he meant the obligatory gathering for her birthday.

"I guess," she said and moved on to hug Lawrence, then Kyle.

She stopped at Hassan.

"Happy birthday, Cake."

Her gaze narrowed to nothing. Cake? Really? Wasn't that a name better reserved for Sandra Jacobs, now? "Hi," she said, arms heavy at her side.

His gaze darted left, then right. "Can I talk to you?" Hassan said.

Edy blinked. "I'd rather you didn't."

Matt let out a low whistle.

"Edy," Hassan said, stiff against the smirks at his back, gaze forward, shoulders taut, determined. "Please."

"There's nothing to say," she blurted. "Nothing

to . . . " Edy shook her head, blinked, and swallowed a thousand times. Then she swallowed a thousand more.

"One minute," Hassan said and held his hand out. Edy looked at it, never wavering, waiting.

Waiting for her.

"One," Edy said and pulled him to the fringes of the dance floor.

At the moment their bodies touched, Matt handed Mason some cash.

~~~

The first time they'd danced together had been ten years to the day on the very same floor. Layers of enveloping pink and a polished tiara had rendered Edy majestic. In true fairytale fashion, he'd insisted on the first dance, prince to her princess. Her birthday, his brashness. Hassan counted on it once again.

But their dance was a stiff two-step. His one hand clasped Edy's in the air, while the other rested fixed, arthritic-like, at her side.

"I'm stupid," he said. "Stupid and sorry."

He abandoned formalities for her waist, both arms wrapping it and pulling her in close. It was only after embracing her that he remembered they were supposed to be dancing.

Edy stiffened in his arms. Rejecting him and his apology. "You don't owe me anything," she said. "Whatever happened—"

"*Nothing* happened."

Except something had happened. But not what she thought. Sandra Jacobs had been a distraction, a convenient, impulsive one, roused in a moment of weakness, frustration, and another night of staring at Edy's window.

She'd called him, wanting to come over. He'd let her. Why had he let her?

He'd remembered Sandra's argument in the hall with Wyatt and saw her invitation as a means to get what he needed. She could be the distraction he wanted and she could tell him what he'd been desperate to know: who was Wyatt Green? Easy enough, right?

So, he'd let her come over. Let her think what she wanted. When Sandra kissed him, he let her do that, too. He'd timed the moments where he'd pulled away, where he'd pressed with one question, then another, only to have her return with those stupid, irritating kisses. She was easy and her easiness grated. He'd thought that something would click, would really rouse him, and that there'd be some primal, overpowering urge, a legitimate response to easy sex with a beautiful girl. But damn if he hadn't glimpsed a picture of Edy on the mantel and shot all that to hell. So, he got straight to his point with Sandra.

"What's Wyatt to you?" Hassan demanded and snatched her hand from his shirt.

Her cousin was what she'd told him. A cousin that she only sort of knew.

"Forget about him," she'd insisted. "It's only you that I think about. You that I want to be with."

Clarity snapped into place. Every mistake that had led to that moment, stood stark for examination. She thought he *felt* something for her. She'd taken his badgering as a mark of jealousy.

She wanted him too, she'd said, wanted him to be her first.

Her words were a wall dropped between them, a hurricane flinging him to the opposite side of the room. What was he doing? How desperate had he become? He hated this girl. He'd used her, manipulated her in the hopes of gaining something. But he wasn't done wreaking damage. The worst had come in the morning.

Rather than sending her home in the middle of the night, Hassan drew blankets from a closet and threw an extra pillow on the floor. He'd sleep down there, leaving her to take his bed.

Edy saw her take out in the morning.

What had she believed? That he had slept with Sandra Jacobs? That he loved Sandra Jacobs?

"She slept in your bed," Edy said.

"I slept on the floor."

She loosened in his arms, relaxing a single degree beneath his touch.

"It's none of my business," Edy said.

He thought he saw something in her eyes. Something more powerful than annoyance, more dangerous than friendship.

He pushed both the thought and the tendrils of hair in her face away. "She's nothing to me. And I wish . . . " His words died in an exhale. Where were his parents?

"You wish what?" Edy said, so soft she nearly mouthed it.

Was it possible? Could she really not know?

A wild sort of funk pressed out the speakers, familiar to the old folks and rousing for the young. The twins whooped from the sidelines when their father swung their mother to the dance floor.

Hassan grinned. "I wish you'd dance a hundred songs with me. But I'll settle for my usual dozen."

He whipped her around and dipped her low, with show enough to earn a roar of approval from a dozen men. Edy flashed that smile of smiles and they were off, for one dance, two, two hundred, maybe.

~~~

Wyatt stared straight ahead, face blackened with fury.

"What the hell?" he said through gritted teeth.

"Hey, I was surprised he took that long," one twin told him and nodded toward a Hassan with not one but two arms around Edy.

"Well, I don't know," said the twin with dreads pulled tight in a ponytail. "I at least thought you'd man up enough for the first dance. Since you had the balls to come at all."

He cut Wyatt a look out the corner of his eye.

"And what did I tell you?" the other one said. "A hundred on Sawn to detonate on the runway. That plane wasn't taking off. No way." He tilted his head toward Wyatt and a sweep of neat dreadlocks brushed his shoulders with the motion.

The ponytailed one pulled a face. "Well, if you were so sure, then you're stupid. You should have made the bet two hundred since you know so much."

"Right." The insulted twin gave Wyatt a once over. "He's the one that's here, showing up at chapter three and wondering why he's a minor character. But *I'm* the stupid one."

"You two talked enough yet?" Lawrence said. "Or are you gonna give the password for the ADT system, too?"

Another song began. Edy made a show of weaseling away from Hassan, only to be reeled back in and close. She laughed, exchanging words with him that the two of them alone would ever know. Was Hassan her date, or Wyatt's? And was he really so easy to forget?

It reminded him of a time with Lottie, back in Rhode Island. Wyatt shoved the thought from his mind.

"I'd never put up with that," the ponytailed twin said. *"Ever."*

"You're right. He should go over there," the other one urged. "As a matter of principle, they need to be straightened out. Now."

Wyatt looked at Lawrence, the sane one from what he could tell. Lawrence shook his head in silent warning. Wyatt turned away with a sigh. He waited through another song, and then another, as annoyance ebbed to rage and rage to chilling realization.

"You're benched," ponytail twin said. "How about we give you a tour of the house in the meantime?"

Had Wyatt been in his right mind, he would have said no. Had he not been distracted—no, dismantled—he would have said hell no. Going anywhere with a Dyson twin was the thing that Wyatt, of all people, knew better than to do. But he was a slack-faced dummy in the moment, standing in old clothes, numbed by his own stupidity.

How had he not seen it before, when Wyatt slept with the feeling, dreamed of it, and reached for it in slumber each night? How many fantasies had Wyatt and Hassan inadvertently shared, yearning, haunted, defeated by the exact same girl?

Except Hassan was a sham, a charlatan, a lie posing as the truth.

Like family, my ass.

The twins began the tour abruptly, leading Wyatt to a frozen-over and barren garden, worked in the spring by their mother and an overweight younger sister he didn't know they had. They took him to one of their bedrooms next and showed him a personal collection of video games and sneakers. A visit to the room opposite meant waiting through a presentation of home-recorded games— of high schools and colleges he'd never heard of, of NFL teams he couldn't care about. And through it all, he thought of Hassan and Edy, arm-in-arm below his feet, unchallenged.

A bathroom followed on their tour, then another, with pantries, linen closets, nonsense and more nonsense. They worked in circles and rushed stairs and flipped lights while laughing, losing Wyatt in shadows and snickering nearby. Wyatt walked in the Dyson house until the new rang familiar and he tore around stumbling on stairs. Eventually, the twins lost interest. When they did, they gave him the relief he craved by showing him to the front door.

"A plate for the road," ponytailed twin said and handed him an aluminum foil-covered dinner. "I wasn't sure what you liked, so there's a bit of everything in there."

Wyatt's stomach somersaulted. He hoped for some of their inch-thick steaks from the grill, flame-split lobster tails, and skewered shrimp, basted with a thickening sauce begging to be licked. Then he saw one of his TV dinners, with its palm-thin chicken thigh and ice-chunked mashed potatoes. Even the weight of this Dyson dinner strained the wrist.

But he didn't need a handout from these guys, especially when said handout came with the warning that he could never be good enough for their girl. Just when Wyatt opened his mouth to tell them so, the door closed in his face.

~~~

On Monday at lunch, Edy dropped down before a sour-faced Wyatt, who refused to make eye contact. She opened a greased, brown paper bag and pulled out *mattar paneer*, an Indian vegetarian curry spiced with Rani's heavy hand. An aluminum foil pouch of *naan* followed it, which she unfolded before jabbing a bit of bread in her mouth.

"I'm sorry," Edy said.

Wyatt jammed a fork into his hamburger.

"I looked for you," Edy said. "They said you went home. That the twins walked you out."

Wyatt shot her a pointed look. "You could say that."

Edy peeled the lid off her bowl and sniffed. Rani's food had no equal. The road to heaven smelled like the Pradhan kitchen.

After a sufficient amount of indulgence, she looked up to see Wyatt's scowl deepen two-fold.

"Give me a break, already," she said. "You were hanging with the guys. You know, like that spiel you fed me in the Don Corleone speech."

He stared. "You've got a lot of nerve, you know. Asking me out, ditching me at the sideline, and then trying to find some way to make it my fault. You think because you're pretty you can treat me like crap. You think I'm soft, slow, a sucker. I'm none of those things. And I won't let you treat me like it either."

Edy blinked. "I didn't know you think I'm pretty."

"It's beside the point."

Wyatt worked the fork back and forth, wedging it from its burrow deep in his burger. "You know, the next time you want to use me for retribution, or jealousy, or whatever game you and Hassan happen to be playing, find someone else."

He was right, of course, absolutely right. She'd been self absorbed, short sighted, thoughtless. As usual, her brain had snagged, unable to get past thoughts of Hassan. But there'd been something else. Something far less innocent. She'd asked him to be her date not because she'd wanted his company, but because he was an outsider, *an other*, a sure way to rattle them.

She'd used him. She'd used her friend.

Edy could scarcely recognize her own thoughts these days, choked in anger, drowning in jealousy and desire. Whatever she wanted with Hassan, whatever existed between them, gave her no excuse for treating people like crap. She had to do better. She would do better, and she'd start with Wyatt. Edy reached a hand across the table and took a deep breath.

"I'm sorry," she said. "Will you please give me another chance?"

He looked up as if surprised.

"Always," Wyatt breathed. "Always."

~~~

Edy's father spent two and a half weeks in Egypt before returning to the states. The first forty-eight hours of his time in the U.S. were spent in D.C., debriefing the feds on conditions in Cairo, Alexandria, El Mansoura, and elsewhere. He arrived in Boston in the manner he departed, by way of a single black sedan and overwhelming silence. Edy and the Pradhans met him at the front yard on arrival, snow crunching underfoot in their rush to meet him. Another legal case kept Edy's mother away.

Sallow eyes, sunken cheeks, shirt flapping in the wind, Edy's father looked rung out and haggard, as if Egypt had banned proper eating and sleep as easy as they did free press.

Edy clung to her dad all the way to the front porch. She had so much to tell him, about how the party went and Ali's dress disaster, and how on attending ballet practice the previous day, she'd been pegged for a part in *The Nutcracker* with the company. Each year, the Boston Ballet chose the best among their students to perform alongside the professionals for one of their biggest shows. Last year, Edy had been the youngest ever selected. This year, with even stiffer competition, she had made the ranks again.

"Daddy—"

Her father glanced over his shoulder, searching, impatient, even though he'd just arrived. It wasn't until Ali showed up that he deflated visibly.

"Did you want to rest, or . . . "

"Only a shower," her father said. "Then we have to get to work."

Edy's father trotted up their abbreviated staircase and stopped at the front door, flanked on either side by her and Ali. For some reason, Rani and Hassan hung back near the fence.

"You're about to work?" Edy blurted.

If anyone had heard her, they didn't let on.

"But our predictions were not so far off, were they?" Ali said. Concern twisted his face.

Edy's father placed a hand on the doorknob and turned. "That's just it," he said. "They were exacting. As precise as a scientific calculation. The timeline of government collapse, the uprising of the people, the bloody social protests. Our estimation of how influential the world's instantaneous technology would be—Internet, cell phones, social networking—became eerily uncanny. And they had no idea you were so involved in the research. They would have insisted on your presence, too."

Ali sputtered, cheeks reddening as if he were an old lady fielding flirtations from a man half her age.

"Oh no, it was an obvious outcome considering all of the variables," Ali said. He dragged fingers back and forth across his forehead, as he always did when weighing a thousand different thoughts. "Vast income inequalities, gross human rights violations, a mimicry of autocratic rule—"

Hassan appeared on the porch with them. "Edy—" he said.

"Yes. Except *we* alone predicted it, my friend," Edy's father said. "Anyway, we'll discuss my observations as soon as I shower, so we can incorporate them into the social movement theory."

"Dad? Tell me you're not about to work. You just got here," Edy said.

Her father squinted at her as if he surprised and disappointed by her lack of decorum.

He turned back to Ali. "Allow me time to freshen up before we meet in my study."

"Agreed," Ali said.

A hand found the small of Edy's back, discreet under the conservative eye of Hassan's parents.

"Come on," Hassan said. "We'll hound them later."

She shot him an impatient look. Yes, she knew how they could be about work. Political science was the topic of discussion too many nights a week at dinner. But his father hadn't been the one gone, the one dangling in the mouth of danger with little more than a pen and textbook to protect him. He hadn't celebrated his birthday without his dad, or Thanksgiving for that matter. She opened her mouth to tell him that and found the words dissolved on her tongue, a lie never meant to be uttered.

He was as close to her father as her, more so in some ways.

Rani stepped up to them and Hassan's hand fell away, smooth. While his father had been radically Americanized and prided himself on progressive thinking, his mother still fretted over the old ways and appearances and took to sweating anytime they were within three feet of each other.

Like now.

"Come over to the house and help me prepare dinner," Rani said and dropped a critical eye to the hand that dangled at Hassan's side. "Afterward, the three of us can play Scrabble."

Edy shot Hassan a look. He was notoriously sucky at Scrabble, known for hopping languages and creating portmanteaus as a matter of convenience. "You have to play right," she warned, already warming to the idea. Cold weather and the smell of Indian spices, an afternoon with Hassan and the fireplace ablaze. Truth told, he could play wrong, and she wouldn't mind much.

"You really should expand your vocabulary before you criticize me," he said, and headed straight down the walkway.

"Simpleton," he mumbled and broke into a run, knowing she'd chase him for the insult.

Edy took off. They sliced her yard in two and hopped the fence that separated their homes, first he, then she, before dashing for the front door, with Rani shouting after them that they needed to act sensibly.

Ten

Time went on, as it had the tendency to do. In temperamental Boston, weather held to no reason. Cold then mild, frigid then gruesome. Edy, in an effort to find balance, in an effort to find a semblance of her old life, concentrated on easygoing evenness. She permitted herself no more lingering stares at Hassan, no more indulgent thoughts hidden under cover of solitude. He was her friend, and she had known long before these wayward feelings emerged, that the future held no more. Old traditions, old ways more powerful than them both meant destiny had eked out paths determinedly separate for them both. It meant that she would watch him grow, love and be happy with another girl, and if she couldn't bear that, then she couldn't bear to have him in her life. But there had never been an Edy without Hassan, never a Hassan without an Edy. She would permit no one to take that from them, not even her.

Like Edy, Hassan fell into his old tiresome self. First at her house for breakfast, he raided the fridge, holed away with her dad to talk football, and blitzed her with pillows if she took her time getting up in the morning. Awkwardness melted away between them, until nothing but old familiarity seemed to remain. He had his new friends—football friends, cheerleading friends, and Edy turned to more time with Wyatt. Wyatt kept her sane and busy when homework and ballet couldn't do the job. He demanded little from her, and on the days when she had only cursory attention and her own uncooperative thoughts, he contented himself filling the silence for them both. Holidays and football marched by this way, hand in hand through Christmas, through winter. South End claimed their first state championship with Edy on the sidelines screaming as a bundled up Wyatt moved brisk to keep warm. Six touchdowns and a new record for most yards transformed Hassan from legend to god in a single year.

Spring thaw swept through, like the opening of rose petals when blooming, like the sweet scent of showers on a warm May day. Fist beneath her chin, Edy stared out the window of her AP English class, mesmerized by the patter of rain. She imagined herself in a field bursting with orchids, bathing in sunlight. Eyes closed, body expressive, she'd be in tune with the pulse of the earth, with the machinations of her heart, as she danced for an audience of one.

A wad of notebook paper battered the back of Edy's head. She whirled to see Mason straightening his powdered wig, a wig borrowed from Edy's father.

"We've been practicing our speech," Matt said. He cleared his throat. "'Tis *freedom* we seek."

"Drop the mic," Mason suggested.

Edy snapped forward again amidst a room full of snickers. A fair assumption would have been to think they had an allegiance to her, or at the very least, that their need to protect her would extend to protection of her pride. Definitely, not the case. Even though Edy's father had expressed his reluctance at having to miss the annual history program because of pressing commitments elsewhere, it didn't stop everyone— especially the twins—from having a laugh or twenty at his expense. Cue the day of the event and her father's noticeable absence. Cue the twins arriving at school, dressed as her father, with one having gone so far as to borrow his wig.

A spitball caught her in the ear, jerking Edy from her scowling. It had come from the seat right next to her. Edy dug it out and careened to face Hassan, the culprit. Before she could open her mouth with something foul, he puckered up as if to kiss her. The smile crept to Edy's lips without her permission. Delayed, she chucked the offending item back. He caught it without looking.

"Show off," she mouthed.

She had planned this time to puzzle over the machinations of appearance and reality in Shakespeare's *Macbeth*. But as Edy shared too much time with a boy who occupied too many of her waking thoughts—and all of her sleeping ones—she needn't a primer on artful deception.

A lot had changed since the birthday party, and yet nothing had changed at all. She was still Edy and he Hassan, two friends and nothing more, even while the girls around him had tripled. Unlike before, Hassan returned their indulgent stares and flirted when they flirted. He made dates and ventured out, while Edy's time with Wyatt had tripled. Star gazing appeared to be his favorite thing.

Not long after the New Year's, Edy auditioned for a spot with the nation's most prestigious summer intensive in ballet. While her initial motivation had been the honor of admittance, each passing day near Hassan brought another wish, that of distance and an ease to her hurt. Only in the shadows of her bedroom did the wounds of the day set in, anguish from another round of heartbreak. Edy imagined that a summer apart would do her good, giving her a chance to get over her friend in what would be their longest separation ever. After all, only she knew the strain of a fictitious smile during the day, book ended by weeping through the night. Perhaps her love of dance could heal that with effort.

Even before the letter arrived, Edy knew she would be accepted to the School of American Ballet, an appendage of the New York City Ballet. She was simply that good. In order for her to attend, Edy and Hassan's mother would spend the summer in New York, living with Rani's sister. Ali and Edy's father would be touring Europe and the U.S. most of the season, anyway, as they were in impossible demand following the release of their new book on the politics of social unrest. Hassan would summer at the Dysons' when the boys weren't touring football camps, and Edy would separate herself from him, as best, and completely as she could.

Summer arrived, and with it, Wyatt's lip trembling tantrum about her going away. While it would have been nice to see Hassan pitch a fit, Edy set off on the four-hour trek to New York with a pinch of redemption. Hassan's mother made for a meandering sort of driver, insisting on pit stops along the way, and Edy found herself peeking at her phone for messages from Hassan only to find it flooded with fractured complaints from Wyatt instead.

They got to New York eventually. Ijay and Kala Gupta lived on the twenty-fifth floor of a gleaming, window-laden high rise overlooking Central Park West. Their bellman, clad in a starched crimson coat and black slacks, tipped his gold-lined cap and greeted Rani by name. "Ted" he said simply with a tap of his badge, before taking both Edy's luggage and Rani's and leading the way up.

Rani's sister, Kala, answered the door. She wore a silk cream blouse that tied at the hip and smart brown slacks, looking every bit the polished Manhattan wife and socialite. Kala grinned perfect white teeth before embracing her sister, skin deep pecan to Rani's butter cream, sharp angles against curves. Not a hair ran out of sync with Kala's tight pin-up, not an off-putting color, nothing overdone, as always her make-up complimented, coolly. Perfection had always been her mantra.

She fussed over Edy and remarked on how much she'd grown before holding her out at arm's length for a good look. Two years, she proclaimed, and Edy would be all the rage. One, if she had a growth spurt.

Yeah. Whatever.

Kala led them inside, albeit hesitantly, fingernails picking at each other suddenly.

The condo remained as Edy remembered it: open-air with big floor-to-ceiling windows that drenched everything in sunlight on a good day. A view of Central Park, Central Park Lake, and a dazzling Manhattan skyline swept them in a panoramic arc from where she stood.

New York, Edy thought with an exhale. Just the place to rejuvenate, renew, and morph into something spectacular. Just the place to meet a million Hassans or forget he existed altogether.

"Edy?" Kala said. "You remember Ronsher, don't you? He'll be here, too."

Ronsher was the son of Rani and Kala's older brother. Edy turned to face him, and not for the first time, was struck by how much he looked like his cousin Hassan. New York, Edy thought, *would* have been the perfect place to forget Hassan, were it not for Hassan's duplicate parked alongside her for the summer.

Only, Ronsher wasn't Hassan's duplicate anymore. He'd staked a claim on a look all his own, a look he needn't worry about his cousin borrowing any time soon.

A full foot taller than the last time they'd met, Ronsher, or Ronnie Bean, was a lean and golden boy aptly named by the twins for his likeness to a beanstalk. He had the smile of Hassan and the glimmer of his eyes, but oh, was he different from what she remembered.

What had once been thick and healthy black hair fell into his eyes in fat chunks of midnight and chestnut. He wore an ocean of eyeliner, had both ears pierced, and his black tee fit vice-tight. Neon letters screamed "Groove, Slam, Move," across his ribcage as his listless eyes roved from Kala, Edy, to the ceiling. "Emo tragedy" were the words that came to mind.

"Hey Ronnie Bean," Edy said, unable to look away from him, even at the risk of rudeness.

"Just Ronnie," he amended with a great sigh.

It was harder to see Hassan under all that, *in that,* but Hassan was still there, in the broadness of the shoulders and the shape of the face, in the mouth that seemed almost identical.

Edy moved to hug Ronnie Bean, then stopped at the look he gave her.

"So, you're here for the summer, too?" she said, falling back into awkwardness.

"More like forever." Bean shouldered her as he passed and made for the hall, dismissing her in jeans so skinny Edy could make out the curve of his ass.

"I hope you'll change your clothing and your attitude while here!" Rani yelled in Punjabi before the door slammed soundly behind Bean.

Edy looked wide-eyed and at the women, knowing their tolerance for American tantrums to be nil. But Kala merely exhaled.

Ronnie Bean had spent summers in Boston. Over time, he'd become one of them, welcomed. He was Edy's friend. Her good friend. Or rather, he had been.

"Ronsher moved in six months ago," Kala said. "I'm not sure how long he'll be here."

Edy remembered Bean's dad, a civil engineer for the U.S. Army with little patience and exacting standards. It seemed impossible that the Ronnie Bean before Edy could be produced by such a rigid man. Obsessed with propriety and beholden to the old ways,

Bean's father held honor and decency, as defined by him, in the highest regard. In short, there could be no end to the ways Bean could have offended his sensibilities, even if he weren't standing before Edy looking like the Indian premiere of MTV.

The following morning, Edy rose early, showered, dressed, and found messages from both Hassan and Wyatt. She gave Wyatt a quick, cursory greeting, but paused long enough to give Hassan the lowdown on Bean. What was he doing in NYC, and why was he suddenly an asshole? When no answer came quickly, Edy rushed to breakfast, gobbled her food, and got ready for the fifteen-minute walk to SAB, the School of American Ballet. On her way out, Edy discovered that Ronnie Bean had been thrust upon her, unwilling escort that he was. He wore the t-shirt and jeans from the day before and pretended not to hear Rani's snort of disgust.

Four blocks into their walk, Bean broke the silence.

"I don't care what you think of me, you know. You or anyone else." He splashed black puddles, mucking the hem of Edy's pants as they went.

She glanced at him. "Okay."

"And I had stuff to do, you know. *Other* than walk the baby to school."

"Then go!" Edy said and cut a sharp left to avoid his splash. "Now stop before I shove you face first in the dirt."

Bean slowed as something like a smile played at the corner of his lips. But as quickly as it arrived, it departed. "Whatever," he said. "And the minute I turn my back, the Central Park rapist pops your cherry and dumps you in the Hudson."

"There's a rapist on the loose?" Edy looked over her shoulder, just in case.

Bean sighed. "Edy Phelps, the Boston bumpkin."

On the next block, he pulled her into a deli and ordered two oversized bagels weighted with lox, tomatoes, capers, onions, and cream cheese. Edy glanced behind them at the door, wondering what would happen if she were late on her first day to the world's most rigorous ballet intensive.

"I die for these things," Bean admitted and tore into one ferociously.

Edy sniffed the fish suspiciously. "I can't imagine why." Her stomach twisted in a merciless vice, earning a grimace from Edy. Bean shot her a quizzical look just as her cell phone vibrated. Edy looked down to find a message from Hassan.

Go easy on Bean, he wrote.

Nothing more.

~~~

For two weeks, Edy's schedule never deviated. Pointe, variations, adagio, ballroom dancing, and character classes, all of it arduous enough to bend bone and crack the back. Despite Edy's vow to put distance between her and Hassan, they exchanged texts each morning and again at night—sometimes all night—and sometimes long enough to line the bookshelves of the world's best scholar. Her texts with Wyatt were frequent more so than long, with him checking in after this class and that one to see how it went and what was happening next. She came to expect and receive his irritation each day, since she only answered his messages at night.

Something was happening with Bean, something that Edy had noticed almost immediately. Though he bellyached about walking her to class and missing out on much-needed sleep each day, he never went home, or even in the direction of home, on leaving her at SAB in the morning. After two weeks of his charade, Edy's mind had run through a whole mountain of possibilities, from Bean getting hooked on some vicious synthetic drug and meeting up with his dealer for a daily fix, to a secret girlfriend of another race. By the time she got up the will to ask him, she'd decided that a girlfriend might be the explanation.

They were back at his deli, him with his bagel, Edy with a safe and rather mild fruit smoothie when she decided to broach it.

"What's her name?" Edy said and took a sip of her drink. She regretted not ordering tea or some other warm beverage. Though the day's weather mimicked a sauna, she told herself the heat would help her near-constant stomachaches.

"Whose?" Bean asked around a mouth full of salmon and cream cheese.

"Your girlfriend. She must be white with all the trouble you're going to." She took in his red shorts, Jordans, and baggy tee before considering. "Or from the hood."

Bean arched a brow. "Girlfriend?" He slung the word back at her, simpering.

"When you leave me at SAB," Edy rushed ahead all the while wanting her words back. "You walk in the opposite direction from home."

"So? I get on the subway."

"And go where?"

Bean snatched her smoothie for a loud, indulgent slurp. He handed the cup back bottomed out.

"Catch you in the p.m.," Bean said and disappeared, insistent on the wrong direction.

The next morning, Edy woke Bean early and told him she needed to be at SAB by eight instead of nine. He grunted and cussed, emerging from bed in the red shorts and "Goin Nowhere" tee from the day before. Bean showered and left his Sonic the Hedgehog spikes damp so that they hung like well-placed highlights accentuating a classically handsome face. The two skipped out on breakfast and headed for the deli, offending both Kala and Rani that morning.

"Let's sit and eat," Bean suggested after ordering.

Edy hesitated. "I have to go in early."

"Two orders of bagels and lox for here," he said and held up a finger to shush Edy's protest. "You're not fat, even if you ballerinas are obsessed with being grotesquely thin."

"We are not!"

"And you don't have to be in early, either," Bean said. "So humor me as if I'm Hassan."

Orders in hand, they took a cramped table in the corner at the back. Edy stared at the bagel Bean had ordered for her, wondering how she could get out of eating it and have strength enough for the day.

"Hassan called me," he said.

She looked up. It made no sense to be surprised, and yet she was.

"Called?" Edy said with forced indifference. "Oh really? About what?"

Bean studied her. "I talk to him every day. Suddenly."

Edy had no idea what to say.

Bean took a gargantuan bite of out his bagel. "You guys are tighter than ever these days. "I assume that's who you're gabbing with when your phone's buzzing all night."

Edy's gaze dropped to her food. Suddenly, gnawing on fish and bagels seemed a damned sight more appetizing than continuing her talk with Bean. Better that than explaining how Hassan was only half her nighttime equation. Better to eat crap smelling fish than explain her odd conversations with Wyatt, conversations where she attempted to convince him she hadn't been gone *that* long and her absence really shouldn't affect his mood so.

"I meet friends on the Lower East Side," Bean said. "After I drop you off each day."

"And?"

"And we dance."

Edy's gaze dropped to his body, and she saw him, really saw him for the first time. Lean, muscular, controlled movements. Hassan had a dancer in the family.

"I'd like to say dancing was what sent my *pitā* over the edge, but really it was his total repulsion with me."

He took another bite of his bagel, appetite unsoiled by his father's rejection.

"Repulsion?" Edy said.

Bean shoved the last of the bagel into his mouth and began to wrap Edy's in napkins.

"Come on. Eat it on the walk. Talking time is over."

Eleven

Roland Green opened the door and sighed at the sight before him.

"You," he said and turned his bottle of Heineken up, swallowing until it emptied.

"Just let me in," Sandra Jacobs snapped.

Her uncle made a sweeping bow and nearly pitched, before righting himself with a quick snatch of the doorknob.

"Right this way, your highness."

Except he went only as far as the shadow swallowed living room before collapsing in his arm chair. A litter of green beer bottles chinked at his feet.

"Well, where is he?" Sandra snapped. She shoved a lock of hair behind her ear and cautioned a glance upward. She wore the look of a girl who expected the ceiling to cave post haste.

Roland Green rummaged through the pile of bottles on the floor, found an unopened one and rid it of its condition.

"Not dark enough for you to be over here, yet," Roland said. He took an indulgent swig of beer. "Can't have anyone seeing you and figuring out you're white trash, too."

"I am not white trash," Sandra spat, trembling with the declaration.

Roland laughed. A hearty, choking, belly aching guffaw that had him swigging beer after to quench his thirst. "Your cousin's upstairs eating his Banquet dinner. Grab one out the freezer if you're hungry."

Sandra stomped up the stairs, only to slow at each creaking groan it earned her instead. The house did look fragile. A few kicks to the wall might topple it.

The dust and darkness overwhelmed her. Up the staircase and a turn right had Sandra easing down a thin hallway. She could run a hand down either wall as she walked. With her heels on, she could touch the ceiling.

Though she knew a string dangled from above somewhere along the way, she didn't bother with the absurd swipes necessary to find it. Already, she knew this corridor, knew the way the floor warped. Sandra eased down until she found the right door and threw it open.

Wyatt didn't look up from his furious scribbling. Seated at a peeling white desk in a plastic folding chair, he worked to fill in the last details of Edy—shadowing in her hair, touching up a subtle smile, easing in curving hips, or whatever. Sandra had seen enough of them not to bother with looking.

"Lottie's home," Sandra said.

That earned a pause of his pencil. Then he started back in, furious.

"She asked about you."

Wyatt's pencil snapped. "Asked who?" he said.

"Only her sister. That's who told me."

Wyatt opened his desk drawer and lined the broken pieces in with an assortment of others. Before he could reach for a fresh one, she put a hand over his.

"I'm sorry I accused you," she said.

Wyatt said nothing, breathing steady, labored.

Quietly, he removed her hand from his arm and retrieved another pencil.

~~~

With the drapes to Edy's window open and the moon shimmering on the shores of the Hudson, Edy lay on her back, legs wide, flats of her feet touching and tucked to touch her bottom. The *Supta Badda Konasana* was a hip relaxing yoga pose she'd learned two years ago in India. Edy held it with ease for sixty slow breaths before releasing, hoping that the stretch and meditation would help with the stomach cramps. She flipped into a smooth headstand and held it, counts and breaths steady till the phone interrupted.

"Hassan," she said, the second she answered. "Tell me how it was."

"It" was a football camp sponsored by running back Earl Rush.

"Oh." Hassan breathed, enraptured. "Crazy intense. And hands on. I even got some guidance from the man himself."

"You didn't."

"I did."

"He called me a show stopper. Said he would keep out an eye for me."

Edy threw her head back and squealed. She shimmied a little too.

"How's ballet?" he finally said.

"Good. Hard, but good."

The silence between them turned heavy.

"Are you staying the whole summer? Seems weird, having you gone this long."

Weird. Interesting choice of a word. Detached, too.

"Yeah," Edy said. "Well, I didn't think you cared all that much."

They held the phone for awhile.

"You've been on my mind," Hassan said and all the air sailed out the window.

She didn't trust herself to say anything sensible, anything safe, so Edy hunched forward and gnawed on a fingernail.

Hassan sighed. "I'd better go."

"Oh."

Oxygen slammed back into her, finally, but the rhythm and ease of breathing had yet to return.

"Call me tomorrow," Hassan said. "But don't tell me what time. Just . . . surprise me."

"If you want."

"I want." He paused. "Night, Cake. Love you."

"Love you too, Hassan."

Edy felt the distinction between his absentminded declaration of love and the unequivocal devotion in hers. Her belly flamed hot in response. Just as she hung up, it was in time to see Ronnie Bean standing in the door, smile unmistakable. He let out a low whistle, tilted the brim of an imaginary cowboy hat and turned on his heel.

Gone, Edy thought. But silent for how long? Sleep eluded Edy, leaving her to toss and turn and wrestle comforters on a cool summer night. 'I love yous' played in her mind like a misfit melody, taunting her, mocking.

She hadn't thought she'd slept at all. Yet Edy woke to a tangle of melded sheets plastered to her thighs, bottoms, and back. She sat up slow, brain fogged and baffled by the contradiction of sweat and cold air. She didn't *feel* feverish. And yet . . . Edy peeled back the quilted white comforter and gasped. Blood stained bedding and body, saturated down to the mattress in a massive arc. Edy scrambled from the bed, feet tangling, pedaling sheets to the floor in her panic to be free. And her mess only spread. Why hadn't all the books she read warned her about how *repulsive* menstruation would be?

On her feet, Edy twisted to glimpse the backside of her nightgown. She'd been stabbed in the back a thousand times, butchered by a maniac, it seemed. *Think.* Of all the girls on the planet, she had to be the most prepared. So, what should she do?

Rani was forty-five and may or may not have entered menopause. Kala was younger at forty-two but childless. Had Edy heard something about Kala not being able to have children? Would that mean she did or didn't have periods? She felt insensitive and ignorant for wondering.

A gush of something sickly sloshed down her leg, and Edy scampered. Down the hall, stomach lurching, as she shouted Rani's name. Edy banged on her door, rattled it in impatience and willed her to hurry up and help. New York or Boston, one house or the other, in crisis, Rani was the one she needed.

Rani emerged, bleary eyed and yawning.

"What's wrong?"

With a morbid whimper, Edy spun round to show the fast spreading red on her backside. Rani gasped, bloodshot eyes sprung wide.

"This is what we've been waiting for! Your womanhood has arrived!"

Edy glanced down the hall, half expecting Bean to pop out and see some of her "womanhood."

"Help me!" she hissed. "*Do* something."

"Come."

Rani grabbed her by the arm and pulled her toward the guest bathroom. She shoved Edy inside, flipped on the light and crowded in with her.

She worked diligently, quietly, taking the time to explain to Edy things that her mother should have. How to clean her clothes, how to combat her bellyaches, how to cope with a tender and sprouting body.

As Edy showered, Rani brewed tea and straightened up. After, the two returned to her room, where they sprawled on her bed whispering about her family half the night. Bean's father, her brother-in-law, had ejected him from the house and disowned his only son. No one knew why. Given that boys were revered in their culture, it seemed an extreme thing to do. Had Bean pushed him so far? Edy couldn't help but wonder.

"He's changed," Rani said in Punjabi. *"You can see that for yourself."*

"We're all changing," Edy said. *"Look at what just happened to me."*

Rani, whose eyelids had been fluttering, went wide awake at her words. She studied Edy's face with unguarded curiosity.

"You are becoming a woman," she said. *"This is as it should be."*

"If becoming a woman means having the Incredible Hulk's temper and agonizing cramps, then yeah, I've accepted the womanhood challenge wholeheartedly."

Rani smiled.

"Is there a boy?" she said.

Horror sliced her to the gut. Edy tripped over a swallow, then another, as her brain flung contrary commands to her mouth. Say something. Say nothing. The wide eyed fright that swept her face was a horror in itself. Rani absorbed it, face unreadable. Finally, Edy found control.

"There's no boy," she said, aware that she'd already blown it.

Rani appeared to comb her thoughts, sorting through each one before deciding to speak. *"What about Wyatt Green? Do you like him?"*

Edy laughed. Leave it to an adult to steer right off the map. *"He's a friend. If that changed Hassan would—"*

Hassan. Jesus Christ.

Rani sat up, and again, she took care in studying Edy. *"Your romantic interest can be of no concern to Hassan. His bride has been selected for him since birth."*

Edy flinched. *"I know that."*

A sting set in her eyes. Tears, she supposed. She willed them away with gritted teeth and sniffed as an old memory came to her. Edy recalled a trip to India. She and Hassan had been nine at the time and pissed about most everything—heat, traffic, the absence of cartoons, and the amount of time it took to get to Chandigarh where Rani's family lived. Like always, the warmest, rowdiest reception swallowed Edy there: the feeling of home jumping up thrilled on the opposite side of the globe, of hugs and kisses set to smother, of love kicked into overdrive. They knew her in Delhi, Ali's home, and in Chandigarh, Rani's, and in little villages where cousins dotted the way. Maybe they all knew her a little too well.

"*Tomorrow, Hassan meets the girl that will be his bride,*" Rani had explained back then, with nails digging Edy's shoulder. "*And she's not you.*"

She'd cut to kill. Like a double edged serrated sword, dragged throat to stomach and twisted back again. Maximum damage inflicted.

Edy hadn't bothered to hide the tears when they came. She let them roll like only a child could, mopping hot drops with the hem of her dress until Rani drew her in and there there'd her. She'd shushed Edy with whispered promises of eternal friendship and devotion and even then, even then, Edy's heart whispered *more*.

Through beaded curtains she'd glimpsed Mala Bathlar, Hassan's future wife. A slight and trembling thing who looked like she couldn't kick a ball, or climb a tree, or skate forward, let alone back. She certainly didn't seem as formidable as she ought to have been. And Edy wondered did the girl even own a bike? As soon as she had the thought, the two were whisked away for supervised alone time.

It lasted three minutes.

A flood of shouting adults returned with Hassan at the helm. Edy had howled before tearing after him. He'd burst out a side door with her on his heels and them on *her* heels. They'd run and run, rounding corners until they'd lost the adults. It hadn't taken long at all.

"No way," he'd said to her. "I cursed them and said I'll never marry her."

Rani's mask of steel said she remembered their trip to India, that she remembered Mala Bathlar and Edy's tears about the girl, and she remembered Hassan's foul-mouthed vow to forever disobey his parents.

"I understand you love him," Rani said.

And the words snatched at Edy's heart with iced fingers. When she opened her mouth to protest, Hassan's mother silenced her with a hand.

"I'm not Rebecca," she said. *"Nor your father, where you can tuck into corners and dip into shadows unseen."* She tilted Edy's chin upward, forcing their eyes to meet. She had Hassan's same gold flecked green eyes. Hassan, minus the warmth in that instance. *"There is no hiding your heart from me. I know you love him. But your feelings don't matter. Accept that he'll never be yours."*

She dropped Edy's face and sat back, as if expecting the tears to come, as if expecting an encore performance from the nine-year-old who needed comfort.

Edy's eyes stayed dry and her mouth kept closed. She didn't have Hassan's heart steady as a promise, but sometimes, sometimes she sensed it, sometimes she felt it. But God, anytime that thought seeped into her mind she couldn't help but question it. Could it even be true? Or was it blatant hope soaring out on the wings of trouble? Hell, his mother thought so.

But so what if she did? And what if Hassan did feel something for her? What then?

"You are young still," Rani said *"Feelings are fluid. What appears certain will succumb to the passing of time. Do you understand, my love?"*

Except this—them—Hassan and Edy—had never felt lax, fluid, changeable. The earliest bastions of happiness placed them side by side, hand in hand, shoulder to shoulder, growing through the years together. Her mantel and his overflowed with pictures of the two in diapers, in need of front teeth, in dozens of countries, and as time passed, with them curling one toward the other.

She could think about that, of course. That and the endless nights he spent in her bed, plus the hugs, and forehead kisses. She could tell herself they meant something, possibly everything. But she knew better than to put her heart through a gamble with the deck stacked against her.

Edith, we must all do what is best for the family. As you grow up, you will discover that sacrifices for the people you love are common, even desirable.

Whatever.

Her stomach cramped again. With the relief of a hot towel on her mind, she got up, gave Rani the obligatory kiss on her cheek to let her know there were no hard feelings between them, and headed straight for the bathroom.

She collided with Ronnie Bean in the hall.

He was fully dressed. Hand on the doorknob across from Rani's room, Bean froze, white stick of a lollipop jutting from the corner of his mouth.

Edy folded her arms. Caught.

"Better me than your aunts," she said.

Bean exhaled. "What'll it cost?"

Edy smirked. "I want to go with you. Wherever it is that you dance."

"Be serious. I—"

Kala coughed in the next room.

"Agree or I scream."

"Dang it, Edy. You're so lame. I don't want to bring you with me."

"That's funny," Edy said. "'Cause I don't remember giving you a choice."

Edy didn't expect her opportunity to come so fast. But that next Monday night, Bean cracked open her bedroom door.

"We leave in an hour."

He gave no word on whether she needed money or how to dress. So, Edy rose, pulled on blue jeans and a

Harvard tee, grabbed a ten-dollar bill, and stood in the hall until Ronnie Bean met her.

"Obvious much?"

He flipped off the hall light, grabbed her by the wrist, and pulled her, yanked her to the front door. They were out so fast. Together, they rushed away.

Bean slipped the doorman a five, and they headed for the subway at Eighty-First Street. B toward Brighton Beach, a transfer at West Fourth, then the F toward Stillwell. It wasn't till Bean asked her if she was keeping a log that Edy realized she'd been studying the time.

"I've never been out so late," she admitted.

"You asked to come. No regrets now," Bean said. He scowled at her Harvard tee and turned away, annoyance jerking his features.

At East Broadway, they exited and walked two blocks on before they joined a queue of jean-clad teens on a trash-strewn sidewalk.

They entered Epic, a suffocating, peeling black box of a nightclub. The sort that prided itself on violated fire codes and poor ventilation, Edy presumed. Packed body to body with sweat-covered adolescents, Epic itself pulsed and strobed to the beat. People didn't dance so much as sway, in limbo.

"Give it a minute," Bean said, "and you'll see what you've been missing."

Wild bass pumped, then froze. A single note pierced the air, then another. The crowd shrieked their approval. A vamped and lusty voice of first one woman, then another, echoed and overlapped.

It happened fast.

A black guy, short and compact, popped onto the floor like a jack out the box. He cavorted to the center, feet gliding, torso snapping, head swiveling in a jerking burst of art. Edy tossed Bean a look of disbelief. Was this what he meant by dancing?

When Edy was ten, her mother caught her watching *Krush Groove* and banished her from the room, promising her that disjointed jerking would lead to a thrice-broken neck. But this boy looked fine. Better than fine, in fact, and Edy pulled Bean in for a closer squint.

"Explain it to me," she said, drinking in every flicker of motion, every flinch of muscle, making parallels to classical form when she could. *"Tell me what he's doing. Tell me why he's doing it."*

"Old school purists call it b-boying," Bean said, ignoring her Punjabi for English. "But you probably know it as breakdancing."

She'd seen breakdancing before, and never had it seemed so curiously frantic, so inexplicably enormous. Never had it volleyed such a crash of emotions, forcing her inward instead of out. What a contrary shock of beautiful ugliness buried beneath the tender parts. Classical dance breathed technique and execution, but this . . .this wanted identity.

She stepped closer, drawn like a child uncertain she'd be permitted to play.

The pit's new b-boy surveyed his crowd with a face-wide smirk, tilted his hat, and mocked the music's snare with a flurry of amped up steps, ultra heavy on the bravado. Cheap strobe lights from a corner illuminated the sharpest of features: a witch-like nose that hooked at the tip and barely there lips that disappeared as the lights sought out a contender. B-boy taunted them for a competitor, beckoning with fingers and booing.

Bean slipped from Edy's grasp and leapt in, spat back the boy's moves triple fast and in reverse, and bowed for the pleasure of his company.

Edy glanced at her shoulder to double check if Bean still stood there.

He didn't.

Bitter, frantic jerks, ensued—first Bean, then the other guy—isolated pops and snaps, followed by disturbing, joint flexing contortions of the body. Edy pushed closer for an examination of their technique, until an Asian chick shoved her back rough and laughed at her Harvard shirt. Slides, glides, mocks of gravity pursued—Edy knew these tricks and yet didn't know them at all, she'd done them and yet never had. It was foreign, familiar.

This *was* ballet, she told herself. But how could it be? No training commenced here. Flourishing and controlled, balanced and bursting, fluid and fire. Ballet, as polluted by life. This was freedom, dance without dictation. While she loved the sculpted beauty and control of classical ballet—this—*this* was life as life came: sudden, rearranged, burned down, and hurled back up.

Life on her terms, whole, bold and unapologetic.

She wanted that.

"Teach me," Edy said the moment Bean returned.

He snorted and looked past her to the dancers.

She stepped in front of him, nose to nose, close enough to kiss.

"I need this, Bean. Please. Teach me."

He looked at her as if trying to determine what she was and when she'd become it.

"First, speak English," Bean said. "We're not back with the villagers. Second, and more importantly, b-boying, krump dancing, it's about anger, frustration, rage—raging *back*. It can't get you into Harvard. It can't get you into City Ballet. It won't get you the family's approval."

They turned back to the pit. This time, a pair of stick figure blondes in baggy jeans and oversized tops whipped and cavorted, both spastic and graceful at once.

"I don't care about their approval," Edy said. "I want to do something for me."

Bean looked at her as if she were the new toy everyone had been raging about.

"Well, well," he said. "You just got interesting."

"Bean—"

He slipped into the crowd before she could say more. Halfway to somewhere, Bean stopped by a rakish blond guy with a neck half as long as his arm. A conversation ensued, maybe even an argument, before the two melted into darkness together.

Three renditions of an 80s hip hop remix later, and Edy's bladder pressed to her belt. She could stay rooted no longer. Maneuvering through stacks of sweaty teens, she kept her gaze trained for a glimpse of Bean as she made her way to the back. Edy found the bathroom near a cushioned bench no one dared use. A turn of the knob and a fruitless shove later had her noticing the out-of-order sign on the girl's bathroom door. Great. Not only couldn't she find Ronnie Bean, but even if she did and they left that moment, she'd pee her pants long before home.

After a surreptitious glance around, she jammed a shoulder in the men's bathroom door. It swung open, and the pungent musk of urine waved hello. The imminent threat of wetting her pants pushed her forward, but her gag reflex revolted nonetheless. Sideways, Edy sidled, heart thumping, as she suppressed an irrational fear of her high school principal snatching her from the stall with her pants down.

Edy grabbed a toilet toward the back, where she could wait and listen should someone join her. Quickly, she snatched down her jeans and hovered over. Never had she been one to sit on a public toilet; she certainly wouldn't start in a pee-stained nightclub.

In the stall across from her, someone exhaled. A groan followed, then a squeak of rubber on linoleum. It wouldn't have been so bad had she not been in a men's restroom. Maybe her heart wouldn't have tried to leave her body in a pitch of fright. Whatever the reason, Edy cut short her peeing, wiped, flushed and yanked her pants up. She wanted out of there. She wanted away from whatever was making that *sound.*

Another groan.

Edy burst out of her stall and hurried to wash her hands. A slip in a puddle of liquid brought her down hard, chin to floor in a head-jarring slam. A burst of pain swallowed Edy's head, ricocheting in blind, unforgiving waves. The stench of urine filled her nose as Edy's vision became one white blur. She rolled onto her back with a whimper as the stall next to hers opened.

Two bodies stepped out.

"Edy. Can I not take you anywhere?" Ronnie Bean asked, sounding resigned.

"She looks hurt," the second boy said. "What do you want me to do?"

Bean sighed. "Help me get her off the floor. I have no idea how to explain this."

~~~

"So, obviously now you know," Ronnie Bean said as they emerged from the subway station. On the horizon, the first rays of sunlight peeked out through early morning haze.

Bean shot Edy a look of loathing just as the last of the roast beef from Nick's All Night Deli slid from her cheek and hit the sidewalk. Whatever. It had warmed too much to be useful anyway.

Edy had already made up her mind that Bean's business was Bean's business and no one would get it out of her. Still, they'd been friends once. Good friends. And she had a question.

"Your father—"

But she got no further, remembering what Hassan's mother once said:

"Homosexuality is rampant in the western world. It's so because western cultures are so experimental, so unorthodox—so rewarding of individuality for individuality's sake. Homosexuality is a road to recognition, nothing more; a quest to seek attention."

Her views hadn't surprised Edy. When they tucked away, just the two of them, Rani pressed on with passion about the plight of women in India, spousal abuse, the dowry system, and female infanticide. She detached from it all though, as if her parents hadn't given Ali's family a dowry, as if her worth as a daughter and a potential had never been the subject of scrutiny. Rani Pradhan hauled double duty as a covert detractor and open advocate of the old ways. Long story truncated, Bean had no allies.

"I'm not ashamed of what I am," he said. "They don't have to accept me. It's just that I—"

"Need a place to live," Edy supplied.

"And food to eat," Bean said.

The plight of every kid everywhere. Not prepared enough to be independent, yet needing it so desperately.

Rani didn't take Edy's face so well. While Kala sat stoic and stirring her tea, Bean did all the talking, telling a tale that looped endlessly and proved no respecter of common sense. Edy, he said, had taken to training on the stairs. Up and down she ran until she grew so fatigued she tumbled face first. Bean, who happened to be checking for mail in the middle of the night—no, he wasn't expecting any—found her, in the stairwell.

To Bean's credit, no onslaught of logic could wither his story. Rani pointed out that she'd seen them both go to bed, that it was absurd for someone not expecting anything to rise in the middle of the night and check the mail, and that Edy had no need for stairwell aerobics when she got plenty of exercise everyday at ballet. Still, Bean remained rooted. Edy, never adept at lying, did her part by keeping up groans of pain to elicit sympathy and a softening of their culpability.

To God be the glory, they got away unscathed.

Bean began to open up to Edy, little by little, day by day. Silent mornings of walks to school turned into long meandering strolls where they talked about everything and everyone, no one and nothing. They made plans for some nights and seemed not to know each other on others—Edy figured those were the evenings he went to dance. She would beg him, of course, for a chance to see the pit and the dancing that haunted her dreams. But Bean wouldn't budge. Not only did he think her interest ridiculous, he didn't even believe she had what it took.

"So, does your mom still treat you like crap?" he said when she asked yet again to accompany him.

"One has nothing to do with the other, Bean."

"You're wrong," he said and swung long legs up on his bed. He leaned forward, eyes dark and intent on her. "The last time I saw your mom, she thought Hassan a king and you the pauper. She thought you were simple and spoiled, maybe even stupid. She thought every choice you made the wrong one and she called you weak and whiny every chance she got."

Edy looked away from him, eyes watering in the suddenness of his attack. "Shut up, Bean. Shut up about my mother."

"Not yet. Not until I figure out why you're never smart enough, never good enough, why no matter what you *do,* you can't *earn* her love—and that fact doesn't even make you mad."

"Shut up!" Edy's arm flung out, smashing a lamp to the floor in her path. The light flickered before tapering out completely. "Just . . . shut up before I kick your ass."

A vortex of blackness swallowed her, wild anger, dominating fury. Never had she wanted to attack someone, but her hands, her body felt raw with the power of fury. She could smash Bean's face, dent him, make him feel the inexplicable humiliation she felt. And yet, somehow, savagery was hardly enough.

"Are you mad at me?" Bean said as she sank onto his bed.

She may or may not have nodded. Eyes on her feet, Edy contemplated his words, how alone she felt, how uncertain. He'd been right about her mother, about her impatience, her hostility, her preference for her Hassan. In the wake of it, in the wake of that truth, she felt like nothing, like less than nothing if possible.

"I'm sorry I hurt you," Bean said. "But it was the only way." Already, he was on his feet. He ushered for her to move from the bed, then began shoving furniture into a corner.

"What are you doing?" Edy said.

Bean grinned. "Continuing our lessons. Part one was helping you find your fury. Part two is showing you what to do with it. Are you ready?"

Edy swallowed. "Maybe."

"Well, ready or not, here I come."

Bean hesitated before giving her a once over. "One more thing. You might want to invest in a sports bra. You've been sprouting like crazy as of late."

Twelve

Summer ended and Edy's father arrived to bring them back to Boston. She hid her disappointment at the absence of Hassan with the smile of her mother, the smile of a practiced politician. But she had missed her father, who had somehow managed to lose even more weight over the months and stood gaunt before her, like a man in desperate need of a fried chicken dinner with all the fixings.

Her new breasts were a non-topic. Edy's father paused only briefly to note them, before sweeping her up in an embrace and a smile. He had missed her; that much was obvious, even if all his time had been occupied by conferences, speaking events and the occasional guest appearance on cable news.

Bean said goodbye to Edy, in that classic, awkward Bean way. He looked past her first, then at her, then past her again, before rushing Edy for a hug. In the weeks following the discovery of his sexuality, they'd come to know things about each other—the secrets that were still technically secrets. His being gay had never been uttered nor her feelings for Hassan, but both understood nonetheless.

"Call me sometime," Bean said. "Let me know how the dancing's going."

And that was the other thing. The new thing. The obsession with street dance.

"Lucky you," her father said as they pulled away from the curb. "To have Ronnie Bean with you for the whole summer."

Edy smiled. She had been lucky. Before Bean, Edy's mother had been little more than an oddity to suffer, a difficult person dismissed by others as such. But Bean had been the first one to see the impossibility of being her daughter. It had done something for her, validated her in some way.

On the ride back to Boston, her thoughts turned to Hassan. Would he be home, waiting for her arrival? She hadn't called, and only a brief text from her to him said that she'd be leaving in the a.m. Obviously, he hadn't been willing to alter his schedule to see her. Otherwise, he'd be in the car. Maybe he'd only see her when it was convenient, at dinner, maybe tomorrow or the next day. She wished she didn't care. She made up her mind not to care. Still, Edy glanced at her phone. He hadn't even replied to her text.

At mid-afternoon, they pulled into their driveway. Edy spotted Hassan, perched on his porch and chugging a Gatorade, his hair like a flag in the wind, longer than she remembered. He stood taller, body weighty and raw with power, muscles like armor. Summer basked him from pale butterscotch to a rich, glistening copper. When their car came to a stop, his mouth curved to the shape of her name.

Edy burst out, sliced the space between them, leapt the fence, and found him in an instant. He snatched her before her foot could hit the porch, whipping her into a crushing embrace. And still, they weren't close enough. Not nearly close enough for an entire season apart. But then he pulled away as suddenly as he had snatched her.

His gaze ran the length of her body and a shuddering exhale escaped.

"Oh," was all he managed.

She flashed hot under the weight of his sigh, lashes lowered, breathing forgotten. Awareness overwhelmed her. Awareness of the single step that would take her back to him, of the air that hung between them, of her pounding pulse and fingers that ached to touch him.

Of words she didn't dare say.

"Edy." His green gold eyes clouded with some complicated emotion. Hassan opened his mouth and let it hang, and then surprised her with his choice of words. "What . . . happened to you?" he said.

That.

An A cup, then a B, then a B pressing over to a C.

Spell broken, she shoved him in the chest, only to find that he didn't budge.

"Pay attention in anatomy class and maybe you'd have a clue," Edy said.

But the sass didn't hold and her eyes were too drawn to the arms of a titan, to a chest carved for a god. Rich golden skin sheathed a body taller, harder and more defined than it had been only months ago. He'd been pushing himself, punishing himself again, and goodness, the results were glorious.

Edy looked up, registered his raised eyebrow, and realized she hadn't been careful enough in her assessment. "Did you give up and finally go for the steroids?" she said in attempt to hide her blush.

Lawrence stepped out the Pradhan front door.

Hassan glanced at him. "His dad tried to talk me into doing steroids like he used to, but I told him—"

"Suck one." Lawrence snatched Hassan's Gatorade and upturned it for himself, chugging out a third. He, too, was bigger than Edy remembered.

"We've been hitting the gym like crazy," Hassan admitted and peeled the bottle from Lawrence's grip. "We need a repeat come fall. And with the twins attracting college scouts this year, me and Lawrence figured we could give them something to look at, too."

Edy looked up to find Lawrence surveying her discreetly. First a glimpse, then another, then a third.

Hassan caught it too. "You all right there?"

But Lawrence only grinned. "Gonna be a real interesting year," he said. "*Real* interesting."

"Well, who asked about your interests? What is this, a questionnaire? Get back in the house, already."

Hassan shoved him. Lawrence stumbled on the threshold, laughing and even chancing a glance back before the door slammed in his face.

When Hassan turned back to Edy; awkwardness fell between them. His gaze dropped, and his hands found his pockets.

"I should go," he said. "More gym time and—"

Of course. Of course he wouldn't change his schedule for her. Her arrival meant little in the grand scheme of things.

"We'll talk later, okay?" Hassan said, still treating her to the top of his head.

"Yeah. Fine. Whatever."

She had other friends to see. Well, one other friend to see. At least Wyatt could be trusted to muster up the proper amount of enthusiasm for her return. Without wasting a goodbye, Edy headed across the street.

~~~

Roland Green leaned against the parched white door streaked in dirt and tapped two times. It rattled with the motion before Wyatt threw it open.

"Boy," he said. "There's a black girl here to see you."

Wyatt's eyes widened at the thought of it.

"What did you say?"

"Black girl. Got a nice little body on her, too. Downstairs waitin' on ya."

Roland grinned. Still, Wyatt hesitated. There were no girls unrelated to him that came to see him, black otherwise. No girls but Edy, and yet his father had made the body comment. Years of suffering his wandering eye and lewd comments had taught Wyatt what his father did and didn't like. Flat-chested girls, no matter how exquisite, were not one of them. Wyatt had no idea who waited downstairs.

"She looked anxious to see ya," his dad said, nudging him and grinning, nudging him and grinning.

"Yeah?"

"Yeah! Now quit lookin' at your old man and get down there, already."

Roland yanked Wyatt from the shadows of his room and pushed him toward the stairs. Wyatt descended a creaking staircase into darkness.

"Edy?" he called.

"Wyatt?"

She rose from the Green family couch, an old leather concoction riddled with lumps.

"Wyatt!" she cried, and he plowed his way down.

On the last stair, he froze. There was Edy. And there was the body. Goodness, what a difference a summer could make.

Edy bit her lip and looked down. "So, they didn't get past you either, huh?"

Shame stained Wyatt's cheeks and forced his gaze down, away. Words fumbled in his mouth for purchase. She had been pretty before, beautiful in a sweet, cherubic sort of way. He'd appreciated her then. He couldn't have her thinking that her body mattered to him. "They're gorgeous," he said.

Oh God.

He choked on nausea and humiliation, both in ample supply.

Calm down. Get away and calm down.

"Let me get you some water. Let me just . . .excuse me." Wyatt ducked into the kitchen, body rattling like a subway station when the train finally blazed through.

"Wyatt?" Edy called.

She even sounded like Lottie. Was that possible? Was it possible that the girl he now loved could be so similar to the one who had ruined him?

Gripping the edge of the sink, Wyatt watched the water drain, willing himself to relax. He was overwrought, his dad always said. High strung, even as a baby.

"Wyatt?"

She stood behind him now. He didn't need to look up to know that. He'd had that connection with her, right from the start. The one that kept her in his consciousness and made him know approximately how close she was at every moment of every day.

"Oh, Wyatt." Edy reached around him and turned off the faucet. "You are making such a fuss. It's nothing. We're friends. I know you didn't mean anything by it."

"Edy, I—"

She peeled his fingers from the counter and laced his hand with hers.

"Forget it. I grew these things and forgot to tell anyone. Even Hassan reacted to them."

Wyatt stood, thoughts cleared. "Did he now?"

Edy shut off the faucet. "He did. And you should've seen my dad. It was like he wanted to get back in the car, circle the block, and try again."

A reluctant smile crept to Wyatt's face. "It's just . . . you were so beautiful before. To see you now . . ." Wyatt swallowed. "Is to want you."

There. He'd said it. The only secret between them: that he was bewitched by her, that a fierceness within demanded her for him, enslaving him to this want. He knew nothing but pain and urgency and greed. She had to see now, what she did to him.

Edy laughed. "You've been in this dark house too long," she said. "Flip on a few lights. Better yet, wait until school starts and you see one of the "it" girls. Then you'll remember the standard for beauty." She pinched his nose.

Always, Wyatt thought. Always so dismissive.

~~~

Leaving again. With a single week until the official start of school, Wyatt stood before Edy, imploring, face contorted in disbelief and inching toward an ugly sort of panic. "What do you mean you're leaving? You just got here!"

He stood opposite her with the fence surrounding his house separating them. He couldn't understand it. They'd spent so much time apart, endured by a single lifeline: a cell phone. Now that they were together, she would leave him again, with a smile mocking his pain.

"Oh, don't be so grumpy." Edy prodded him with a finger. "We're just going to the Cape for a few days—"

"*Seven.* You're going for seven days."

"Fine. Seven. But we haven't been to the summer house in forever. And I could use a vacation. SAB was brutal." Edy shrugged. "Anyway, Daddy brought it up—saying he needed a respite and what with Hassan's birthday coming up . . ." She took in his pouting face. "You can't blame me for wanting family time."

Family time, Wyatt thought, as his gaze lifted to a mammoth-sized Hassan chucking suitcases in the trunk of his father's Benz. Hassan looked up, locked a mocking gaze with Wyatt—and smiled.

Low life. He had good luck in droves.

Edy's father stepped out of Hassan's house and went to help with the luggage. A few words were exchanged; both had their attention on Wyatt.

"If we didn't go now we'd have to wait a whole year," Edy said. She grabbed Wyatt by the arm, seized by excitement. "Oh, and wait until you see what they're getting him for his sixteenth birthday. You will *not* believe it."

"I'm sure I would," Wyatt said.

Edy's father stepped to the edge of the Pradhan yard. "Sweetheart? Come here for a minute." His tone was even; warm, despite the scowl he wore. Hassan stood next to him, unreadable, waiting.

Edy shot Wyatt a look of apology. "Daddy?"

The lines in his face deepened. "I don't believe I've properly met your friend. And I do believe I just asked you to come here."

Edy started forward, glanced back at Wyatt, and tilted her head for him to follow. Panic seized him in rigor-mortic fashion.

"No! Why?" he hissed.

"'Cause you're a boy. Come on. If you hesitate, he'll think you have bad intentions."

"But Hassan's right there."

"Which is why you need to come. To him, avoiding Hassan is nearly the same as avoiding him. Now hurry." She cautioned a glance at her father. "Tell him your name and give him a firm shake. Look him in the eye when you talk. It'll be okay."

She bustled across the street.

Wyatt smoothed his clothes and took a deep breath. This should have been what he wanted, the next natural step. Meeting a girl's father was a good sign, a sign of seriousness. He should welcome the opportunity.

Wyatt walked over.

"Hassan tells me that you all spend a great deal of time together and have done so for quite a while." Edy's father looked directly at her. "He also says that neither he nor the boys know Wyatt very well."

Wyatt caught it. That flash of scalding anger as it crossed Edy's face. She gave it to Hassan and made him hold it. This wasn't an introduction, that look said. It was an ambush.

"The boys don't know Wyatt well because they don't want to," Edy snapped.

"Perhaps there's a reason for that," her father said.

What had been said before their arrival? What sort of seeds had Hassan planted? Or had he said little, leaving Edy's father to drag together pieces that didn't quite fit, to leap to his own conclusions?

Edy's father eyed Wyatt in increments, scrutinizing and analyzing, storing away.

Suddenly, Edy's advice nudged at him.

"Mr. Phelps, my name is Wyatt Green. I go to school with Hassan and Edy. You're right. I should have come over and introduced myself sooner. I accept the blame for that entirely." He offered a hand, willing his voice to steady.

Her father shook, firm.

"And what is it your parents do, Wyatt Green?"

He should've expected that question. But he hadn't.

"My father works at an auto parts store," he admitted. "And my mother's a cashier at Shaw's."

The longest of pauses followed.

"I see."

He shot a look at the Green house, dilapidated, yes, but still worth a formidable sum.

"And what are your grades like, Wyatt?"

He stood up straighter. "Very good, sir. My father says he doesn't know where I get it from."

He probably shouldn't have said that. But then Mr. Phelps laughed, uproariously so, and it made Wyatt smile.

"I like to meet Edy's friends sooner rather than later," her father said. "At your leisure, schedule an evening for you and your parents to come over for dinner, so that I can meet the people my daughter is being exposed to. Likewise, you'll have the opportunity to meet my wife. We'll do it on a Sunday, since the Pradhans are over, and it's festive then." He cast an absentminded glance at Hassan. "Until then, until we've all had the opportunity to meet, my daughter won't be venturing over to your property, nor do I expect to find you on mine. And even after we're acquainted, I don't expect to find you on my premises when adults aren't around. Do I make myself clear?"

"Yes sir," Wyatt whispered.

Nathan Phelps would wait forever for the chance to meet Wyatt's parents. Forever and a winning lottery ticket later if Wyatt had his way.

Edy's father strode back into the Pradhan house.

"Jeez," Hassan said with a derisive eye on Wyatt. "Why not pee yourself and get it over with?"

"Shut up, you," Wyatt snapped and headed back for his house.

He went no further than his yard, where he stood watch in silent suffering. Edy and Hassan, teasing and laughing, slipping into one house and tearing out the other. No boundaries, no limitations on either. Edy and Hassan, a touch here, a shove there, fingers laced, a smile. No notice of Wyatt, both close and far, watching until the moment they departed. Edy in the backseat of the Pradhan car with Hassan, without a wave of goodbye for Wyatt.

Thirteen

The Pradhan-Phelps vacation home was a pea green windswept clapboard, two stories of rickety wood in the old Cape Cod style. Buried deep in the tangle of brush, rock, and high beach grass, the old house tilted east, threatening to slip into the sea with a strong enough wind. But like the houses around it, it was old—older-than-America old, and would no doubt be there long after them.

The layout of the house was simple. A steep set of stairs led to an elevated front porch, and the porch right to the foyer. The entrance dumped into a den, often ignored in lieu of the spacious accommodations upstairs. Exiting that den, a turn left would head for a quaint dining room with fireplace, the kitchen, and finally, the back porch. The view from the rear porch was that of high grass followed by a steep drop to their own stretch of beach, and beyond that, the Cape Cod Bay. From the front, it was the Atlantic in the distance. Bedrooms on the first floor belonged to the parents—Ali and Rani's on one side, Nathan and Rebecca's on the other. Once upon a time, the Phelps occupied the first floor and the Pradhans the second, but as the children aged, the commotion kept up was cause enough for a change.

With a haphazard toss of her suitcase to her bed, Edy hollered at Hassan that it was time for a swim. She fought with the latch on her bag, nearly shredding her nail, before throwing open the lid and rummaging for her one-piece. Once found, she changed in a rush of hands, eager to catch the last bit of rays before nightfall. As children, they'd douse themselves in New England waters and knew of nothing that felt more like home.

Edy had a new suit, a halter variation that ran black, smooth, and taut against her body. Her old one, a peeling and yellow standby, had no space for new breasts, nor the tidbit of bottom she'd earned. Barefoot and ready, she thundered down the hall to Hassan's room and shouted at the sight of him. He stood in swim trunks at the window, gaze on the rough terrain below.

"What are you doing?" she cried. "Let's go, you sack of nothing!"

Edy pounced onto his back, giggling, giddy as she wrapped arms around his neck and legs around his waist, beating him like a dead horse.

Hassan broke from whatever daze he'd been under and stumbled, laughing. Twisting as if to peel her straight off his back, he pawed to free himself. But with each swipe of long, strong arms, Edy bounced and bounded to stay clear. He would not evict her so easily. Eventually, he went still.

"Edy, stop. Come on. Get down."

"Uh uh. Since you didn't get me once you were ready, we're going out like this. We won't get separated again."

She hollered "giddy up" and smacked him upside the head, bouncing up and down on his back. How rare and delicious a thrill to have the upper hand.

"You're not listening. Get off me. I'm not kidding."

She didn't care if he was kidding or not. Edy belted a "yeehaw" before he careened to one side. Laughing, she clung to him, body molding to his back in desperation to stay aboard. He was used to being the stronger one, the one in control, but he simply couldn't shake her free. She clung to his neck, flattening his back. Who knew when she'd have a moment like that again, a moment to subdue the mighty Hassan Pradhan?

"Damn it, will you get off me?"

He pitched to one side and slung her to the bed, rough, and she bounced off in a roll to the floor.

She looked up into dark and furious eyes.

"The next time I tell you to get the hell off me, you get the hell off!"

Hassan stormed from the room, cursing, and slammed the door on his exit.

When Edy found Hassan again, he sat at the shore's edge, staring out at foaming waves beneath a cobalt sky that stretched on to oblivion. His arms wrapped his legs and his knees touched his chin as a light and fanciful breeze danced in his hair and sprayed his skin with Cape Cod Sea. Edy stood, transfixed, taking him in, reluctant to approach. He'd never yelled at her. A lifetime of broken possessions, mutilated clothes, things taken, and he'd never yelled at her. Yet, never had he looked so beautiful.

Hassan looked up, sensing her, and offered a faint smile. When she returned it hesitantly, he patted the stretch of sand next to him.

Edy sat. "I'm sorry, Hassan. I should've listened. I should have got off when you—"

"Forget it. I'm a jerk. I'm the one who's sorry."

Their world turned in silence, waves lapping, stars twinkling. They were far from home, and home was exactly where they were. Her home wasn't a place. It was a person. It was there with him.

He leaned back on elbows, face to the heavens, and gave way to the heaviest sigh. It looked like he'd been holding it forever.

"I'm supposed to believe in reincarnation," he said.

"You don't believe in a lot of things you're supposed to. Not in their way, at least."

The corners of his mouth quirked, making Edy want to snatch his smile and pocket it.

"Have we always known each other?" Hassan said.

Edy looked at him. "Uh, yeah. You know that."

He turned back to the stars. "I mean, before now. Before this life. Did I know you then?"

She considered. Considered the possibility of something other than what she'd been taught. Considered the possibility that the tether between them was timeless, destined, irreversible. And once he'd given life to the idea, nothing else seemed possible.

"Yes," Edy whispered. "I think so."

Hassan covered her hand with his. "Yeah," he said. "I think so, too."

They contented themselves with the soothing sounds of the shore.

~~~

Hassan rose at dawn and ventured to his open window. Thin white linen billowed from it, no match for the seaside wind. From his bedroom, he had a half view of a craggy, sloping shore, overrun with knee-deep wild grass. On that morning the sky hung like steel, a listless, uniform gray as the first of drizzle began to fall.

Reasons existed for everything, his father would say. For the earth turning just so, for a flower blooming there instead of elsewhere. For them having names like Ali and Hassan, despite their being Hindu.

A reason even for the rain he saw now.

It was good, his father would say, even if he couldn't see the how or why in the moment. All things worked to a purpose, he insisted.

The distance from their property to the lighthouse was a mile. Since he could do that without sweating, Hassan decided to head for Pilgrim Lake, adding two miles of running along the bay's edge.

When Hassan headed out, it was with a steady pace, an easy gait, and an appreciation for the morning breeze and the gentle, unassuming rainfall.

A decade ago or more, he and Edy would catch mussels, clams, and oysters at Pilgrim Lake. Their mothers used them for stews, curries, and chowders, sometimes the dads ate them raw. They'd dig them up by the fistfuls, Edy and he, and back then, for Hassan, even that was a competition. He'd get three for her every one, announce his superior shell fishing skills, and then hand them over when her eyes began to teem with tears.

Edy.

Damn her. Even her name was a loaded word. But then again, it always was.

Hassan had had his first fight at age six, when a guy named Joey grabbed Edy's behind. When he found Joey, he lodged fists in his mouth, making sure there were tears in his eyes, too—despite the kid being two years older and two inches taller. On that day Hassan realized two things about himself, and they were the only two things he ever knew for sure. One was that he would protect Edy no matter what. Two was that he had one hell of a temper.

There could be no counting the number of fights he'd started in the name of Edy Phelps, whether she wanted them or not. A misspoken word, a wrong touch, her tears for any reason, and his fists swung without question.

Time to redirect. Thoughts of Edy, wrong thoughts of Edy, were exactly what neither of them needed. Yet, he returned to them constantly. And not because of the teasing curves she'd sprouted in her sleep. He was worse, far worse off than that. He only wished hormones could explain his problem.

When Edy had left for the summer, his mind had gone rogue. Twice, he thought of calling and demanding she come home. But home to what? Him messing with other girls? Tripling up on the running, the weights, the desperation of it all? More girls, more drills, more parties, more anything, anything in the hopes of drowning out her.

But it didn't work. It never did.

By the time Hassan returned home rain fell in sheets, blinding him, dead set on drowning him. He regretted pushing for the lake as the sky darkened, yet he remained too stubborn to veer from his predetermined path. Stubbornness was his mantra and the difference between a damned good running back and a guy soon cut from the team. Thankfully, any son of Ali Pradhan would be both pigheaded and unreasonable, the unquestionable fruit from the vine of his father. Knowing everything had its perks.

Hair plastered to his scalp as the rain soaked through to the boxers. With his clothes clinging and dripping, Hassan retreated to the upstairs bathroom to change. Once there, everything he wore fell to the floor with a plop.

Shivering, he turned on the shower, cranking up the heat for relief. When he stepped in, liquid burned his feet, so he retreated long enough to adjust the temperature. He found a decent medium, returned, and let the water stream over him in heated currents, warming and cleansing as he relished the warmth. Eyes closed, he scrubbed his face and neck and back with thick foam, and before long, began to croon a sultry, begging R&B tune he'd heard on the drive up. Something about spending all his time loving the pretty girl on his mind. He got into it, hitting notes but mostly missing, scatting and moaning as if in concert. The bar of soap became his mic, the drops of water his audience. Only when the shower ran cold did he end his performance and step out.

He looked around for a towel and saw he didn't have one.

Great.

With a swallow, Hassan peered into the hall, first left toward the bedrooms and then right toward the common area. It was early, maybe seven, but seven wasn't early enough to guarantee that no one would see him. He was on the second floor, which was a good thing, since he and Edy had it to themselves. Hassan imagined his father discovering him in the hall, naked as he swaggered for the bedroom. He'd be torn between reluctance in attacking his nude son and a pressing need to shake him till Hassan fell still. No doubt he'd choose the assault.

Safely tucked behind the door, Hassan cupped hands around his mouth and hissed. "Edy! Edy!"

Maybe she'd be tired. Sleeping in. Eating breakfast. Cooking breakfast. Anything other than cavorting down the hall at the wrong freaking moment. But if she was awake, she could just bring him a towel. And if she wasn't, he could run. He had speed. But speed meant nothing if he took off at the wrong moment.

He called her twice more before she stuck her head out. She had a cell phone at her ear, first thing in the morning.

"What is it?" she said.

"I need a towel."

Her mouth spread into a smile. "Are you *naked*?"

"Who in the world are you on the phone with?"

"Hold on," Edy said into the phone. "Of course, it's Hassan. Yes, he's na—just *hold on*."

"Edy," Hassan said, pressing back the irresistible urge to bend something. "Lose the spare and bring me a towel."

He said it loud enough for his voice to carry.

"I'll call you back, Wyatt." Edy paused. "I said I'll . . . I don't *know* where my parents are. I —later, okay?"

She hung up the phone and her mouth spread wide. Devilment lit her eyes.

"Towel," he said, stone in his voice.

She disappeared into her bedroom.

Hassan exhaled, cool air catching him wrong. He shifted from one foot to the other, wondering if he could make a stab for the linen closet. When Edy reemerged, her lips pursed.

"Sorry for the delay. Had to put the phone on the charger. Battery's low." She went to the linen closet and pulled out a washcloth. "This good?"

She held it out low, as if offering him a loincloth.

"Come on, Cake. Steam's only gonna keep me warm so long."

Edy returned to the closet as if rummaging desperately. Perfectly good towels fell to the floor, large towels, plush towels, but she rummaged nonetheless.

"Ah. Here you go. How about this?"

A pillowcase, this time.

"Just forget it."

Hassan stepped out and strode toward the closet, tracking footprints in his wake. In the center of the hall and right next to Edy, he grabbed an oversized towel and dried himself. He made no effort to shield his junk or the delight it took in having her for an audience. Once he'd rid himself of moisture clear down to the bottom of his feet, Hassan tied the towel loose around his waist.

"What?" he said.

Edy's blinked a thousand times. "N-nothing."

"Breakfast then," he said. "When I change."

Dressed in a black t-shirt and basketball shorts, Hassan ventured to the kitchen for breakfast. Since he and Edy seemed to be the only two up, he put on a bit of instant oatmeal for the both of them. Thinking they could use some fruit, he rummaged till he found strawberries, a kiwi, and a batch of blueberries. He threw the kiwi back, remembering that they were Nathan's favorite, and grabbed a bag of bagels instead. With those in the toaster, Hassan whistled out the R&B tune from the shower as he fixed up the two bowls of oatmeal, careful to count out Edy's berries. Done, he ventured to the bottom of the stairs and shouted for her to join him.

"You'll wake the house," Edy said and dropped into a seat at the breakfast table.

He poured her a glass of milk before sitting down with a cup of water for himself.

"So," he said, cutting right to the point. "Were you up on the phone with him all night or just up really early, eager to hear him?"

Edy stared at him, stiff. "We were on the phone a long time, yes. He couldn't sleep—"

"He couldn't sleep," Hassan snapped.

"Yeah. So, he texted me. You know how those things wake me up."

"Yeah. Right. Whatever."

"What's with you?" Edy said. "What difference does it make?"

Hassan burst from the table, went for the bagels, and found them scorched, which pissed him off even more. But two were burned worse than the others, so he dumped those before Edy. She giggled.

"You are *so* mad at me," she said.

He opened the refrigerator, grabbed butter and cream cheese, and tossed them both to the table, not caring that they bounced.

"You're not even thinking straight. I was up most of the night with you, remember? And not that it's any of *your* business, but he called me upset. His parents were fighting again."

Didn't she say he woke her? Who the hell fought first thing in the morning?

Hassan dropped into his seat and shoveled a spoonful of oatmeal in his mouth, finding it too hot. But he chewed anyway, allowing the heat to fuel his anger and incense him more as the food clung to his tongue. Even the way she looked at him pissed him off, gentle-like, as if mocking him while simultaneously wanting to make amends.

"Eat your food," he snapped.

She lowered her gaze to the oatmeal and smiled at the blueberries. "Twenty?"

"Should be. Count them."

When they were kids, her father had taken a trip to El Salvador to study conditions following the civil war. For twenty days he was gone, each marked with a blueberry in her oatmeal, placed there by Hassan.

"Nineteen." She pouted.

He went to the fridge, retrieved one, and hurled it in her bowl.

"You can't help yourself. You try to take care of me even when you're mad."

So she was mocking him. She plopped a berry in her mouth and smiled.

Hassan watched her chew, fascinated with the contours of her mouth and the way it moved, despite trying to hold onto fast melting anger.

Edy stuck a blue-stained tongue out at him and the last of his will dissipated. Hassan reached for it, as if to snatch it from her mouth. She giggled and swatted him away.

~~~

She'd seen Hassan naked. Completely naked, with not a thread to hide behind. She'd seen the contours of his abs, the carving of his thighs, and parts of him that made her blush and hide even when alone.

She'd seen every inch of him.

He sat across from her, wolfing down a proper brunch, oblivious to the staining of her cheeks.

"Hassan, you must be so excited about the upcoming season," Edy's father said. He placed a few slices of Canadian bacon on his English muffin and topped it with a poached egg. Edy's mother handed him the Hollandaise sauce without looking up from her cell phone.

Across from him, Hassan's father, Ali, was busy earning stinkeye from Rani for the fistful of sugar-glazed bacon he munched on.

"The season. Oh yeah," Hassan said. "Should be a good one."

He sounded as if he were trying to get his bearings, trying to emerge from whatever thoughts he'd submerged into.

Meanwhile, Edy's cell buzzed. She didn't want to look at it, not in front of him, not when everything Wyatt-related seemed to irk him, not when they'd spent a whole summer apart either and seemed somehow closer because of it . . . as long as Wyatt Green didn't come up.

The phone vibrated again, and Edy slipped a hand into her pocket, covert, to silence it. She thought of that same hand, under Hassan's the night before, and of the assertion that they had always been linked, eternally, repeatedly, forevermore.

"West Roxbury has a new middle linebacker," Hassan said and stole bacon from his father's plate. "Me and Lawrence peeked in on him at a practice. He's a beast."

West Roxbury and South End met mid-season, two meteorites colliding in the atmosphere.

"We'll see if we can find some footage online of him. Break down his style, his mindset, get at the heart of his weaknesses," her dad said.

Hassan looked doubtful.

Edy brought a slice of mango to her mouth with a frown. "What's the guy's name again?"

"Leahy," Hassan said. "Robert Leahy."

"That guy?" Edy scoffed. "What a slob. Kinda slow in the head, too. I've seen him on YouTube." She had, of course, never, ever seen him. "You'd get past him every time."

Hassan laughed. "He's actually pretty fast. You'd know that if you'd seen him."

She brought apple juice to her lips, considering how quickly he'd honed in on the lie. "You've been training, haven't you?" His body certainly argued the case.

"Yeah?"

"Well, let me see." Edy hurled the juice into his face and bolted, upturning a chair as she fled for the shore.

Hassan hurdled over the toppled furniture, leapt the stairs, and swallowed the space between them in a measured sprint. He snatched her with a scoop and barreled onward for the water. Edy shrieked, wild, laughing, thrashing to get free. She caught an earful of his mother's shouting before landing headfirst in the bay.

Four years ago, on a trip to India, they'd visited the beaches of Goa, where cows and sunning bodies shared the same sand. A moment of teasing and tussling had ended the same way, with a scandalized Rani professing her utmost shame before taking Hassan and Edy back to the hotel. She fussed about what her parents would say if they had been there, what her brother would say, her sister. She wasn't raising Hassan right, Rani insisted, if he could be so indecent and not care about how it affected the family. A female had no business being touched by a man who wasn't her husband or son, and, clearly, they were neither. They'd been provocative, unforgivable.

Edy now emerged from shallow waters, sputtering and laughing, to find Hassan looming over her, large. She knew he'd be impossible to tackle head on, football players found that out routinely on Fridays. So, she used his saturated polo to pull herself up before a wave made her tumble. Smile smug, he lent a hand on her scramble up but found she used it as leverage to tickle him. Hassan fell into the waves, his laughter uproarious, on the defensive, and pushing Edy away. They tangled and fell into the water as one, his mother fussing in Punjabi the whole time.

Ali always came to their defense, usually, with some well-reasoned premise posited by a sociologist he admired. Stuff about gender, expectations, identity, and cinematic constructs in the Asian Indian diaspora. No one dared argue with him. One, because he was the final authority in his family, and two, because no one knew what the hell he was talking about. But this time when they emerged, drenched and dripping, Ali said nothing, eye on his son, attentive instead.

Love Edy

Fourteen

Edy lived for their days on The Cape. Snapshots in time they were, frozen moments, where the laws of the outside world didn't apply. It was an impossibly positive place, bursting with memories, brimming with promises.

The spot where their land met the beach was roughhewn. Tufts of wild grass and rocks jutted in unexpected places. Edy balanced on a massive one, arms arched and extended in classic *demi* second. She placed weight on the back leg and offered a *demi-plié*, opposite leg bent, then straightened in a sleek slide forward. A clean turn, a pirouette, and a *grand battement* followed, leg thrown up in the last so that it paralleled her head. The crashing of waves was her music, the howl of wind her beat. Below her was a drop. But if she was good, it wouldn't matter.

Applause shattered her concentration.

"I haven't seen that in awhile. I'd forgotten how perfect you were."

Hassan scaled the rock, crowding her so that dancing was no longer possible.

"I was trying to shift into something new. Bean showed me *something* and I . . ." Edy sighed. She'd been unable to seize the caustic fury from the pit, unable to morph it and make it her own. Though she'd absorbed every technical detail she'd been exposed to, she couldn't rattle her muse. All this time, all these years, she'd been a parrot of dance, enslaved to choreographers and instructors. Everything she attempted on her own felt stilted and tepid. Bean had warned her though; she would find no focus until she abandoned fear for courage. Choreography was nakedness. Edy wondered if she could ever embrace it.

Hassan took a seat on rock, and she dropped next to him, watching him as he examined its surface.

"This is the right one?" he said, gaze still searching.

She nudged his side and he shifted, revealing the thing he sought. Their names, carved on the underside, long, long ago. No dates, no hearts, nothing so complicated. Just "Hassan", then "Edy", like always.

"I'm going to tell your father that you exposed yourself to me," she said, eyes on her bare feet, dangling above water.

Hassan grinned. "Exposed myself? I should've charged you for a show that good. You saw me and you liked it. You know that."

The heat returned, hundredfold in its fury, painting her face and body, leaving her nowhere to hide. So, he'd seen her. Not just looking but gaping, wondering what he felt like.

But he couldn't know, couldn't know the extent that he'd affected her, no matter how hard he kept on grinning. And even with the thought, she saw the smile and saw past it, to their days beyond the Cape. What would happen when they returned to school, when football started, and he went from being hers to being theirs once again?

"What?" Hassan said, smile drooping at the edges.

Edy turned from him, horrified by what pooled in her eyes.

"Nothing." She hesitated, knowing he would never be satisfied with the answer. "I only wish I didn't have to share you."

Centuries passed in a second.

"Share me," he echoed.

She couldn't understand the irritation in his voice. With his eyes clamped shut, vulnerability sharpened his features and heightened his intensity. It painted him in stark relief.

His face turned to steel.

"You've got it wrong," Hassan said in a voice that made Edy want to shrink into herself. "You've always had it all wrong. Look at the way you are with my parents, with my mom especially. Our lives change the second we do. A brick wall goes up and it doesn't come down. You know what happens next?" He gestured between them, eyes narrowed, voice raw with bitterness. "They take us. We don't get family like we know it; we don't get *us* like we know it."

He dragged a shaky hand through his hair, trailing sand and exhaled mightily. "And for the record you don't share me," he mumbled. "Not even close."

Edy bore the weight of someone expected to speak. But the words wouldn't come. What good was love with an expiration date? What use was inevitable heartbreak? Yes, he cared and she could cherish that, but to what end, to what purpose? Predetermined paths waited for them both; his laid out and hers what she made of it. She had nothing but leftover crumbs when it came to Hassan. Loving him was a waste.

"Edy?" he said. "Talk to me. Please."

She didn't have the words for this conversation. With fingers pinched to the bridge of her nose, she shook her head and concentrated on breathing. At first, his glare draped her, bathed her, willing her to bend to his will. But this life, their life together, didn't contort to anyone's will.

So Hassan retreated, Goliath on the football field, something else with Edy.

~~~

Fourteen phone calls unanswered on the "eve" of Hassan's birthday. Why Edy felt the need to call it that was beyond him. Was it some great big holiday, a day of reverence, of devotion? For the mighty Hassan Pradhan, every day was a day to prostrate oneself before his altar of muscles.

What a jerk. What a scheming, greedy, hoarder. As if the girls at school weren't enough, he had to show his naked body to Edy. And what for? In the hopes that she acted like them, that she'd throw herself at him like them?

Wyatt shoved aside his Banquet TV dinner of fried chicken and sighed. He drummed fingers on the surface of a rickety pine table. The lamp perched on its end provided the only source of light.

Calling her would do no good; all day Edy's phone had gone to voice mail. Texting her got no response. Seven of those already and not a single one in reply. It was selfish of her, shallow of her, *cruel* of her to treat him that way. But, Hassan Pradhan was in her midst, and of course, she couldn't resist.

"Put that damned phone down," Wyatt's father said. "You've been staring at it for two months."

Two months. Two months of loneliness.

His father popped open another beer and dropped down across from him, eyes laughing.

"I want to make a phone call," Wyatt said.

This time his father did laugh.

"You haven't got anybody to call," he said. "Nobody that'll call back, that is."

Wyatt's jaw set. He knew someone who would call him back. Someone who had asked for him by name.

"Maybe I'll call Lottie," he said.

His father set aside his beer, all pretense of amusement now gone.

"That's not part of our deal," Roland Green said.

Wyatt swallowed. "Maybe I don't like our deal."

His father snatched him by the forearm, upturning his bottle of beer so that it ran a river from table to floor. Four of his fingernails dug into the tender flesh of Wyatt's forearm, blanching it under the power of his grip.

Wyatt gasped. "Dad . . . stop. You're hurting me."

"I'll do a lot more than that if you go off the rails again." His father hurled his arm. It bounced off the table, elbow first.

Wyatt cursed.

"Eat," his father said and shoved the TV dinner back at him.

The lamp on the table flickered. Either the bulb needed replacing, or his father had forgotten to pay the bill again. A minute later, Wyatt received his confirmation, when he and his father were drenched in darkness.

~~~

When Hassan woke to their final day on the Cape, his birthday, it was only because he'd grown tired of Edy nudging him.

"*Why* won't you let me sleep?" he moaned.

"Because I can't take it anymore. Get up. You *have* to get up."

She leapt atop him, straddled him, then shook him with vicious enthusiasm.

Hassan let out a torturous groan. "Edy! You have *got* to stop jumping my bones. Now, get off. Please."

He covered his face with a pillow and shifted his top half to one side, away from her. It was the best he could manage with Edy on top.

"Hassan, come on! It's our last day here and—"

She fell back, fell silent, withdrawing in more ways than one.

"And what?" Hassan said, moving the pillow from his face.

He knew 'what', even if he couldn't put it into words. 'What' was the thing that happened between Boston and the Cape, between Edy and Hassan alone and Edy and Hassan out there, when the rest of the world imposed.

"Nothing," she said.

He looked up at her, took her by the arms, and willed her for once, just once, to say the thing that neither of them had been able to.

He imagined pulling her down to him so that their lips met, so that they kissed. What would she do? Pedal away, shocked and confused and trying to figure out how their sibling-like relationship had gone so wrong?

Except they'd never been like siblings. Not to him.

Edy stared down at him, with those gaping, glistening, wide, brown eyes—and inside, he felt his will begin to wilt.

"Look outside," she said.

Hassan sighed and released her.

She got up so that he could stretch to the window, pull back the curtain, and take in the coastline. What in the world could she want him to see? Sunrise? It was too late for that.

His birthday. Hassan's gaze skated closer to the house, finally falling on the driveway, where he stopped.

A sable Mustang wrapped with a gleaming red bow —a convertible—beckoned with the top down.

He cursed. "Is that mine?"

"Hell yeah!" Edy cried and yanked him by the arm.

He pitched from the bed, and the two scrambled, hand in hand, sliding on parquet, barreling downstairs, about to smack into the front door.

Hassan shoved it open, and only dimly registered their parents before they spilled out into the front yard. He let go of Edy, to cavort left, then right, desperate to soak up every line and curve of the his beauty, unable to slow for a proper inspection. At the back of the Mustang, he registered the Massachusetts tag with "Hassan 27", and a howl ripped from his throat.

He bolted to the driver's side and yanked on the handle. Since it was locked, he turned for the house where Edy and his parents filled the doorway.

"Gimme the keys before I bust through the window," Hassan said.

Edy's mother looked at his parents.

"I told you she couldn't hold water," Rebecca said.

Hassan's father held out the keys like an offering, only to have them snatched in a hurricane of movement. Hassan turned away, then doubled back to swallow his dad in a hug. He squeezed first him, then his mother, and tearing off for the car.

"Our gift's inside!" Nathan called as Hassan pried the door open.

"Are you kidding me? There's more?"

Nathan descended the stairs. "Well, I know how you young men like sound systems, so . . ."

Hassan shot Edy a look of frightened curiosity. He couldn't fathom what a sound system from Nathan might look like, and apparently, neither could Edy. She came down and joined him on the passenger's side. Nathan made his way around to the driver's side door.

"I'm not exactly sure how it all works. It appeared to be a very complicated process. But the gentleman assured me it's quite common among young people to place the speakers in the trunk."

Hassan and Edy turned to each other, wide-mouthed, before diving from their seats.

"Holy crap. This thing is tremendous!"

"Satellite radio," her father continued, prouder now, posture straighter after his gift's enthusiastic reception. "Twenty-four hour football commentary on three stations all year round."

Football. The thing that anchored him, that made sense even when thinking was an ordeal. Only Nathan knew and understood and had felt it for himself.

Hassan swept him into an embrace before remembering Rebecca and going to smother her too.

His gaze turned back to the car, where he absorbed the beauty of it all and the power hidden just beneath the hood. He had no idea how long he should stand there, looking thankful. "So, um, can we go somewhere? Maybe get some bread or something?"

"Bread." Rebecca hooted and messed up his hair.

"Around the block a few times," Hassan's father said. "Mind the posted speed limits, the stop signs, etcetera." He looked his son over once more. "And when you get back, dress properly."

Hassan looked down at the tee and pajama pants he wore, noted the absence of shoes, and grinned.

"Bye," he said and grabbed Edy by the hand.

A few minutes later, the two eased down the unassuming streets of North Truro, wild grass, sand dunes, and slung low houses on either side of them.

"Unreal. Beyond unreal," he muttered and adjusted his mirrors at a red light. "I don't think anything could make this day better."

"Well, I have something for you. I mean, it's not a Mustang or a sound system, but . . ."

"You do? Why didn't you tell me?" Hassan pulled over.

Edy reached under her seat and pawed around before returning with a slender, baby blue box wrapped with a sleek white ribbon.

Tiffany's.

He shot her a look, drawing a blank as to what it could be. Nonetheless, Hassan took it from her and tugged at the ribbon.

"Where'd you get Tiffany's money?" he said as he unwrapped his gift.

"You know I get a few bucks to spend for your birthday each year."

"Not Tiffany bucks." He looked up at her.

Edy blushed. "I've been saving my allowance. Walking home instead of catching the bus."

The walks home with Wyatt. They didn't mean what he thought.

Hassan lifted the lid, revealing a pair of sterling silver dog tags engraved on one side. He picked them up and squinted at elaborate font.

To Hassan,

My favorite guy,

In this life and the next.

Believing in you even when you don't.

Edy

He looked at her.

"How could you—"

"My secret."

Her words meant a million things at once, the way everything between them did. And yet, it surprised him when his vision blurred. Hassan blinked away tears.

"I love it." He cleared his throat. "It's perfect. Really." He closed a fist around the tags and enveloped Edy in his arms, holding her closer to his heart than anyone ever.

Fifteen

Wyatt knew sophomore year would blow. He knew it the moment Hassan pulled into the driveway with the top down on a $32,000 car, name hanging on the back, Jay-Z cranking from the speaker system. He knew it the moment Hassan leapt from said car, sleeves rolled to reveal massive biceps, only to go around and help Edy out as if she were some bruised rose petal. And he knew it the moment the two sauntered into her house, arm in arm, without a look his way.

Her father had been so abrupt to Wyatt. Not rude, but barely tolerating. Didn't he see what was right under his nose? He was so busy worrying about what might be he couldn't see what was. Hassan and Edy on the verge of something more. Maybe already there.

Things came easy for Hassan. Looks. Athleticism. Girls. Edy Phelps, however, wouldn't come so easy.

She didn't know about the summer, about the wild parties and endless stream of girls. She didn't know how Hassan had spent his weeks apart from her. But she would. Wyatt would make sure of it.

Monday morning, Wyatt stood curbside before his house as the caravan got organized. And by caravan, he meant the twins in the SUV with Kyle and Lawrence in tow, plus Hassan in the Mustang with Edy. Chloe was absent, though it was no surprise. Two weeks earlier, she'd shouted Lawrence down in the street about skanks, so they were Splitsville. Funny how Wyatt had an ear to all of South End's drama, right there from his stoop.

Another day of Edy not noticing Wyatt began. On the first day of school she wore this billowing white sundress with spaghetti straps that lifted and accented perfect cleavage. A fuss was occurring on the sidewalk. It appeared that the twins wanted her to change. Edy flipped them off and climbed in the car with Hassan.

Up to this point, Wyatt had had little control over his encounters with Edy. From the last day of school to the first of their sophomore year, her every moment had been scheduled so as not to coincide with him. While he didn't think it purposeful, it certainly *felt* as if it was. But a new school year had arrived and with it his day to see and spend time with Edy. Excitement stuffed itself in his mouth and threatened to inflate, carrying him off on a horizon of anticipation. He would see her in an hour, maybe two. Better still, the moment when Wyatt would reveal Hassan for the deceiver he was drew close. The thrill of anticipating *that* could undo him. So, Wyatt set off to school with enthusiasm in his step, whistling a feisty tune the whole walk there.

~~~

Mrs. Applebaum, Edy's new homeroom teacher, was a short, pallid woman with heavy-lidded eyes and deep curves, despite the presence of a waspish waist. She was young, no more than thirty, and had a watery, brown gaze that flitted about, unable to sit still. When Edy entered the class, Mrs. Applebaum pointed to a chair in the center.

"There," she barked.

"Assigned seats? Really?" *Welcome to first grade.*

Mrs. Applebaum turned to the dry erase board, already on to something else. With a sigh, Edy marched for her chair.

"Nice pair, Edy. I see you caught on that they grow by fondling," Shane Mitchell said.

She stopped just as he guffawed in that obnoxious way of his, doubling over and wild with the spectacle. But he had no idea how absurd he looked, wedged in the second seat of the second row, knees knocking wood in a desk-chair combo too small for the basketball team's starting center. "Yeah. Well, from what I hear, fondling doesn't grow much on you."

A collective roar was let out from the half dozen present, just as heat crept through Edy's cheeks. Why had she said it? Lord knows she had endured Shane Mitchell's crassness since grade school. Never had an outburst been warranted.

"Nice one," Chloe said from her seat in the center.

"Thanks," Edy said.

They hadn't spoken since their walk home with Wyatt. Now that she felt a little saner, an inkling of remorse tickled her.

"If you're done with your acceptance speech," Mrs. Applebaum said, "I'd recommend you take your seat."

Of course.

Edy dropped into her assigned chair behind Chloe and went to work getting organized. She had six A.P. Classes, including human geography, which sounded absolutely nonsensical. But her mother had insisted on it. Homeroom with Mrs. Applebaum would be followed by calculus with Hassan, then environmental science with no one in their right mind. Edy thought to compare her schedule with Chloe's, which no doubt would have things like drama and art, if for the sole purpose of living vicariously.

"Oh no," Chloe whispered.

Lawrence Dyson ambled into the room, three inches taller than memory served and rippling with muscles.

"There," Ms. Applebaum said, pointing to a seat up front near Shane.

Lawrence chuckled and dropped down behind and to the right of Edy.

"Edy," Chloe said, stiff as her head tilted just so. "Tell your friend not to even *try* talking to me."

"Okay," Edy said. "But—"

"Edy, tell *your friend* that paranoia is the first sign of drug use," Lawrence said.

Chloe whirled around. "I am not paranoid!"

Edy lifted a finger. "Personally, I would have denied the drug use—"

"Shut up, Edy!" Both cried.

Edy looked from one to the other. "Have you guys had some sort of fight?"

Chloe faced forward in a huff. Lawrence rolled his eyes. "Moron," Lawrence said.

"Slut," Chloe hissed.

Mrs. Applebaum inflated blowfish-style and sputtered as she weaved down the aisle, thick hips bumping empty desks wayward. She stopped in front of Lawrence. "What *is* your name?"

He sighed. "Dyson. Lawrence Dyson."

A hoot of cheers rang out from a far section of classroom, no doubt praise for the previous season or predictions for the next.

Mrs. Applebaum opened her mouth and shut it before hastening to the front of the room, bumping desks at double speed in her rush to snatch paperwork from her desk. "You're not on my roster. You don't even belong here!"

"Sure I do," Lawrence said.

She stared at him, trembling, furious with her disbelief. "If you don't leave, I'll call security," Mrs. Applebaum said, eyes wetter than ever.

Lawrence grabbed his backpack and reached inside. She jumped as if she were expecting a weapon. With a half-smile, he pulled out a sheet of paper, printed with a signature at the bottom.

She glared at it as if expecting it to coil up and hiss. "What *is* that?"

Lawrence held it out but said nothing. Eventually, Mrs. Applebaum snatched it.

Edy turned to Lawrence.

"What is it?" she whispered.

"Letter from the principal. They hijacked her homeroom and decided to put a bunch of football players in there. Good for team moral, they say. Whatever can bring home a second championship."

Edy pursed her lips. "Special treatment."

Lawrence shrugged. "Not special. Deserved."

Mrs. Applebaum looked up from the letter, face doughy and devoid of color. Meanwhile, a crowd crammed at the entrance—a pressing mass of swollen and chiseled out boys interspersed with what had to be the rest of the class. People took any old seat, jocks at the back, geeks at the door, students funneling in to line the walls.

"No, no, no!" Mrs. Applebaum cried. "We will *not* have chaos! We will *not* have mayhem!"

She rushed forward, only to get swallowed in the procession, absent in a wave of confused faces. Edy imagined the scene a microcosm of the world, as the bigger, stronger kids pushed through to choice seats and the smaller, kinder ones looked around in wonder. Hassan got through, of course, and found a seat toward the back on Edy's left. To her surprise, Wyatt found one on her right.

"Edy," Wyatt said. "I've been trying to call you. I—"

Mrs. Applebaum jostled her. Apparently, she'd found a system to combat the chaos, one that required her to bustle up and down the aisles, rudely demanding names and using Lawrence's letter to insist people go to their proper place.

Edy twisted to see past her rump and caught a glimpse of Wyatt's arm before Mrs. Applebaum ushered him out. She went through the class that way before turning to the hall. In the end, the room looked drastically different.

"It's like a team meeting in here," Chloe said. 'Yuck."

Every guy in the room was a tenth grader and player on the football team—Hassan, Lawrence, and Kyle were included, every girl like a random fill-in for normalcy. Except it didn't quite work.

Mrs. Applebaum gave up on the assigned seats, stopping instead to survey her class. Jason Mann, team quarterback, was hovering over Kendra Robinson, openly begging in his hundredth attempt to win her back since cheating. Onlookers booed her. Meanwhile, Tommy Kent and Kelly Lighthouse made out in the back, as Liam Williams shouted into his cell. Reggie Manning was up and Crip-walking again, undeterred by the gobs of paper that flew his way. Finally, Hassan, Lawrence, and the rest of the boys were arguing viciously over a play from last year. When Kyle went to the dry erase board in an effort to illustrate his point, Mrs. Applebaum rushed to the hall and screamed for security as if she'd been molested.

"Well," Edy said to Chloe. "This ought to be an interesting year."

~~~

It wasn't until third period that Edy saw Wyatt again. She took a seat toward the front of the room, and, when he entered, watched him take one next to her.

He stared forward momentarily, fingers drumming on the surface of his desk.

"Wyatt?"

He turned to her, mouth flattened. "What the hell, Edy? You haven't had a word to say to me since Hassan got naked for you."

A collective gasp stole the air in the room. Fiery embarrassment choking her, Edy attempted to survey the damage, only to find everyone staring straight back at her.

"Wyatt, I—" She shook her head. There was nothing to say. Nothing that wouldn't feed the rumor mill further, nothing that would make the moment go away.

"I'm sorry," she said, which sounded like a confession on further thought.

"Whatever." He faced forward again.

Edy slumped down in her chair. God, they'd come off as some overwrought love triangle. She hadn't even denied Wyatt's accusation, and in high school, that was the same as a confirmation. She needed a hole to sink into and a good friend to shovel dirt on top. Never come out again, that good friend would tell her, for the rest of your short, short life.

~~~

Edy saw Hassan just after fourth period, when she slipped her human geography book into her locker, closed the door, and found him standing behind it. Hassan leaned against the metal slab next to hers, arms folded, and winked.

"So. I hear we're official now."

"Yeah." There was no way to explain it, so she didn't bother. "Sorry."

"Does that mean you don't want to have my baby?"

"What! I never said that!"

He grinned at the furious way she stammered. Around them, people slowed.

Hassan glanced over his shoulder, leaned forward, and switched to Punjabi.

"You never said what? That you didn't want to have my baby or that you did?"

Edy stared at him, too confused to answer his question head on.

"If I didn't know any better, I'd think you were coming on to me," she said and flashed a nervous smile. *"Bad idea, right?"*

"And if I was?" he said in English. "Then what?"

Then I'm all in if you are.

Edy swallowed, heart pulverizing her ribcage with the thought. Somewhere, anywhere, she'd find a stray bone of sensibility left in her. Not by looking at those fire-lit eyes, or the lip he bit until it blazed. She'd look at her books, think of her future, and focus on more than fairy tales.

Except, she stared at him. And he stared right back, assessing, weighing, drinking her up as if thirsty for every drop. She felt the tug, always his irresistible tug, and felt she might plummet without moving a muscle or taste his smile, well, because. That last thought brought an inferno to her cheeks, stoked when he brushed fingers to her face.

"Think of me," Hassan said and headed off to class.

Edy's heart went into retirement. It packed its bags, headed for the door, and flat lined at the exit.

The last class of the day, seventh period was American History, antebellum era to present. On approaching the door, Edy spotted Lawrence standing outside it with Kyle. With a few minutes to spare, she decided to join them.

"I don't know where the twins'll go," Lawrence said. "And I'm tired of people asking me."

Edy frowned. Matt and Mason were seniors, blue chip players already neck deep in the college selection process. Despite playing on a mediocre team for their first two years, they'd been among the top defensive players in the state, coveted by some of the best teams in the country, which meant going south. Edy wished they had options closer to home.

"Everyone knows where they'll go. Georgia's come sniffing, end of story," Kyle said.

The University of Georgia was the alma mater for two generations of Dysons. A few years ago, the school retired his father's number. A flicker of irritation crossed Lawrence's face. It deepened till Edy followed his gaze.

Talk of Georgia wasn't the problem. It was Wyatt.

"Edy." He stepped up to her, with his back to Kyle and Lawrence. "We really need to talk."

"No," Lawrence said. "You don't."

She shot him an impatient look.

"You put her on blast in front of the whole class and now you want a private audience?" Lawrence said. "Get lost before I smash you."

Edy gave Wyatt a once over. Red blotched his cheeks and rimmed his eyes. She took a step to one side and shot Lawrence a silent warning. He raised a brow but said nothing. Wyatt came to her, shifting his back for the illusion of confidentiality.

"What is it?" she said.

"I'm sorry. For what I said and for the way it was taken. I know you wouldn't give yourself away so cheaply just because a guy is good with a football."

"Wyatt."

"Sorry. That's all I wanted to say."

"All right. Then thanks, I guess."

She wasn't sure if it was much of an apology, or even if she deserved one. As far as she was concerned, people took his words the wrong way, as people liked to do in high school.

"All right?" Wyatt said. "Is that really all you have to say?"

Edy blinked in surprise. His hostility had blindsided her. Wasn't it her name stuffed into everyone's mouth on the first day of school? "I, uh, don't know what you want from me," she said "Or why you're being so loud."

He touched her arm, delicately as if afraid she might break, fingers brushing. "Edy . . ."

There was something too intimate about that touch, too foreign, too not Hassan. She flinched. "I should go. I have class."

He grabbed her by the arm. "A second. I only want a second to—"

"Buddy? You have a problem?" Lawrence stepped forward.

Wyatt dropped her as if she'd burned him. "No. Of course not."

"Then don't touch her. Ever."

He was overreacting, of course, and drawing a crowd while he did so. For Lawrence, the ever silent one, this was out of character. It spoke to Edy in a way that no one else's anger could have. It meant that the verdict on Wyatt had been rendered. Her friend would never be accepted by the boys.

Lawrence stepped up, close enough for them to draw the same breath.

"Lawrence, please," Edy said. "Quit being a jerk. He didn't hurt me, he only—"

"Grabbed you," he said.

She decided to try a different tactic.

"You're making a scene," Edy said softly. "You hate to make a scene."

It was as if she hadn't even spoken.

"Come on," Lawrence said, nose to nose with Wyatt. "I'm in your face. Let's dance."

Wyatt said nothing.

"Leave him alone," Edy said. "You know he doesn't want to fight."

Lawrence smiled. "Touch her again," he said. "And I'll peel your face back from that mug you call a head."

No motion, no movement. Satisfied, Lawrence disappeared into a class across the hall. Wordlessly, Kyle followed.

"They're just protective of me," Edy said in a rush of breath. "They've known me so long and—"

"Yeah. I know," Wyatt said. "They don't let me forget. Ever."

It was true. Everything that flowed from Hassan and the boys to Wyatt had been off putting, on the offensive from the start. It had never been about Wyatt as a person, or Edy for that matter. No, it was about protecting their girl—from him.

She brooded on it all through history, but tried to shove it from her mind by the end of the day. Their protectiveness was irksome, meddling, but borne of love she knew. Doing without them wasn't a viable option; getting them straight would take a century. Perhaps she bore some of the blame for them being insufferable. After all, she relished every dirty stare she got from the "it" girls when one of the Dyson boys or Hassan fussed over her. In some ways, she might have encouraged this world she lived in.

After history class, Lawrence waited in the hall.

Kids streamed by like two rivers running in opposite directions. Cheerleaders, dancers, football players, all on their way to practice. Edy dug in so as not to get swept up.

"I don't like that dude," Lawrence said in greeting.

"I noticed," Edy said. "But I don't think that has much to do with him."

Lawrence cocked a brow.

"Anyway, you were bullying him," Edy pressed on. "You were bullying a kid that you know is harmless. Not cool."

"Who's harmless?" Hassan asked as he appeared behind Lawrence.

"Wyatt," Lawrence answered. "Though you couldn't tell it by the way I had to defend her."

He slung his backpack on and slipped into the flow of rushing kids. Halfway down the hall, Lawrence shouted, "Practice in fifteen!" and disappeared around the corner.

"Defending you? What's he talking about?" Hassan took a step closer.

Wow. This thing just escalated.

"It's not like it sounds. Lawrence is the one who flew off the handle. I was talking to Wyatt and thought we were done. He sorta grabbed me when—"

"Grabbed you? Grabbed you how?"

"Not 'grabbed me' grabbed me," Edy laughed nervously. "More like . . . took me by the arm. I don't know how else to put it. It wasn't rough or anything. I—"

"You what?"

His coldness froze her.

"Nothing. Can we drop this?"

"No. I need to know what's up with you and this dude. Is there something between you?"

"What? No!" she looked around, horrified, only to find that the day's end crowd had begun to peter out.

"Why would you even say that?"

"Because he feels like he can touch you!" He took a step closer. "Tell me if he's done it before." Voice low.

"Done *what*?"

"Touched you."

Her tongue thickened in astonishment.

They were *not* having this conversation.

His eyes darkened. "Edy. You haven't done something with this guy, have you?"

Wounded. He had the nerve to look wounded. After Sandra Jacobs climbed out of *his* window. Well, that was it. The tip top of her freaking limit.

"No. You don't get to . . . not after you—" She broke off, choked by frustration. "Get away from me."

Edy shoved Hassan, only to find it worthless, him unmovable and absorbing the blow. He stared down at her with that same hurt and demanding expression. Him with the gall to want answers, after all this? She rounded him in her rush to get away.

"Edy! Wait."

Quick strides brought him to her in an instant, despite the distance she'd made. When she didn't stop, when she refused to stop, he grabbed her by the arm.

"You see that?" She whirled on him in impatience. "That's what he did. That's the way it was. But according to you, it means there's something between us. It means there's everything between us, since you feel like you can touch me." She snatched her arm free.

"And that's the same to you?" Hassan said. "When he touches you and when I do? It feels the same?"

"No," she whispered, the word escaping in a breath.

"No," he echoed. Uncertainty made such a tiny word swell to gigantic proportions.

"Fine," she snapped. "To know me so well, you're as blind as a horse's ass when it comes to my feelings!" Edy said. "Now get out of my way. I have ballet."

Hassan did get out of her way, and when she cautioned a look back, he stood where she'd left him, looking dumbfounded.

~~~

Dinner was a silent affair that night, with only Rani, Edy, and too much food. Ali had a late night on campus for an event he was speaking at, while Edy's father and Hassan had their food holed away in the study. Apparently, footage of the West Roxbury middle linebacker had been found, and the two were eager to dissect it. Meanwhile, Edy's mother was busy with some focus group. She planned to announce her bid for a senate seat in the coming days.

Edy ignored Wyatt's text messages and faked small talk with Rani. All those seemingly innocent questions about the first day of school were loaded, so Edy feigned stomach cramps and stayed clear of anything that included Hassan.

Hassan. They were having his favorite that night, barbecued chicken. He could take almost anything barbecued, an old hat, he once said, so long as the sauce was right.

Any thoughts she was capable of having circled back to him and their moments together in the hall. His touch. Damn him for telling her to think of him. Edy already floated on daydreams, warmed on fantasies, and heated with words she delivered in her dreams. Dinner felt like rubber on her lips. She stared more than ate and glanced down the hall.

When Edy's cell phone buzzed for the umpteenth time Rani let out a sigh. She hated phones at the table, newspapers, or anything that took away from family life. Sometimes, Edy found her warm, comforting, like one of the surest reminders of home. Other times, she thought Rani needed an introduction to the twenty-first century.

Edy excused herself with a claim of too much homework. She went upstairs to her room and called back the only boy who ever dialed her phone frantically.

"Yes, Wyatt?"

"You're angry with me," he said. "About the way things went at school. About people thinking you and Hassan are together now."

"It's all right," she said. "It was bound to happen."

Did she really just say that?

"I mean . . ."

Nothing. Not a single word came to her rescue.

A muzzle. She needed to invest in one.

"Edy." Wyatt hesitated. "Is there something between you two?"

Is there something between the sun and the moon? Between the stars? "No."

"I don't want to see you hurt," Wyatt said.

Hurt. Oh shut up, already.

"This summer," Wyatt said. "You weren't the only one who had fun. Hassan spent his time with a lot of girls."

Edy's lungs stilled. For awhile, she heard only his tortured breathing.

"Edy?"

Girls. Of course. Why would that stop? What was she, stupid?

No doubt, he could hear it in her silence, the hurt that clouded with even the insinuation of there being someone else. In this case, a million someone elses.

It was out before she could stop it.

"Tell me what you know," she said.

"There were parties," he said "Three, four, five times a week. The Dyson brothers, Kyle, and Hassan, they went everywhere. And they always had girls with them. Beautiful girls. Hardly ever the same ones twice. I mean, these were the sort of girls who—"

"Never mind," Edy said. "Please stop."

There was no way she'd cry. She had the thought even as the tears started. She was not his girlfriend; she was his friend and a victim of her own foolishness. So, he was close to her. He may or may not have flirted with her—it wasn't the equivalent of a blood oath. If anything, his reluctance to pursue her—assuming he wanted to—had everything to do with the importance of their family and friendship. They could never look forward to a forever. Any romance they attempted came stamped with an expiration date: the date his parents selected his bride.

"Edy. You deserve—"

"I should go," she said. She wasn't up to the "better boyfriend" talk when she hadn't a boyfriend to begin with. "Homework, then bed. See you tomorrow."

She hung up on his response.

~~~

Edy climbed into Hassan's Mustang the next morning with a backward glance at the twins' Land Rover She wondered why the Dysons even bothered to stop by, if the conclusion had already been reached that she would ride with Hassan everyday. The year before, the boys made a point of peeking their heads into Edy's kitchen or Hassan's to grab leftover breakfast before school. Now, their sole purpose was to honk and tell them to hurry, like a pep squad ensuring they weren't late.

"What is it?" Hassan said, catching a glimpse of her looking their way.

Her mind went to the summer and to the girls she never saw. How many could there have been, when time and fatigue were the only constraints? What had they done? How often had they done it?

"You never told me about your summer," she said. "I told you all about mine, but apparently, you left out some crucial moments in yours."

He stared at her. She waited for annoyance, defiance, anger. After all, they were nothing to each other in the throes of love. She had no right to question him. Right?

Hassan's head fell back, hands grasping the steering wheel, and he sucked in all the air.

"I spent the summer running from myself. I made stupid choices. Constantly."

"What does that even mean?"

He looked at her. "Just say it, Edy. *Please.* Say what you want and it's yours."

He couldn't do that to her. Not once he'd dumped three thousand girls in the mix and she didn't know how to feel. He made her want to snatch her hair out in patches, or better yet, choke him out until he slumped.

"Drive, you bastard," was what Edy said.

"Fine," Hassan spat. "Let's just go to school."

They peeled off in silence.

Sixteen

Fall at other schools in the city meant a bunch of things, depending on the point of view. But at South End, fall had only one meaning: football. All else was a derivative of that.

Football season had officially begun. The season opener against Brighton was a massacre worthy of intervention. Big numbers for Hassan and the Dyson boys meant bragging rights for Steve, who claimed credit through the summer regimen he'd put them through. Big numbers for Hassan meant more time huddled in the study with Edy's father, who analyzed football with the same passion as he did political conditions in a developing country.

West Roxbury barreled toward them too fast, but only Hassan seemed to feel it.

At the start of the year, the papers argued that Leahy was stronger, maybe even faster than Hassan. But hadn't they seen Hassan against Eastie? Brookline? Charlestown? *Everyone?* He was far from the hopeful freshman vying for a few minutes of limelight. He was force and fury, fire forging steel, welding outcomes in their presence. He was bigger, stronger, faster, better than Leahy and more so every day. But that was fine. All adversaries—all—fell quick and hard to Hassan and his teammates. And as they stood amid the crux of a fierce winter, Hassan knew that Leahy would find domination like the rest. That was what he told himself until game day actually arrived.

"You can do this." Edy a ran hand through Hassan's hair. "It's just like all the others. It's yours already."

Hassan heaved into the toilet in response.

The vomiting was nothing new. He saved it for big games and that night was the biggest: he would face Leahy in what promised to be a sold out stadium. Scouts would be there. Hassan's rise—or fall—would be legendary.

He chucked his blueberry pancakes into Edy's toilet and hovered, face hidden.

"God," he moaned. "You'd think I'd be better than this by now."

Edy tucked away his hair, dangling near danger, and returned to rubbing his back. Slow, concentric circles, ran heat through his body, soothing away even thoughts of the game. When she ran fingers through his hair, Hassan leaned into them, ever tamed by the ebb and flame of her touch. A new weakness found him, one that had nothing to do with his game.

"I could let you do that all day," he said, voice echoing in the bowl.

"Then you should," she said.

He ruined it by heaving again, a violent lurch that raised him from his knees and forced him to clutch the toilet, though little more than spittle emerged. Edy's hand drifted lower, to his back, where her hand found bare skin under his shirt. Eventually, Hassan's ragged breaths eased, finding all the calmness he could with her touching him there. Edy stood and ventured over to a linen cupboard.

"You've got an extra toothbrush in the medicine cabinet," she said.

Hassan used the toilet to get to his feet but rose only so far as the edge of the tub, where he took a seat.

Edy wet the towel and handed it to him. He washed his face and handed it back.

"You okay?" she said.

Hassan looked up. "I can't stop thinking of all the ways I can lose the game."

She hung out the rinsed towel, flushed the toilet, and joined him. "That's crazy. I know what's going to happen tonight. Don't you?"

He shook his head. She was always so sure of him. Even when he couldn't figure out how to be.

Edy reached into his shirt for the dog tags she'd given him. He wore them always, even in the shower.

"You and Leahy are going to face off," she said, running a thumb over the tags' beaded necklace. "It'll be the toughest game you've ever had. You'll have to push harder and run faster and be smarter than you've ever before, because Leahy has earned his name. But when you do, when you find what's deep down in here," she traced a hand to his abdomen, "he'll be smoke to your fire, trailing you to the end zone."

Edy kissed his forehead, tucked away the tags, and stood. When she held out a hand, Hassan snatched it, not to pull himself up, but to pull her in for the fiercest of hugs.

He was ready.

Ready for anything.

~~~

Below-freezing weather for the night of the game, that was what they predicted. Hassan and his teammates were quarantined that day, remaining at school for dinner on through till it was time for the bus ride to West Roxbury. At the Phelps' house, the excitement was palpable with everyone jostling about, shouting for hats and gloves and scarves that might have been there, next door, or in one of five cars.

With the fall of night, Edy bundled in a sweater, jeans, and black goose down coat. She painted the palms and backs of her black gloves, the fold of her black skullcap, and the tips of her black scarf all with a white "twenty-seven", Hassan's number. She then gave her cheeks the same treatment.

Edy told herself that she wasn't nervous. On the drive back to school with her parents, on the climb in the bleachers to their seats and as a massive Robert Leahy, prodigy of Boston's mean streets, trotted out to the field, she told herself that she was not nervous. She didn't care how good Leahy was, or if they said he was the best. This was Hassan's night. It was *theirs*. She sensed it.

"You okay, kiddo?" Edy's father placed a hand on her knee and squeezed.

He placed a finger on her forehead where a white "twenty-seven" sat, pressing with a smile that reflected her own anxiety.

"This is the beginning," he told her. "The beginning."

Certainly, she could feel as much. Though the beginning of what, she couldn't be sure.

Time for kickoff.

West Roxbury won the coin toss, and with it, opted to receive instead of kick. The game began like a scuffle set to mute, with neither team retreating nor advancing. Helmet to helmet, pad to pad, cleats grinding into grass, offense and defense clashed in a stubborn assault, from which neither gained an advantage. And as the minutes of the first quarter ticked on, Edy scowled at an unchanged scoreboard.

Things went wrong in the second. Six plays set at a furious pace and West Roxbury found themselves within kicking distance. Unwilling to take a chance on a failed touchdown, they opted for the field goal and put points on the board for the first time that night. Murmurs wafted from the crowd. Mutiny, Edy thought. Already it sounded like betrayal.

Time dwindled on the first half. Eventually, South End's quarterback, Jason Mann, hurled a pass, only to have it picked off by West Roxbury.

They ran it back for a touchdown.

Edy stood at the close of the first, gaze scanning South End's team for a glimpse of twenty-seven. Shoulders after shoulders slumped, heads lowered, helmets pulled off with the unmistakable look of the lost. And the crowd wasn't much better. Behind Edy, a fat man in a padded navy coat with a dollop of mustard high on the breast, promised everyone within ten decibels that Leahy would be the top player in the nation come senior year, how he knew that a school like South End, with soft and pampered kids, could never match up against a beast like West Roxbury. They were tough and hungry, he went on, sloshing toppings from his hot dog, and no rich kid could change that.

"Oh, shut up," Edy snapped. "You haven't even figured out how to keep the food off your breasts."

"Edy!" her father cried. But her mother laughed.

"You little brat," the man snarled. "Watch your mouth or I'll—"

"You'll what?" Edy's mother interjected. "Threaten the daughter of the district attorney?"

Her mother's gaze fell slow, taking in the increasingly widening girth as if she could melt his fat like butter under heat. When she looked up again, another lump of toppings splattered onto his lap.

"Get a bib," her mother said. "Or better yet, keep your damned mouth closed."

Her mother faced forward again, dignified as ever, amidst the choking chuckles of Ali. She gave him only the hint of a smile.

Never in her life had Edy's mother spoken up for her. But before she could point that out, a roar erupted from the crowd.

Hassan had attempted a run, only to get mowed down by Leahy.

A loss of three yards.

"No tears," her father warned, even as Edy felt them bubbling upward. "This is exactly what he needs."

Fury made her forget the cold as she contemplated how her father could say such a thing. He hadn't seen Hassan. He hadn't seen the fear, the vomiting, the uncertainty. Edy turned away from her dad and refused to look at him again. Lips pursed, she stared at a distant point just past the marching band but found she couldn't ignore his words.

Mostly, football had come easily for Hassan. After a slow start, he blossomed into long yards and big plays, his right in the wake of talent and hard work. Last year he'd set records; this year he'd do the same. Despite that, people thought Leahy better. Why?

Because Hassan had never tasted the abyss.

That was what her father meant.

When the South End football team trotted out for the second half, Edy leapt to her feet, electrified. "Get your head out of your ass, Hassan, and kill him!"

"Edy!" Rani cried.

Dismay echoed all around.

She would deal with her punishment later. But at that moment, Hassan needed her. She took to a battle cry, something wild and incoherent, a frenzy of shrieks and stomps and whistles that she could carry for as long as he needed it. *She* would be there for him, there in the abyss with two quarters of game play and glory to be had.

The second half began like an omen as South End's kickoff returner stumbled out of bounds on catching the ball. He hit the ground in a tangle of feet, and a collective groan seeped from the crowd.

The end seemed near. South End was unraveling from all edges. Quickly.

Hassan's team lined up like the bow of an arrow. Edy spied them and frowned. A glance at her father told her he couldn't read the play either. They were in ace formation, with Hassan in the backfield and two receivers on the ground. They could pass or could run, but neither seemed good given the setup. Hassan's blocker, Kyle, was absent from the play, with two receivers on the ground in his place. The long pass seemed a fifty-fifty shot with the setup, while Hassan's sporadic performance had probably zapped the coach's willingness to rely on him, so Edy bit down on her knuckle and waited.

The ball snapped, and two walls collided in the night. Breath held, Edy's heart beat out the tune of her impassioned fear. Helmets smashed, thrashing followed, bodies tangled into a monolith—a single horrible giant with arms and legs of an endless variety. No one boy could get free from another, and yet she needed them to. Desperately. Where was he? Where was he? *Where was he?*

Hassan appeared, slipping from the monster smoothly, like melted butter poured out. Two steps, no more and Leahy crashed out, dead on him in wild pursuit. Arms tucked, feet pounding, form perfect, Hassan split the field—fast, faster, impossibly so, as if harnessing light and sound, fire and fury, the very shrieks that decimated her throat. Leahy couldn't keep up. No human possibly could. She hollered it, knowing he could hear. And in the end, Hassan toppled into the end zone, rolling back over belly, unable to slow down even once on his feet.

He was back.

Mayhem ensued.

Seventeen

Victory. He had claimed it for his own. Not from the jaws of death, as people liked to say, but from the lips of naysayers, the throats of doubters. One touchdown alone couldn't do it, so Hassan grabbed two to seal the game.

Duffle bag over his shoulder, he crossed the darkened parking lot as he headed for the bus that would take him back to South End. Soreness beat at his shoulders, back, and limbs, though it played distant second to a game with Leahy on the losing end. In his ears, teammates jabbered about this play and that, about the party at the Dysons' in a few. They whooped and jostled, piling atop each other with elation only winners could have. Later would bring the pain of battered limbs, the agony of bruises and contusions. But that night they would celebrate their victory. Hassan's gaze scanned the crowd.

"On your left," Lawrence said.

Hassan spotted her, quick in her steps to meet them. He gave Lawrence a once over and saw a conversation long overdue and a friend willing to wait a little longer. Edy broke into a run, and Hassan forgot all that, dropping his bag in his eagerness to scoop her up.

How could he tell her? There was no way she knew what she'd done for him.

Edy stood on tiptoe, arms wrapping his neck before she whispered in his ear.

"I was with you," she said. "I was with you the whole time. You could feel it, right?"

He exhaled and let the parking lot melt away. "Yeah, I could."

She looked up at him, face lit by the moon, brown eyes wide, hair billowing from a cap with his number painted on. He touched the "twenty-seven" on her cheek and allowed the thumb drift from it to the pulse behind her ear. He tilted her chin upward and she leaned into his touch. This girl was all he'd ever need.

"Sawn!" Lawrence snapped. "Pay attention."

Parents.

Eyes closed, he pressed lips to her forehead, knowing that if his mother saw, he'd be answering for that kiss in particular.

"Find me at the party," Hassan said.

Edy pulled back. Not away, just back.

To his right, a procession of teammates chanted, "Rocky! Rocky!" in a wide berth processional to him. She looked from the team to Hassan.

"If you want me to choose," he said, "you'll win."

Edy sighed. "Dyson house?"

"Dyson house," he said and chanced a thumb against her cheek once more.

"Pradhan!" boomed the team coach.

Oh boy.

Hassan spotted him filling up the doorway of the team bus with his body.

"Pradhan, you sonofa—! Get on this bus! I've got a wife and two kids at home!"

Hassan looked around, blinking at the sudden absence of friends.

"An hour," he said. Hassan snatched his duffle bag and trotted for the bus.

Inside, the doors swooshed closed behind him and the darkness engulfed. Hassan took a step forward, only to stop as Mason leapt to his feet.

"Ohhhhh, you dog!" he hollered. "Don't you take advantage of that girl tonight!"

The bus roared in approval.

~~~

People cramped the Dyson home to fire-code capacity that night. Football players, dancers, jocks, and wannabes crushed in alongside Leahy and a dozen or so other West Roxbury players, jovial despite the loss. Hassan respected his nemesis more for the disposition; he didn't think he had it in him to do the same if he were the loser.

Steve and Tessa Dyson were away, the agreement on condition of a South End win that night. As Hassan sat on the living room couch, vaguely aware of thumping hip hop as he sipped a beer, he imagined what it would have been like to have American parents like his friends, ones that did things as normal as let them throw parties and have girlfriends.

Next to Hassan was the Dysons' twelve-year-old sister, Vanessa, a lump of a girl that rarely abandoned the television. That night, she wore blue shadow on her eyelids and a glob of red gloss on her lips, as she stared up at him with eyes distressingly full of adoration.

"Tell me what you like to do, Hassan. Besides football, I mean."

Most of the time, Vanessa was a non-issue, holed away in her bedroom or the theater or some other place Hassan could avoid. But that night she was there, eager to celebrate his victory. Celebrate with him, apparently.

Vanessa placed a hand on his knee. He removed it with two fingers and dumped it on her lap. In a nearby corner, Matt and Mason nudged each other and pointed, winded and wheezing from laughter. No help would come. None ever did.

"I know you like football," she said. "And you should, because you're so good." She leaned forward, plump hand once again on his knee. "Better than my brothers, even."

She batted eyelashes at him, forcing him to shift back for space.

Hassan had two options. The first entailed getting up, which would invite over scores of girls, eager to share the limelight of his win. Alternatively, sitting there would mean enduring his best friends' kid sister. He told himself the second option was best, even as Vanessa Dyson dragged a manicured finger across his arm.

"You know what?" she said. "Your eyes are so pretty."

"Go to bed, Nessa," Lawrence said and pulled her to her feet.

She pouted, only to stomp off after one stern look from her brother.

"Thank you," Hassan mouthed.

Lawrence sighed. "She promise herself to you again?"

Hassan turned up his beer and found it empty.

"Not yet," he said, with a glance to the can.

Lawrence grinned. "Guess I should've waited a little longer then."

He disappeared before returning with a fresh beer. Hassan took it, mumbled thanks, and looked around. "Sawn. You and Edy—"

"I could use some air." Hassan said and headed for the back porch.

He weaved between a throng of cheerleaders in uniform near the door. One grabbed his wrist and pulled, forcing him to pause long enough to pry her fingers from him without being forceful. A hand gripped his bicep; lips brushed his ear in invitation. Freedom found, Hassan slipped into the cold of the night, grateful.

Another half hour passed before Edy's arrival. He spent it on the back porch, staring out at the skyline, and above it, the crescent moon.

She used to call it a fingernail moon when they were kids. Just a sliver of whiteness suspended in the sky, the rest hidden but still there. They were the same way, he supposed. A sliver of what was real in view, the rest hidden but still there.

The door behind him opened.

Edy.

"I was starting to worry," he said.

"Sorry. I had to climb out the window."

Hassan grinned. An easy task for a girl with all jocks for friends. He reached out an arm to her, impatience melted away.

"Come here, already," he said and pulled her in.

She came to him, natural as breathing. When she folded into his embrace, their bodies melded—it was always the same. His lips found her forehead and pressed. Her arms wrapped his waist and squeezed, slipping beneath the fabric of his coat.

She tilted her head up to look up at him, smiling. He took her hand from his waist, cool to the touch, and brought it to his chest, at the place where his heart beat beneath. "Feel that?"

Her fingers spread, eyes wide. "It's beating so fast," she whispered.

"Do you know why?"

Edy lowered her gaze. "The game?"

"Try again." He captured her mouth with his.

Their foreheads touched, their noses, their lips, and he whispered Edy's name like a last exhale. In the ice of winter the whole world froze, except him and her in that moment. He kissed her again. Swallowing, devouring, moving in deeper, pressing closer with each passing second.

Everything. That's what he aimed to give. Hollowed out and emptied from his soul into hers. Edy clung to him, opening, purring, and reeling him in, weakening Hassan by her ready reply, scorching them both with hunger. This kiss . . . oh . . . this kiss. He had his tongue in her mouth, thrusting. Edy met it with a moan.

"Oh. Wow. Okay."

They looked up to find Lawrence staring at them. He blinked as if trying to burn the image away.

"Twins are about to tell the team that they're committing to Georgia. I know you already knew, but they wanted you there and stuff."

"Okay," Hassan said.

"Okay." Lawrence shifted, looked awkwardly from one to the other, and then ducked back into the house.

"Well," Hassan said. "Let's go give 'em something to talk about, huh?"

He held out his hand to her.

When she took it, Hassan swept her in.

"Leave your window open tonight," he said. "I don't plan on getting interrupted again."

~~~

Edy slipped into her room just after one in the morning, the silence of a sleeping house engulfing her. She hesitated, back at the window, listening for a sound from her parents.

Nothing.

Leave her window open.

That was what Hassan had said and that was what she thought about, with the taste of his spearmint gum still sweetening her mouth.

He wanted to come to her, uninterrupted, with the promise of finishing they'd started.

Edy looked back at her bed.

The feel of his body lingered on her, the pressure of his lips still there. She could smell him, taste him, touch him still, it seemed. But there was no way she was ready to sleep with him. Her pounding heart said maybe.

Edy turned to find him scaling their tree. She stepped back, giving him space enough to swing in. Avocado eyes met hers, heavy-lidded and weighted. Exhaustion, definitely. Maybe even regret.

He kissed her before she could ask.

Tendrils of heat licked through her, tempting with all the possibilities, of kissing, of hands pulling her in tight, of hardness flush against her.

He slipped an arm around her waist, pulling her in. The smallest breath escaped her before he stole even that in a kiss. And there it was again. The thing she couldn't name. The thing that curled and stirred at his touch, slight from day to day, but like a vortex suddenly.

"I don't know if I'm doing it right," Edy admitted, even as their lips met.

"Hmmm." Hassan grinned. "Let me check." He kissed her as she giggled. And when he pulled away, he shook his head in mock disapproval. "See, you're not supposed to laugh. But we'll work on that later."

He turned from her, closed the window, and peeled off his jacket before cinching her in again close. They paused, shared an exhale, and warmed the space between them. Brushed lips, hip to hip, and in the space of one whimper—hers—Edy realized.

"How long would you have waited for me?" Hassan said with a ghost of smile on his lips. "How long would we have waited for this?"

Edy heated to the roots of her hair. "Maybe forever."

"Yeah," he said. "Me too I think sometimes."

His lips returned in a series of slow nips before following with a procession of more, behind her ear and straight down the pulse of Edy's neck. She shivered, pulled him up by the scruff of his hair, and cut off his laugh with a hungry kiss of her own.

They stumbled into bed without the kissing having slowed. Her under him with her heart running the Kentucky Derby. His ran right alongside hers, looking for a first place finish. Standing up, her hands had been everywhere: in his hair, on those rugged shoulders, running fingers over those iron-like pecs. But once they collapsed in bed with him atop her, both froze.

Hassan rolled away. "Let's catch some sleep. A few hours, though, and I climb across the yard."

Edy looked at him and flushed. She looked at him wondered. Where had he found the self control? Five minutes ago, she might have given her virginity to him. She'd been willing, even though she'd not been ready. Before, she had prided herself on being far more practical than the boys, but now she wondered. Meanwhile, he was still Hassan—still as loving and sheltering as ever. He was still on some quest to protect her, and he would always protect her, even if she needed protecting from herself.

Eighteen

Hassan woke to the sound of his cell, shrill and far too close to his ear. He groped for it, nearly toppling the Patriots lamp at his bedside, before closing his hand around it. He'd spent most of the night at Edy's, arms wrapped around her, fading in and out as he listened to her sleep. Rest had eluded him.

"Yeah?" he said into the phone.

"We need you to come over," Lawrence said. "Mom has us moving stuff and we need an extra pair of hands."

They were rich and could hire help. But there was no point in stating in the obvious.

"I'm asleep," Hassan said.

"I noticed."

Hassan rolled onto his back, eyes shut in an attempt to catch the last remnants of rest.

Lawrence grunted. "Listen. Just . . . come over and give me a hand. *Now.*"

He hung up before Hassan could respond.

Half an hour later, he dragged himself out of bed, showered, and hiked the three blocks to the Dyson house. After getting no answer with the doorbell, Hassan nudged open the front door and watched it swing into darkness.

"Hello?" His voice carried with the echo. He could have been sleeping. He could have been reviewing the playbook. He could have been scarfing down pancakes or something. His stomach grumbled in agreement.

They'd better have breakfast.

"Hello?"

A blast from the side floored Hassan, toppling him at the exact moment he realized people were near, in the shadows. He took a slap at the back of his neck before sharp, stinging jabs rained down all over his legs. And it occurred to him. He was getting his ass kicked.

Hassan struggled to his feet, only to be snatched down by his shirt. Both twins grabbed hold of his arms, subduing him so that only his legs could kick.

"Ow!" he hollered and attempted to twist around.

Above him, Lawrence came into view.

"Go, Lil' D. Get a lick in. We know you didn't hit him," Mason said.

"Man, come on. I called him, like you said. Why should I—"

"Either you hit him, or you're next. And Sawn'll probably help since you didn't help him," Matt said.

Lawrence sighed. He knelt down on a knee so that he and Hassan were eye level. Then he tagged him in the arm. A punch with no fire. A love tap.

"Hit him for real. And hurry up. He's strong."

Hassan strained against the weight of their hold only to have a sharp yank on either side still him. Lawrence blasted him in the shoulder.

"Ow!" Hassan cursed. *"Kutiya."*

The twins released him and stood.

"You okay?" Mason said and offered Hassan a hand. He slapped it away.

"You can't be mad," Matt said. "You agreed to this."

Hassan clamored to his feet, wondering what his legs would look like when he removed his pants. Rubbing the spot where Lawrence tagged him, he scowled at his attackers.

"I'm pretty sure I never agreed to getting attacked."

"No. But we all agreed years ago that we'd beat up Edy's first boyfriend, whoever the sorry sucker happened to be." Mason threw an arm around Hassan. "And now that that's done, we sit down and have a nice long talk."

Hassan took a seat on Matt's king-sized bed, drew up a leg, and let his back hit the wall. Across from him, his three closest friends in the world scowled as if he were the intruder who had just been caught. He suddenly realized just how brave a man Wyatt Green had to be.

Mason flipped around a chair from Matt's desk and straddled it, eyes on Hassan. He leaned forward so that his arms folded along the top before resting his chin on his fist.

"Did you sleep with her?" he said.

To outsiders, there was no telling Matt from Mason. Both had long, lean, dark frames and devilish sort of grins. They were known for their wit, their hijinks, and their carefully construed indifference. But Hassan knew another side of them: the one he was seeing now.

"No."

The room filled with exhales.

"You been in love with her a long time," Mason noted. "Maybe even always."

Hassan lowered his gaze. It wasn't exactly a question, and he didn't exactly have room to argue.

"What are you gonna tell Nathan?" Matt said, from where he leaned against the wall.

"Nathan? What about his mom? His dad? Or Edy, when the chick he's supposed to marry shows up on the scene?" Mason said.

Hassan exhaled. He was sixteen. Sixteen and American. As American as any blond-haired, blue-eyed boy from Topeka, Kansas. He didn't want to worry about arranged marriages, race, religion, or any other differences adults liked to get tangled in. But like all children of immigrants, he balanced on a tightrope, hovering between what was and what is—pockets overflowing with pressures from each.

Hassan's phone vibrated. He peeked at his phone in what he hoped was discreet fashion.

A text from Edy.

Having a problem.

His answer was immediate.

???

Can't stop thinking about u.

Nothing could stop his idiotic grin.

Lucky me.

When Hassan looked up, all eyes were on him. He sighed, unable to shake the feeling of having more to grapple with than what was fair for a boy his age.

"Look. You think I've got all the answers?" He jammed away the phone. "No one does. Not me, not Edy, and definitely not our parents. But I can tell you this. I'd rather be sitting next to her with all the problems in the world, than trapped in a room that smells like monkey balls and skunk piss, while acting like I care what you guys think."

The twins grinned.

"That just earned you more face time with the floor," Mason said.

"We'll see." Hassan stood. "This time, I get Lawrence."

~~~

Edy grabbed a khaki knapsack off her desk, stuffed an endless assortment of nothings in it—including tattered receipts and chewing gum—took the chewing gum out, thought of Hassan, and threw it back in with a blush. Halfway down the stairs she remembered her coat, ran back, and set off again.

"Sweetheart, you don't think it's odd to go skating at night?" her father ventured, following her to the door. "It's a festive activity, best handled under the light of day."

"Daddy, please. What difference does it make if it's light out or not when we'll be indoors?" Edy turned on him long enough to catch the rare pursing of lips that meant he'd been stumped. She erased it by standing up on tiptoe and kissing his cheek. "Hassan, Lawrence, and the twins will be there, so yes, the answer to your next question is that I'll be safe."

His frown tilted only a tad.

"You could do something closer to home. All of you could crowd in here like you used to and—"

"Daddy."

"Edith, Dorchester isn't safe at night!"

Edy sighed, reminding herself as she rummaged through her knapsack for keys that his worrisome nature was a sign of love, not distrust.

"I'm more capable than you give me credit for. And anyway, we'll be fine. We're skating, not heading to a knife fight on Blue Hill Ave."

The twist of his face had her regretting the words, so she kissed his cheek quickly, certain that her path to escape narrowed by the second.

"Be safe," he said in a voice a little too soft, a little too serene.

She shot him a single inquisitive look and left.

Edy peeked into the SUV idling at the curb and scowled at the sight of Chloe. Mason was driving with Alyssa Curtis in the front passenger seat. Matt and Lawrence sat like bookends in the back with Chloe in the middle. Jessica Wilson sat on Matt's lap.

Alyssa and Jessica were the two upperclassmen who Edy always assumed attended her birthday parties under duress. Seeing them so clearly attached to the twins forced Edy to rethink their motivations for the annual attendance. It conjured up images of all the girls who used to compliment her shirts or chat her up enthusiastically, in the hopes of gaining sway with her boy of choice.

"Nice sweater," Alyssa said in greeting.

Edy's eyes narrowed to nothing. Never had the girl spoken to her before.

"It is nice," Mason concurred from behind the wheel. "Sawn pick that out when you two went shopping for curtains?"

The Dysons snorted with laughter.

"You shut up," Jessica said. "*I* think they're cute. Always have been."

She shot Edy a reassuring smile.

"I forget your name," Edy said sweetly. "Or the last time we spoke for that matter."

The laughter snuffed out.

"Do me a favor and dial back the Cruella de Ville," Matt said.

If he thought for a second that his friends wouldn't be subjected to the Wyatt treatment, then he—

"Beautiful view back here," Hassan said.

Edy jumped, turned to face him, then flushed horribly, as latent understanding found her. He'd been looking at her backside.

She groped for something clever. "Hey," she managed.

"Hey," he said. "Haven't seen you all day."

"Hadn't touched her all day" was what came to her mind. That he hadn't wrapped arms around her waist or pressed lips to hers all day. Him slumbering with an arm beneath her head felt like eons ago. Was it really only the night before?

"Stare at each other on your own time," Mason said. "Meet you at the rink."

Their group met at the rink's entrance and queued for shoe rentals. When it was Edy's turn at the counter, Mason flanked her right and Matt her left, whispering in her ear about a pierced and pudgy man, whom they likened to a walrus in a leotard. Wasn't he her type?

Didn't she want his number? They'd make sure she got it if she wasn't nicer to the other girls.

With only a pout that mimicked hurt feelings, she promised to say nothing more. Absolute silence was what she'd give those girls. That wouldn't stop her from searing glares though.

As the group laced up on benches, Jessica and Alyssa traded barbs with the twins about their exes, slicing words that cut, despite bright, deceptive smiles. With each comment, irritation snaked through Edy, promising to tip her temper to the point of words. So when Matt whisked Jessica onto the rink and kissed her, Edy's scowl followed them round and round, turning circles that should have made her dizzy.

"Starving," Mason announced. "Gonna make Lawrence buy me something. Be right back."

For some reason, he snatched Hassan by the arm, steering him away. Edy looked around, wondering how she'd come to be left with Alyssa Curtis. Where were the others? Even Chloe would have been preferable then.

Alyssa was staring at Edy. "Am I really that bad?"

Edy couldn't keep her word to the twins and answer her, so she decided to pretend she hadn't heard.

"Wow. It's as bad as everyone thinks. You're an absolute jerk," Alyssa said.

Edy's mouth fell open. "And you're only talking to me to get somewhere with Mason!" There. She hadn't meant to say it, but she'd been provoked.

"You're either painfully conceited," Alyssa said, "or you enjoy playing the victim. It's their fault though, with the way they orbit you like the star of their solar system. Are we all supposed to treat you like that? You go on and on about when and under what conditions certain people to you. But just as easily as I can talk to you, you can talk to me, too. I've seen you every day for years. In the halls, on the street. I've seen you walk right by me. Why don't *you* talk to me?"

"Why would I do that?" Edy mumbled.

"Oh, I don't know! Maybe to thank me for one of the birthday presents I've gotten you every year for the last six years."

Edy shot her a sideways look, heat creeping into her cheeks.

"The boys have nothing to do with it," Alyssa said. "People don't speak to you because you don't like to be spoken *to*. You act like we're the snobs, but you're the biggest snob of them all. You and yours are too good for everything and everyone."

Edy paused, mouth pregnant with a protest. It reminded her of the time Ali had spent all afternoon professing to be a consummate diver, fielding the laughs of his wife, Hassan, and Edy. He'd climbed shirtless onto the diving board at their resort in Belize, abdomen hairy and formidable, arms extended. A pause ensued, weighted and silent, as they considered—only briefly—that perhaps they didn't know all there was to Ali Pradhan.

And then he swan-dived into the pool.

Things weren't always what they seemed to be.

"If I'm so unbearable," Edy said, "then why do you come to the parties?"

She didn't think she wanted to hear the girl's answer.

Alyssa hesitated.

"Mason loves you," she said. "So I do too."

Edy considered the possibility.

She'd seen them horse playing in the hall and exchanging the occasional hug or touch. But nothing more. "I never knew you two were so serious."

Alyssa shrugged. "As serious as anyone can be with a Dyson."

It occurred to Edy that being romantically involved with someone who was all tickles and giggles had to be difficult. How could you separate sincerity from situational comedy? She pictured Alyssa leaning in to kiss Mason, only to have her most vulnerable moment turned into fodder for laughs. Edy had always thought her boys too good for the pickings around them. Never once had she considered their shortcomings.

She hadn't known that Mason and Alyssa were an item, for example. Yet she'd seen him with other girls in the hallway as readily as she'd seen him with Alyssa, grinning, flirting, and cutting eyes as their bottoms sashayed past. Were Hassan to ever treat her that way, Ali and Rani would have to bury him piecemeal.

Mason appeared.

"Matt's trying to show us up," he announced and held out a hand to Alyssa. "The bum thinks he's Don Juan the Figure Skater."

Alyssa gave Edy a tight smile and whisked away with Mason as Hassan showed up.

"You didn't get food?" she asked, blinking away lingering thoughts from the conversation just passed.

"I ordered fries for us, but Mason licked 'em." Hassan shrugged.

"Ready?" he said and pulled Edy to her feet.

He gripped her hand, eager, led her to the rink, and then shot like a bullet. She whipped in alongside him, ready for his punishing stride.

Back when Edy's mother was a lowly assistant D.A., she and Tessa Dyson would take the kids roller skating. The women used to harbor a fanaticism for the sport that sucked them all in, making their childhoods as much about strobe lights and blading to disco as it was about football, family, and friends. But though that was long ago, skating bonded them still. They managed a competitive streak that outsiders couldn't quite get.

Music pulsed and jolted as a dizzying array of strobe lights streaked the rink. They circled at a blast, fingers laced, hair flapping, bodies slicing in flawless sync. Edy leaned in, leading, and shot him a wolfish grin.

"Keep up," she warned.

His eyes lit with the deliciousness of her taunt before he kicked into overdrive, yanking her forward into breakneck speed. Edy shrieked in approval, then heckled as they passed a meandering Mason and Alyssa circling the rink at a crawl.

"Come on. I like your thinking," Hassan said, and they whipped around the rink again, twin minds of a single devilish nature, racing toward the source of their next amusement. And when they arrived, they circled Mason and Alyssa as if they were prey, grinning at the winding way they moved. All jerks and lurches from Alyssa's inexperience with Mason's jaw clenched in his impatience.

"I'd say you should glue her to you," Hassan said, "But I doubt she can hold you up much longer."

They swept off at the barb as Mason cursed, crooks on the lam, laughing, chancing a second look. Together, Edy and Hassan shot at triple speed, stockpiling velocity, feeling invincible. This was them, them as they'd always been.

His arm slipped around her waist. She was still getting used to that.

A day. It was all the time that had passed since he'd pressed her hand to his heart and his lips against hers. All was the same, and yet all was different, as if viewed through a kaleidoscope of colors, ignited.

When the music slowed, he pulled her in for an easy stroll to the up-tempo music. She relaxed in his embrace, molding like seams stitched together, gliding, anticipating, intuitive. Had they always fit so perfectly?

Yeah. They had.

Nineteen

School.

From the front passenger seat of the Mustang, Edy stared down at her palms, palms creased with lines Hassan could trace by heart—had traced by heart. He took one of her hands in his.

"Ready?" he said.

She didn't answer, instead allowing the warmth of his hand and the familiarity of his fingers to coax her to steadiness.

Not ready. But it wouldn't matter.

He slapped a kiss on her cheek and bounded from the Mustang before coming around to let her out. When Edy slowed on climbing out, he bent and stuck his head into the car, mouth close to her ear.

"It'll be okay," he said. "We are what we are. No regrets, right?"

That much she knew. Her back straightened with the notion.

But her eyes swept the parking lot. Kids clustered on the right and left, some by cars, others on bikes, a few with skateboards. At least one car had its trunk open, hip hop bounding from it. In a moment, all eyes would be on them.

"It feels fake," she said. "Like putting on a show."

Hassan pulled a face.

"So, you're acting when you're with me?" A smile played across his lips.

"No, but—"

"Then get out and kiss me already."

He took her hand and pulled her from the car. The moment she stood, he embraced her, and like always, she became instantly aware of him—*painfully* aware of him. Aware of the space between them, of the shared air they breathed. And like always, she wanted to push straight through it.

"Did I ever tell you that I like theater?" he said.

Edy smiled, tilting her chin up expectantly.

"Me too."

He leaned in closer, blotting out the school, parking lot, and onlookers from her mind. Briefly, Edy wondered if he could sense the wild pound of her heart, the shallow breaths she had to try for, the sweat that formed on her brow. Then he kissed her and all was forgotten.

With his hand against her cheek, his mouth moved over hers, earning a flush of her face. Every place they connected ignited her at his touch, beckoning her to boldness. She lifted her hands to his waist and ran them to the small of his back, reaching beneath the jacket and sweater for a feel of smooth skin and taut muscle. The kiss ran deeper, and she stood on tiptoe, not caring that her back was pressing into the side mirror of the Mustang. A whimper of want escaped her. Then the school bell rang.

Hassan cursed. He broke off from her, leaving her to the chasm of his absence. "We'll be late." He said it with a too-dry throat, pushing it out as if the words cost him pain.

With her surroundings reappearing, Edy remembered their goal, with the success of it painted clear on shocked faces. Both Edy and Hassan had staked a claim in what would become a well-documented kiss, staving off innuendo in the hopes of conveying a clear message.

"They were together," that message said. And while they hadn't quite figured out how to address their "togetherness" to their parents, they did know one thing. There was no room for ambiguity at school, even if home was a different matter.

She didn't have long to wait. They were on her before lunch, sullen and salty beauties with gazes that burned and scowls that promised wrath. Wax-smooth skin and wintertime tans were their mark, as lush, full-bodied locks hung around faces so beautiful even their anger seemed a derivative of attractiveness, a model of what the rest should aspire to. They bumped her in halls, sneered in corridors, and muttered insults about her clothes, her appearance, her nothingness.

But they were tragically mistaken.

They thought her as delicate as the daises that bloomed in the spring, dipping with the wind, bending with pressure, petals aflutter. It was what ballerina meant to those who couldn't know, who had never known the broken bones and the fire of competition.

Twenty-six bones comprised the feet, knitting together with thirty-three joints, delicate bits of bone that shuddered in duress and shattered with abuse. Aches, breaks, gritting teeth, and pained smiles—that was the truth of being a dancer. Joy mistaken for meekness and flames mistaken for smoldering cinders, she had passion fused down to the soul and cells, passion that ruptured on stage. To think Edy Phelps weak was their mistake. It was a mistake with consequences, though.

~~~

Wyatt stepped into the boys' bathroom and a wad of wet paper plopped upside his skull. He looked up to see dozens of similar clumps, all affixed to the ceiling with little more than water and a strong throw. Given the course his luck usually took, it seemed appropriate that all of them should rain down on him at once. That was life for Wyatt Green, one more blow when he was down, ten more when he could take no more.

Edy. Hassan. *His* Edy with Hassan.

Not for the first time that morning, he bit down on his bottom lip, hoping to supply real pain in the place of heartbreak.

"Don't cry," he whispered to the face in the mirror. "Not here. Not now."

The face looking back at him made a different claim, that he could do nothing but cry. So, He let it happen, the shudders racking his body, the tears flooding and spilling over, one after another until the trickle became a river.

This was the way it had happened with Lottie, the way he'd lost Lottie.

There could be no bearing that again, that rupturing and emptiness, the aching, utter despair. He'd do anything to avoid it.

He had nothing. He'd always been the boy with nothing. Parents that couldn't care. Bills they couldn't pay. Loneliness that never left.

As a kid, he made peace with his bitter existence, with nights too cold and blankets too few. He'd never tried for more, never even thought he could have more—more than loneliness and hunger pains and words of impatience.

But then Lottie had come, with a smile for him and hugs for him, and endless hours of walks and talks all *just for him.*

Then the other guy came and they weren't for him anymore—Lottie wasn't for him anymore.

The accident happened soon after that. The terrible thing he couldn't explain, the need to just *be* with her, the fog in his brain, the screams. Nothing else.

They'd had to move.

No one accepted Wyatt's version of events and he and his family *had* to move.

By the time Boston came, he'd given up on smiles, hugs, walks and talks, given up until the moment he saw Edy. Even a flicker of that smile had told him what he hadn't been able to believe: that life, love, even loving were all still his to have.

But then Hassan showed up. The boy who had everything wanted even her for himself. Hassan wanted his share, and Wyatt's share of Edy, even when Wyatt had so little to give.

He couldn't have it.

He absolutely couldn't have the one thing Wyatt had left.

~~~

Grateful for the bell that signified escape from trig, Edy filed into the hall and stopped at the sight of Chloe and Lawrence blocking her locker. She braced herself for hysteria. Since there had been none at the skating rink, she expected double the next day. They were warped that way.

"Hey, Cake," Hassan said and wrapped an arm around her in greeting. Around them, the hallway swelled to capacity.

"Aren't they gonna fight?" she said.

"Probably not today. They've been back together for a week or so, so it'll be another few days before they fight."

"But about what?" Edy said, as she followed him in a short shot to his locker.

Hassan spun through his combination and threw open the door.

"Now I wouldn't be a good friend if I told you that, would I?"

Lips pursed, Edy eyed the couple. Chloe giggled about something, and Lawrence shifted, leaning in as if wanting to be closer without detection.

A thought occurred to Edy. "Was it about what went on this summer?"

Hassan stiffened. "Tell me. Are we talking about Chloe and Lawrence or me and you?"

"Hassan."

"Listen." He switched over to Punjabi. *"This wasn't the easy decision—you and me. I fought it, and you know how stubborn I can be. Everything we know tells us this'll never work. Centuries of history say that we'll have to grow up, that we'll have to accept who we are and what we're not meant to be."*

"But?" she said in English.

He turned to her.

"But I haven't thought about anything more than I've thought about being with you." He hesitated, as if considering how to proceed. "Whoever I'm meant to be," he said, switching over to gentle English. "Whoever I'm meant to grow into—that person is supposed to be with you. I know that."

He'd said it as if it were some bare minimum, as if his being with her weren't the thing she craved like oxygen. Words tangled like brambles in her mouth. She gave up on speaking and threw her arms around him instead.

"Mmm," Hassan said. "I should have said that back when I was naked and looking for towels."

A burst of laughter tore from Edy, and she shoved him, though his body didn't budge.

"If you two are done . . ." Lawrence said, appearing at their side. "I'd like to go. I'm starving."

Hassan slammed his locker shut. "We're done. Just waiting for you two to finish rubbing noses and building your nest or whatever it is you do."

Lawrence scalded him with a look. Beneath it, though, embarrassment reigned.

"Relax," Hassan said and threw an arm around his best friend. The words that followed were masked in a low baritone. When Lawrence shoved him away, both were grinning.

"You never shut up, do you?" he said.

"Not when I can help it," Hassan said.

Lawrence, Hassan, Edy and Chloe started down the hall, only to have their path staved off by Wyatt.

"Oh. Hey," he said, as if his meeting them was accidental, despite the obvious intention in his cutting them off.

"Hey," Edy said when it became apparent that no one else would answer. "How are you?"

What was with the thick feel of awkwardness? The sudden weight of needing to apologize, though for what, she couldn't be sure?

"Well, I heard the news about you two. I just wanted to . . . come over and say congrats, I guess," Wyatt said.

Hassan raised a brow.

Edy frowned. "But I thought—"

"I was being overprotective." He shot a smile at Hassan. "Turns out you guys don't have a monopoly on that after all."

Hassan and Lawrence exchanged a look, faces like granite. Wyatt's smile melted.

"We got off to a rough start," he continued. "And I'd like to try again. You'll find I'm not half as bad as I look."

He extended a hand to Hassan. A covert glance left and right told Edy they had more attention than they needed.

With a sigh, Hassan accepted Wyatt's handshake.

"Alright," he said. "Second test drive. Sit with us at lunch. We're heading over now."

The five of them took off again, picking up the twins along the way. Seamlessly, the Dyson brothers and Hassan fell toward the back, where remnants of whispers wafted forward. She heard her name and Wyatt's more than once.

It turned out he'd have to do a lot more than shake hands to be one of the boys.

~~~

Edy hated lunch. She'd hated it ever since the first day of junior high, when she'd sat down with Hassan, the Dysons, and Kyle, and Sandra Jacobs had asked if five boys were at the table, or six. It was a stupid thing, the equivalent of calling her a tomboy, Hassan supposed, but Edy'd cried just the same. He'd always meant to ask her why. Now, as Sandra Jacobs approached with Eva Meadows and the redhead in tow, Hassan knew one thing: there was no way in hell they were sitting with them. Not when he was just getting somewhere with Edy.

Lawrence and Hassan exchanged a wide-eyed and desperate look, but the twins were already on it. They stood and slipped into the girls' paths, mouths splitting with the width of phony smiles. The group took another table a few rows down, made up of the twins and those three girls. Kyle brought the twins' lunch trays over and returned without a word. It seemed Hassan wasn't the only one who remembered that day.

Hassan looked up, mouth grim with the promise of what might have happened, only to find Wyatt watching him. He made a note of it, filing it away for later contemplation as the group ate in silence.

One of the earliest lessons Hassan's father had taught him was that man wrought consequences for all his actions, whether they came in the moment or delayed until later.

As it was, the consequences of lunch barreled straight toward them, or rather, straight for the twins. Mason's gaze cut left long enough to recognize the danger before he took a step toward the boy's bathroom.

"Don't you dare try to get away, Mason Humphrey Dyson! I will come in that bathroom after you!" Alyssa Curtis yelled.

Kyle mouthed "Humphrey" in amusement as she sliced the distance between them, looming despite her slender stature, jet-black locks like windshield wipers with each furious step she took. All around them, people stopped for the show.

"Alyssa. Let me explain." Mason glanced at Hassan. "You shut up!"

She rushed Mason, only to blast him upside the head with her backpack, books hitting the floor as she struck him again. Mason threw up his arms, fumbling and tangling in backpack straps in the worst attempt to protect himself, as the boys around him gave her the widest berth. Only Hassan, who knew that he was inadvertently responsible for this attack, stayed planted, as if his presence might somehow lessen the embarrassment in the end.

"Would you stop playing already!" Mason hollered. "That hurts!"

"You think I'm playing?" Alyssa cried. She tanked him with another blow. "Didn't I tell you that if you ever hurt me again—"

"It was *lunch*! And you don't own me." Mason straightened his posture in an attempt at decency and fare, laughter wavering at the edges of his mouth. "Anyway, I'm a free agent. I can do what I want."

"Oh, you little tramp." She hurled the bag in face, but he swiped it away before she took to beating at his chest like a wild woman.

"Lawrence," Mason cried. "Matt? Hassan? A little help here!"

"We are *done*," Alyssa hissed. She grabbed her bag and began hurling stuff into it. Edy, who had stood a safe distance away across the hall, came over to help.

"Fine," Mason said. "We're done. You see I don't care."

Alyssa stood, her mess of books forgotten, with a face like the Maine lobsters they boiled in the summer.

"Don't try and call me when no one's listening. Telling me you love me. That you've always been in love with me. To hell with you, Mason Dyson."

Grinning, Matt bent to hand her a book only to have it snatched out of his hand.

"And you," she said. "Don't think I'm not telling Jessica about how the two of you got all chummy with the skanks at lunch. Every week you're begging her to come to Georgia with you, you trash. And to think we almost went. Both of you can get lost."

She filled her backpack, slung it on, and shot a glare at Hassan that made him step back. Alyssa cleared a path for herself by shoving Lawrence into a locker.

"Mason—" Hassan said in grinning apology.

"Shut up, you coward," Mason said and turned away from the stares of a too-swollen crowd.

Four periods sat between lunch and practice at the end of the day. Hassan spent them contemplating the handshake he'd shared with Wyatt. How many ways was it possible to turn over a single gesture, examining it for the truth beneath? There were an endless assortment of possibilities, it turned out, and reflection was what he did best. The cultivation of anticipation was what separated him on the field from others, what made him able to read tea leaves on each play, anticipating every possibility like some master of divination.

People didn't speak truth so much as wear it, cloaked in veiled gazes, draped in deception. Wyatt Green had extended a hand of friendship with a smile that started too late and a palm damp to the touch.

Hassan's initial reaction had been to slap the hand from his face and call Wyatt for what he was, a sneak on the aim to get closer to his girl. But it would have left him looking like the jerk in what appeared to others to be a genuine gesture of friendship.

He decided to take another approach.

After the final bell, Hassan stepped out into the hall where he waited for his new friend. Fingers drumming the straps of his backpack as he wore it, he considered the sort of fool Wyatt Green took him to be. Slow enough to miss deception when he saw it. Dumb enough to not know when a man wanted his girl. Naïve enough to let him try something.

It occurred to Hassan to break him, to lift the boy whose body resembled driftwood, snap him over his knee, and toss him in the Charles River. His jaw tightened the moment Edy and Wyatt emerged from class. The two weaved over.

"Long day, right?" Wyatt said. "A.P. classes plus football must be a killer."

The verdict was in. He definitely took Hassan for a fool. No matter, they'd straighten that out in a second.

A steady backwards count in Hassan's mind reeled in the last vestiges of nastiness. He replaced it with a grin.

He was ready.

"Let's take a walk," Hassan said and clapped him on the back. "Just me and you for a second."

The sunshine façade Wyatt wore fell away like papier-mâché in the rain.

"We don't have much time," he said. "You'll be late for practice."

"There's time enough."

Wyatt did away with the pretenses and shot a look toward the main office behind them.

"Security's on your right," Hassan said, low enough so that only he'd hear. After all, he still had a hand on the boy's slight shoulder. "We'll keep them in view. Now let's go. You don't want Edy thinking you're afraid of me."

Hassan looked up to find hesitation in Edy's expression. He disarmed it with a raise of his brow.

"We'll only take a minute," Hassan said. "If you can stand our absence that long."

It worked. Edy broke into a smile.

On the way out, they passed a pack of upper-
-classmen shouting greetings to their star running back.
He steered Wyatt, grip tightening on his shoulder as he
pretended not to notice the slight pull of resistance.
Once they exited the chain-link fence that lined the
student parking lot, they crossed the street, and Hassan
released him. Wyatt shot a look back to the security
guard booth outside.

"No point in running," Hassan said. "You know I
can catch you, like you know I can beat the hell out of
you before help arrives."

The sudden slump of Wyatt's shoulders served as
quiet acknowledgment of the facts.

"Great," Hassan said. "Now that we've got that out
the way, tell me your goal with Edy. And if you feed me
some crap about platonic friendships, I'll hammer you."

Wyatt withdrew; face a blank slate, blood drained
from the truth.

"Don't you have a practice or something?" he said.

"I'm willing to be late for you," Hassan said, voice
tender as if flowers and chocolate might follow.

"Then I'm honored," Wyatt said.

Hassan glanced at his watch. "Let's try this again.
This time, note the impatience painted plain on my face.
"What-is-your-goal-with-Edy?"

"Whatever it is, it's more realistic than yours!"

Hassan managed a deep breath before strangling
the urge to dive on him. "Okay. She know that?"

As expected, the indignant look slid straight from
Wyatt's face. "What difference does it matter?"

Hassan snatched him by the shoulder and they
started down the street together, for a conversation that
required distance from so many ears.

"You love her?" Hassan said.

Wyatt's face twisted in a grimace. "Does it matter?"

"You know it does," Hassan said.

"Then no. I don't."

Hassan stopped. Looked him over. "You know better than to say it. You know that if she understood what the ice cream dinners, hugs, and thousand text messages a day really meant, you'd have nothing to hold onto but your own worthless memories."

Wyatt's Adam's apple dipped quick down a long, pale throat.

"But I can't prove you're only pretending, can I?" Hassan said. "My saying so would jeopardize our new relationship. She'd think I'm trying to run her life. The overprotective boyfriend," he paused, surprised at having used the word, but knowing it to be the right one. "The over protective boyfriend coming between her and a friend. She wouldn't believe it if I told her you were a common snake."

Hassan bent to pluck a jagged rock from the ground. He ran a thumb over its contours as he contemplated.

"I don't have many options," he admitted. "But neither do you. So, you know what I'm going to do? Pretend right along with you. As of now, you're a stand-up guy, not the creep next door trying to get lucky."

"What? But why?"

"Because me and you are gonna play the same game. But we're gonna play to different ends and see who comes out on top."

Wyatt frowned thoughtfully.

"Equal parts brawn and brain," he said. "Pradhan gets in the game and in the mind of his opponent while other guys are still suiting up in the locker room."

"September seventh, *Globe*, Special Edition," Hassan said. "Glad to know you're a fan."

He tossed his rock away and took off on a shortcut to practice.

They were equal now, he and Wyatt, both having recognized the other as an opponent. Now, their game could begin.

Twenty

Dinner that night was a fabulous concoction of curries, meats and breads, pressed over and running with plenty because of the *Purnima* or full moon fast Hindus observed intermittently.

"I made your favorites, samosas, because I know you haven't eaten today," Rani said to Hassan as he took a seat at the table.

Except he had eaten, breakfast, lunch, and an oversized coffee roll from Dunkin Donuts, so far as Edy knew. Anyway, he hadn't fasted on a full moon since fainting at peewee league practice almost a decade ago. After hearing about it, Ali had excused him from skipping meals—without letting Rani in on it.

"Thanks, Mom," Hassan said.

The second his mom turned from the table, he shot Edy a wink that had her blushing and grinning like crazy. It turned him to thinking of bedtime and whether how bad he wanted to join her again. They hadn't done anything that night and yet her touch had him walking in circles.

With his mother tinkering around in the kitchen, bringing out dishes one by one as if she were in the world's longest wedding processional, and with his father still holed away in his study, Hassan's hand flexed open and closed on the table before he walked his fingers halfway across to where her hand rested. Teasing. Threatening to touch. Her fingers inched forward and he beckoned them. *Come on. Take a chance with me.*

His mother returned and they jerked at the sight of her, burned by the fear of suspicion. She wielded a tray stacked with pulses, an assortment of beans alone. But she was all busy hands and idle chatter as she arranged the table to maniacal standards.

"Homework?" she said.

"We did it," Hassan said. Jeez, his heart beat like he'd run back a touchdown. Damn if he'd admit to anyone though.

"Football practice?" she said.

"Good."

She gave him a warning eye. He knew that she hated the way he tended to answer in English, no matter what language addressed in. Rani turned to Edy.

"Ballet practice?"

"Long but good," she offered in accented Punjabi, earning a smile from his mother. When Rani headed for the kitchen Hassan snorted.

"Brownnoser," he said and stole a samosa, shoving it into his mouth before his mother returned.

Hours later, Hassan stretched out on his bed, arms folded behind his head, eyes upward on the ceiling. With dinner heavy in his stomach and his mom snoozing in bed before the Bollywood musical *Ready* for the umpteenth time, Edy slipped into his room and leaned against the door to shut it.

He had a Martha Stewart sort of room, if Martha Stewart slung a football all day long. Stark against otherwise white walls, life sized navy silhouettes sprung to life with pigskin in hand. One stretched, form flawless, his muscles tested in a gallop for his life. Another stiff armed with a ball cradled tight, while a third, his favorite, featured a fearless dive into the end zone. All this, of course, was in crisp contrast to the show room furnishings his mother adorned the room in.

Edy flopped onto her back next to him. He hadn't been able to help the way his arm curled round her, nor the way the corners of his mouth eased up as she snuggled in. He listened to her breathe—in, out, in, out, until her chest synched with his, their rising and falling soothed him with a sense of security, teasing him with how basic and human they both were.

As if life could be that simple.

"How many Hindu gods can you name?" Hassan said. More than me, I bet.

His mother snoozed on the downstairs couch, volume amped on reruns of her Bollywood soaps. She would wait on his father's arrival, feed him, then bypass Hassan's closed door without issue. An adolescent boy required privacy, both parents agreed. Sort of.

"What are you really asking?" she said and turned so their noses grazed.

He claimed her mouth in what should have been a gentle kiss, in what started as a brush of lips, but morphed when Edy mewled and hauled him in tight by the shirt. When Hassan extracted himself, every cell in him thudded with hard, hot blooded protest.

"Well?" he worked out, despite lungs deflated to the size of pebbles.

"Well what?" she said.

He rolled on his side to face her again. "How many?"

He . . . needed this answer. Theology never settled quite right with him, like a broken bone that wouldn't set. Whenever it came up, which was rare, it was the mask used to hide another. Digging out the true thought, the true question, was something that few could do but Edy.

"I don't know. Maybe twenty."

"Out of what?" he said. "Thousands? A million?"

"Maybe."

He drew back, so that he pressed against the headboard, a knee up to prop his elbow.

"To devote to one thing is to sacrifice another," he said, still breathless.

"Who said that? Nietzsche?"

He looked at her. "Edy Phelps."

Eventually, she drew him to her and ran a hand through his hair. Even that, gentle as it was, stoked his flames a second time over.

"You're a good son," she said, "who loves his parents and has his own mind. Why does that have to be divorced? Accept truth in whatever way it comes, whether in the Vedas or your own self-reflection."

Hassan snorted. "Spoken like the daughter of an Ivy League hippie." He shot her a smile. "Enough with the jabber. Kiss me so I can stop thinking about it."

She did as she was told before pulling away.

"What?" he said and puffed a breath of air into the palm of his hand. He smelled garlic, which was bad, but she'd had the same dinner as him.

Her nose wrinkled, gaze skating the length of his room. She set the headset on his dresser and sauntered to his walk-in closet.

"Neither," she said and placed a hand on the handle.

A flash of sweat-fused uniforms and concussion heavy helmets k.o.'ing Edy had him slamming the door as she yanked it.

"Um, something I can help you find, Cake?"

She looked past him, then back, nostrils flared, lips thinned. "You have so much *stuff*," she accused. "Things you never use."

He had hoped her journey to his closet had been about some shirt she wanted to model for him, maybe some tee she could tie up and strut around in. What she was talking about had him wading in blind.

"Okay," Hassan said.

"You have coats you've never worn," Edy said. "Shirts, pants, sweaters you hate, stuffed back there, with tags still attached."

"Even shoes," Edy said. "I know there are sneakers Rani buys that you refuse to wear."

That time she did snatch for his closet door, only to have him yank her back at the onset of the avalanche.

"Mind telling me what this is about?" he demanded, slinging his helmets in one corner. He returned for the funk-strewn practice uniforms as she disappeared into his closet and retrieved her by the wrist when the mess had been cleared.

"Wyatt," she said.

His fingers unwrapped from her arm one by one until he withdrew from her.

"Hassan."

"Edy."

"You've seen him, Hassan. You've seen the way he dresses. It's not right. And . . . and I thought if there was anyone I could come to for help, it would be you."

He wanted his headset and Xbox; he wanted the Edy before Wyatt Green. What he didn't want was this.

"I've seen plenty that's not right," he muttered and collapsed on his bed.

His girl. *His* girl digging in *his* closet to hand *his* clothes over to some slick smiling snake that couldn't even make a secret of wanting to bonk her. In a justified world, no court would convict him for maiming Wyatt Green, or at the very least, going Jigsaw on him for a few hours.

"Hassan, please?" Edy said.

And he looked up to find not the fierceness of a girl readied for closet battle, but the huge brown eyes he drowned in, over and again, endlessly.

Eyes he never hoped to conquer. Hassan exhaled.

"He won't wear them," he warned. "He won't even appreciate what you've done."

Edy's face split with a grin.

"He's nowhere near my size," Hassan tried. "You'd be better off trying your own closet."

She threw her arms around him in a squeeze he returned despite his better judgment. This girl could lead him to the heart of trouble, if she wanted. Hassan would follow, right off a cliff.

~~~

Edy's fingers flexed in their strain to maintain her burden. One, two, three seconds of silent confusion lapsed with nothing but the wind licking at her neck.

"What do you mean 'no?'" she asked Wyatt. A careless look behind her said that Hassan had gone back indoors.

Wyatt stepped out on the porch, shutting the door on a muffled television and ghostly array of shadows.

"You don't get it, do you?" His gaze held no one destination, darting from the two overstuffed bags Edy propped against the wall of his house, to a hundred other minutiae, eyes glassy. For whatever reason, he wouldn't meet her gaze.

"Did I come at a bad time?" She probably should have called. She'd been so psyched about the coat, sneakers and half dozen other goodies that she hadn't considered etiquette or—

"Edy, you can't expect me—" He swallowed. "You must know . . ."

"I know they aren't a perfect fit, but it's the best I could do."

"You can't be this stupid!"

Edy stood, sure that her eyes had doubled in size, even as icicle winds battered them.

"What?" she whispered.

"Edy, please." When he reached for her, she yanked clean of him.

"You need clothes," Edy hissed. "Take them and leave it at that."

She started for the stairs. This time when he touched her arm, she stopped. Exhaled. Took time to catch her breath.

"Edy, please."

Please was right. She'd come there for a purpose. So, she lined the bags neatly on the porch railing, careful to keep her overburdened contents from spilling.

"Talk to me," Wyatt said. "If you'd only give me the time of day. There are so many things I need to tell you."

Edy stood and scanned Hassan's house and hers for witnesses. Once she'd confirmed that no eyes gaped, she fled, ignoring Wyatt's cries to come back him.

Twenty-One

The next night, the Phelps family had a meeting, all three in attendance plus the campaign staffer feverishly scribbling in the corner. "Meeting" was hardly the appropriate word, however; as mostly Edy's mother talked and mostly they listened.

Her campaign was now underway.

They could expect changes around the house.

She'd be available less.

She would expect more from them.

Their family, as a whole, would be held to a higher standard. Therefore, the very highest level of decorum was expected.

She stared straight at Edy for that one.

There would be travel. A tremendous amount of travel, meaning that she would be away from home more often than not. Sometimes, she would require their presence, but she would make every effort to ensure this happened as infrequently as possible.

The press conference to announce her bid for Senate would be held in two and a half weeks, on a Saturday.

"My birthday?" Edy said.

It was that time of year again.

Her father, who had been staring off into the distance, sat up straighter.

"Rebecca, you can't expect . . ."

The staffer stopped scribbling. And Hassan burst in.

"Hey, you guys! Guess who got free passes to—"

He froze, eyes darting from Edy to her mother to her father. Finally, it rested on the staffer.

"Who are you?" he said.

Edy burst out laughing.

It was absurd, really. The family meeting with the court stenographer, Edy wounded by the notion of having no more loathsome birthday parties, and Hassan bursting in like the main attraction at a bull fight, running and blurting the question they all should have asked.

"Hassan, please," her mother said.

Whether "please" meant "please get lost" or "please settle down," Edy couldn't be sure. But Hassan dropped down next to her all the same.

"Rebecca, we've been doing these birthday parties for Edy since she was a year old," her father said.

"All the more reason why missing one shouldn't be that big a deal," she said. "Missing two if we're talking about you."

Hassan leaned over and whispered to Edy. "What's happening, Cake?"

Quickly, she explained.

"Claudia?" her mother said.

The staffer stood. "Meeting opening followed by schedule expectations, expectations concerning proper decorum, brief overview of travel demands, and advisement regarding candidacy announcement in two and a half weeks." The staffer looked up.

"Excellent. On the day in question, we'll have breakfast out, in a very visible way, as a happy, smiling family. Then we'll travel over to the Old State House, where I'll make the announcement, with my doting husband and beautiful daughter by my side. We'll follow that with a rally, then a fundraising dinner."

Edy lifted a finger. "Is it possible to—"

"My fundraising dinner is being hosted by a *very* gracious governor and being attended by a number of city elites. The date was chosen by people with far more substantial interests to consider than a child's birthday party," her mother said.

"I was only going to ask—"

"Meeting adjourned," her mother said and strode out of the room.

The staffer scrambled after her.

"Edy—" her father began.

She didn't know how to feel. On the one hand, her mother had solved the dress problem. But on the other, her father stared back at her with eyes that said he'd been mortally wounded. She hated that look, hated what it meant: that the parties had been his way of holding onto an escaping childhood, that he was unanchored without them, lost in a sea of adolescence. She didn't always mind being his little girl. Sometimes it wasn't all bad.

"I was getting too old for the parties," Edy blurted, unsure of she started talking. "I've been wanting to do something different."

It was better that way. Better for them both if she swept the old ways out of sight. After all, there was no coming back from her mother's pronouncements.

"Have you?" her father said, voice small.

"Of course. I'll be sixteen. Old enough to date."

She exchanged a tiny smile with Hassan.

"I see," her father said and left the room.

~~~

Edy stood to the right of her mother and father and to the left of Kyle and his father Cam, her mother's right hand man in politics. They crowded together on a roped-off section of State Street, with their backs to the historic Old State House. Rain swelled the sleek sheet of

November sky as twitches of lightening illuminated it. A distant storm made a fast approach. Not that it mattered. With the cameras on her mother, there could be no moving, no delaying, no deviation from the plan. Even the Four Horsemen of the Apocalypse would have to hold on Line Three once Edy's mother got wind of an opportunity to give one of her "Mean Nothing" speeches. Pressed to the gills with platitudes and pregnant pauses for applause lines, her speeches had ways of being both ambitious and empty, promising nothing, all the while implying everything. Somehow, it seemed appropriate for her.

Under the glare of flashing bulbs and the frigid slice of winter wind, Edy allowed her thoughts to drift to dance. Ballet had been neither here nor there for her lately—neither the passion nor the disappointment that came with strong emotion. Instead, she found herself memorizing style and substance, as committed as ever to the punishing exactness of the classical variation, even as she warped it in her mind, molding it to the pops and snaps and gyrations of the street stuff she'd never dare do in public.

She thought about New York, often. About Bean and his father and rejection and the anger of krump dancing in the pit. She contrasted it with the grace and sculpting and exactness of classical ballet, fusing them in her mind like a Franken-scientist gone mad.

They were clapping. People on stage, in the audience, everyone around applauded with a vigor that told her she'd missed something important. Her mind fumbled with the faux pas before setting her on track again. Edy brought her hands together just as the noise of the crowd petered away. It occurred to her that her display might have been captured; daydreaming might have been captured, not just by local papers, but by national media as well. How long did she have before her blank stare became fodder for *The Daily Show* or *Late Night?*

But she was a kid. No one cared what kids did.

Following the close of a fire-filled speech crammed to the throat with buzzwords, Edy's mother fielded a dozen or so questions before exiting in the same way she'd ended their family meeting. After a moment of confused loitering, Edy followed her parents and the others, head lowered, determined to blend in as well as a teenager could amongst the most powerful adults in the state. It was her birthday, of course, and part of her wondered if she could at least be afforded the option skipping some of the grind. Maybe she could catch a movie with Hassan or go bowling with the twins. Anything had to be better than impersonating a mannequin for her mother.

They paused at the entrance of the limo, where a rapid back-and-forth took place; first, between Cam and a staffer, then Cam and Edy's mother. Afterward, they piled into the limo and pulled away from the curb.

"There'll be consequences for the next person that stands behind me looking less than enthusiastic," her mother announced.

The eyes and ears of Rebecca Phelps were as plentiful as the grains of dirt on the ground. Favors were the currency of politics, and even small ones had their value. Telling on Edy brought a reward.

There would be no movies with Hassan, of course. No bowling with the twins either. For Edy's birthday, she had the distinction of being ushered around alongside her mother all day, smiling like the world's most well-behaved child, all the while imagining herself collapsing on her back like an upended turtle and burrowing into her shell.

Hassan texted her during the fundraising dinner at the governor's private mansion. He wanted to know how she was and when she expected to leave. She didn't know how to tell him that whatever hopes he harbored for an evening together were a waste. A seven-course menu and politicians who salivated at the sound of their own voice promised that.

When Edy made it back to her room, it was a quarter to eleven. Her feet throbbed around the permanent cramp of pumps while the clock on her nightstand ticked out the final minutes of her birthday.

"Happy birthday," she whispered.

No dress hung on the door. No three-tiered cake waited at the Dyson house. Instead, she was just Edy, as she'd always wanted it.

So, why did her heart feel so heavy?

Edy pulled out her cell phone and reread the happy birthday message from Hassan. Three words were the closest she'd come to hearing his voice that day.

"Happy birthday, Cake."

She looked up to find Hassan's head jutting through the window.

"Hey!" she cried and tossed her phone aside, the ache of her feet forgotten as she threw her arms around him.

He laughed, latching onto her with an arm as he tilted precariously. "Let me in, okay? I promise to hold onto you all night."

She stepped back, smile broad with the deliciousness of the thought.

Hassan swung a leg in and unfolded to full height, into hard-bodied broadness that pressed at the seams of his fabric.

His hand found hers to pull her in close, communicating with eyes that never hid his secrets. The smile from him was brief, sweet, tiny with the humor of their new world. Them. Together. That was what his face said before he kissed her, wiping away the possibility of thought. When Hassan drew away, it was with a sigh from both. "I have company," he admitted.

Edy stole a look at the window just as another leg slipped in. One after another, her room filled under the silence of stealth as Matt, Mason, and Lawrence piled in.

"Did we really have to do this here?" Lawrence said.

Mason peeled off a backpack; Matt pulled off another. As Hassan locked Edy's door, all three Dyson boys went to work emptying bags.

Refreshments emerged from one of the Jansports. Twinkies. Guacamole. Salsa. Tortilla chips and a bag full of Lil' Smokies. Another of Rice Krispies treats. Trail mix and Gatorade. So distracted was she by the hodgepodge assortment from the first backpack that she missed what emerged from the second. Hassan and Lawrence tacked up yellow and baby blue streamers to the walls. Matt blew up balloons.

"Alyssa made these pinwheels," Mason explained as he pulled out the last of these treats. "They're better than they look."

To argue as much, he held up a mashed and half empty bag.

Alyssa. His on again off again "it" girl that she hated without knowing why. Alyssa, the girl that kept trying nonetheless, as if being Edy's friend somehow meant something.

"I've been stupid," she admitted.

"I know," Mason said. He gave her a long and skeptical once over before opening his arms. She went into them. When Matt stopped to look at them, she pulled him over, too.

"I promise not to be a jerk anymore," she said. "If that's who you lo—"

"Forget about it, okay?" Mason said. Abruptly, he vacated the embrace. Matt followed suit.

"How about you put it in a Hallmark, Edy?" Lawrence knotted purple balloons to a string.

Matt pulled out an iPod and speaker dock, the last of the goodies in his bag.

"You probably shouldn't—"

She glanced at the door. But Matt pressed a finger to his lips.

"We'll keep it low," he said. "Quiet storm stuff."

The twins were known for a lot of things, but silence wasn't one of them. Nonetheless, the first song was sultry and acoustic. A brush of violin. A hint of piano. Rumbling waterfalls and crashing waves.

Hassan held out his hand.

"First dance?"

Always, she thought. Forever and then one more time after that.

Edy placed her hand in his and allowed herself to be drawn into his arms. He smelled of winter leaves and apple cider, love and nothing else. She pulled him closer, willed him closer, and found that close enough wasn't even possible.

Lips brushed her forehead and dipped lower, grazing the button of her nose before settling on her mouth. Arms she'd always known encircled her, fierce in their entrapment, as his lips tasted, drank, swallowed every breath she had.

Somewhere, a throat cleared. Hassan stepped back, dropped his hands, and sighed.

"I'm pretty sure I had at least half a minute," he said.

"You did. But my stomach didn't," Matt said.

Hassan dropped onto the bed with a snort. Edy joined him. The music shifted brazenly, from gentle innuendo to braggadocios hip hop warped on acid. Despite its low timbre, the rowdiness barred none.

"I wanted you for myself," Hassan said. "But they insisted on coming. 'A party's not a party with only two people,' Matt said. But something tells me we could have had a party all our own."

His fingertips traced trails on her skin, his mouth kissed shivers through her body. She wanted the party he promised; she *craved* that party.

Matt snatched Edy up. She clamped down on a yelp before crashing head to chest into him. He dove into spasmodic, lurching hip thrusts that only mocked the beat, face contorting to suggest more rigorous work than that what was actually being done. Mason came behind her for a violent sort of sandwich, both twitching and bumping, closing in on her space. Laughter ruptured from Edy despite pains to stifle it, and she dissolved into a mess of giggles.

When she refused to dance like them, the twins declared Edy worthless and tossed her toward the bed. Hassan caught her with a smile.

"I don't think they actually needed you for your birthday," he admitted, adjusting her so that she shifted from the rumpled lump in his lap to sitting up in the bed.

His gaze fell to her lips, petering her goofy smile to nothingness. Only he could erase her thoughts that way; only he could render her senseless. An upturn of full lips and glimmer of gold-flecked eyes turned her bones to pudding in her body.

Hassan cleared his throat.

"I owe you an apology," he said. "We uh, started making you this dress, you know, as in keeping with the birthday tradition. But the ostrich feathers, duct tape, and pink shag carpet felt understated when compared to your usual look."

She shoved him, knowing it to be the equivalent of taking a running start into a brick wall. He fed her a grin as broad as the sky above and took the same hand she'd used to assault him to trace circles in her palm.

"I want to kiss you," he said.

"Do it."

He looked up, grin broad and emboldened by her frankness. "I used my one freebie," he told her. "I don't think they can stand us making out."

Edy waited. Eventually, his gaze dropped to her lips, up again, then down before his Adam's apple bobbed.

He moved in, mouth drawn to hers, and Edy pressed to meet him—hand to chest, drinking in contours and hardness with her fingers.

She could taste his scent, smell his touch; her mind garbled from the feel of him. *This.* She thought. It was the only word she could manage.

A blast of pillow to the head sent both of them reeling. "I'd tell you to get a room," Matt said, pillow still in hand. "But if you did, we'd beat you to dust, Sawn."

Hassan's face split into a massive smile before he leapt, tangling with the twins. Lawrence scrambled to his defense, like always.

Too much noise.

Four oversized football players, trying and failing not to topple furniture, crash into walls, and bring down the curtains would be more than her sleeping parents could stand. She could think of but one way to stop them.

Edy helicoptered in. Diving from the edge of her bed, she landed partway on Matt and partway on Lawrence like a pan full of hot grease, scalding them so they jerked away. No one would dare throw a punch. No one would risk harming sweet, sweet Edy.

In the end, she rolled onto her back, guffawing at having done something no one man could accomplish: breaking up a room full of football players in a tussle.

"You'd better run," she said. "'Cause I was *that* close to cracking skulls."

Edy tucked her hands behind her head and closed her eyes, marveling at how plush the mauve carpeting was, even after so many years. Somewhere near the closet was a splash of carnation pink, where Chloe had spilled nail polish remover half a decade ago.

The first pillow blasted her square in the face. As Edy's eyes flew open, a torrent of blows followed. Pillows —her pillows—assaulted her from every direction.

Her feet fumbled an attempt at uprightness, only to get snatched out from under her altogether. Then the fingers started. Hundreds of them, *thousands* of them, tickling, as she arched her back and kicked her feet in vain, making her whoop like a hyena.

The hand that covered her mouth was Hassan's, seconds before his face hovered over hers.

"Next time you dive into a fight," he said. "Pick a side. You know, so you don't get jumped, skull-cracker."

She caught a glimmer of teasing in smiling green eyes and couldn't help but return it. Hassan leaned in and licked his lips.

"I need to take a leak," Lawrence announced.

"You can't," Hassan said. "You know you can't."

He rolled onto his back with a groan.

"I go in here or elsewhere," Lawrence said. "Either way, I go."

"Call his bluff," Matt said. "Make him piss his pants."

"No!" Edy leapt to her feet, images of her attempting to explain a urine-soaked carpet—minus a pet to her parents. Her mother would claim it to be but the latest evidence of her overwhelming incompetence. *See? She hasn't brains enough to find a toilet, let alone think for herself. How can we get her into Harvard now?* Her father, on the other hand, would leave no academic journal unmolested in his search for a reasonable explanation. *She's experienced a regression to the anal stage of Freudian psychosexual development. It's all right here.*

"This way," Edy said, eager to take the risk over the alternative. Still, she slipped into the hall, lungs shrunken to stones in her chest. She didn't dare breathe; no way she'd risk the slightest sound. She jerked a finger in the general direction of the upstairs bathroom. Lights out, door slightly ajar. Across the hall from it, her parents' bedroom looked similarly safe.

It had been a long day, she told herself, and they were middle-aged. They had to be resting.

Lawrence disappeared. It literally happened that fast. Soundless, he whisked away, leaving her mouth agape with a promised warning of caution, undelivered. The bathroom door closed behind him.

And she waited.

Never had the hall looked so long.

Never had her parents' room seemed so close.

And never had her heart galloped like a herd between her ears.

One. One one hundred. Two.

"Jesus, take me," Edy whispered.

When they were kids, Steve Dyson had had an English cocker spaniel named Hugo, a proud and glorious hound that had walked the streets as if the very trees should bend to his will. And why not? He'd enjoyed weekly spa visits, deep tissue massages, pawdicures, and all-natural treats regularly. He'd spent his days lazing about and his evenings dining on beef ribs, succulent T-bone, and specially made sausages from a local deli, all of it supplemented by organic fruits and vegetables.

One day, Hassan and all three Dyson brothers had decided to give Hugo a makeover. They'd shaved him down to the pink, leaving only a thick strip of fur running from crown to tail. They'd adorned him in clip-on bangles, thick rouge, and a crudely painted replica of the New England Patriots' cheerleading uniform. Edy, who had served as lookout outside of Matt's room, had managed a thick sheen of sweat on her arms. Their signal for the arrival of a parent had been so cumbersome and confusing that she'd shrieked at the sight of their father, bolting down the hall and shouting like Paul Revere with the British on his heels. They'd been caught. And while they would have been found out whether Edy had taken to hysteria or not, her reaction had all but confirmed Steve's suspicion that the boys had been up to something.

This felt like that moment.

Lawrence emerged. His steps were swift and weightless, as if time and gravity were mere figments of her imagination and he could float away on dust. But as Lawrence arrived, Edy realized they had a problem.

She could hear the boys in the hall.

"If that's a six pack, then you need remedial math," Hassan said.

"You don't have muscles on your back!" Matt said.

"I do six-thousand sit-ups a night," Mason bragged.

"When? Where?" Matt said.

"Maybe on your girl's face," Mason spat.

She wanted to run, down the hall, down the stairs, and out the front door. But it would do no good. There was nowhere to run.

"Look at this," Hassan said. "And this. And *this*. I've got muscles flexing muscles. You dream about this."

Lawrence and Edy exchanged a wide-eyed stare, faces mirrored in horror. Edy shoved open the door and the both of them entered. But she stopped. Lord, did she stop. And think about backing out her room again.

They were naked. Almost naked, with boxers as the only barrier between skin and sight.

No shirts. No pants. Too loud.

"All I know is that I look better than both of you," Matt said.

"We're identical, you moron!"

Hassan stepped back. "Let Edy vote. She'll make the right choice." He winked at her, as if she might need encouragement to make the "right choice."

"That's fine," Matt said. "Get your feelings hurt. 'Cause no girl can resist—" he gestured to his taut body. "All this."

"Edith!" her mother shrieked.

Hot oil. Hot oil down her back followed by a sheet of cold ice.

That was her mother's voice.

"Edith, I'm talking to you!"

She wished she wouldn't. If there were anything she could have, anything at all, it was for her mother to turn around, march back to her room, and *not* talk to her for the next few lifetimes.

Edy turned on her heels, slow, in a measured about-face. Behind her, Mason, Matt, and Hassan stood in an arc, frozen and in their underwear.

"Mom, we—"

"Who saw you come in?" she blurted.

"I—wait. What?" Edy said.

Her mother marched over to the window and yanked the curtains shut. She went back to the door, closed and locked it.

"You must have come in through the window. Were you seen? Did anyone see you?"

Hassan shook his head.

"Then get dressed. You'll not be leaving here tonight. I can't take the risk. Lawrence, you'll have the couch. Hassan, take the sofa in the study. You two will have to figure out the guestroom. We'll have breakfast in the morning and you'll leave in a respectable manner. Understood?"

"Mom, I—"

She held up a hand. "I don't want to know. Goodnight."

She slammed the door behind her.

~~~

Edy woke to a breakfast that might have been catered. Poached eggs on smoked salmon. Silver-dollar pear pancakes with caramelized figs and berry compote. Turkey bacon, Canadian bacon, Irish bacon, and brown sugar bacon piled high around ham, smoked salmon, chicken, and pork sausages. A pile of fluffed biscuits stood in the center like a crowning achievement, accented on all sides by a jubilee of mixed grapes and cheeses. She stood at the swinging door of the dining room entrance, watching as the boys crammed their mouths with meats and cheeses, piled their plates with breads, and washed it all down with a colorful assortment of juices. Edy's mother looked up from her end of the table, chewed momentarily, and turned to a tall glass for a sip of orange juice.

Dismissed.

The word curled through her limbs and curdled her blood until nothing but the fire of fury remained.

She thought nothing of Edy.

Less than nothing of Edy.

Hardly worth the trouble of worrying over when found in a room of half naked boys. Who could want Edy? One by one, Edy's fingers curled until they resembled a fist. Two fists. She marched into the kitchen with them at her side.

"Who cooked?" she said on passing her mother. "Certainly not you."

Her mother paused, lips parted in anticipation of a sliver of Canadian bacon. A table's worth of eyes stared back at Edy, motionless, waiting.

"You're right," her mother said, after taking a survey of the table. "Breakfast is compliments of Sullivan's Catering Service. They work on short notice."

Edy ventured over to the buffet cabinet to retrieve a plate and piece of silverware. She helped herself to the fruits first before retrieving a cut of salmon.

"Where's my father?" she said.

Her mother snorted. "Somewhere penning his ninety-seventh book about why people overthrow governments. As if the answer weren't simple."

Simple. Everything was simple with Edy's mother. Horrifyingly simple, brutally simple, in fact.

"So, tell us then," Edy said, knowing the words that would follow could upend her mother's career. But then again, half of what she said in private could upend her career.

Her mother sighed. "Fine. People do things because they can. Everyone wants power. Dominion. But they're stupid. Left alone, most would be reduced to hungry, cowering creatures, quaking and yearning to be loved." Her mother laughed and before treating her to a crawling once over.

These little jabs, when she made them, were hot stabs just for her. Stupid. Left alone. Yearning to be loved. What a Lifetime movie pair mother and daughter made: one merciless district attorney who squeezed power by throat, the other a ballerina so shy she couldn't tell her best friend and lifetime crush she'd probably been in love with him only forever.

But more stood between them than contrary personalities. More even than differing takes on life. Her mother acted as if she'd been bested in some way by Edy, as if she held some grudge against her, as if Edy had outmaneuvered her in a loss she couldn't quite get over. But none of that made sense. Her birth came years after her parents' marriage and her mother's career was absolutely admirable as the first female and African American district attorney. She would forever be remembered. Maybe it all did boil down to personality.

From across the room Edy caught Hassan watching her. He followed her with his gaze as she continued preparing her plate. Fruit. A bit of toast. Jam. Edy took a seat.

"Plate's a little thin," her mother said. "Trying to lose weight, I take it. Not that I blame you."

Edy gripped her fork, poised to spear the smoked salmon. A thousand thoughts went through her mind, of being too thin, too fat, too broad in the hips for classical ballet. She strained against a false image.

Edy wondered if her mother had never felt it. The gnawing hole of imperfection. The aching doubt. It seemed both possible and impossible.

"Edy's beautiful already," Hassan said. "Perfect."

When her mother took him in with a raised brow, Hassan met her with an even stare.

"Is that so?" she said.

"It is." He sat up straighter.

Edy looked from one to the other. What was happening? And why?

"Yeah" Mason said. "Everyone says that." He looked around for affirmation. "Edy's perfect. Gorgeous. A real stand-out. Right boys?"

"No doubt," Matt chimed in.

The table turned to Lawrence.

"Well?" her mother said.

"She's a'ight." Lawrence shoved a cluster of berries in his mouth. His eyes studied the stripes of the tablecloth, the swirls of a wooden floor, the particles of air, perhaps.

"Careful, Lawrence," her mother said. "Much more and she'll swoon."

Edy snorted on a laugh. It caught just there, between her nose and her throat, thrashing and desperate for relief. She shook with the force of the laugh, tears welling with the effort. It burst like water from a detonated dam, spewing until she trickled to nothing.

When it abated, even her mother smiled.

"I had a fascinating conversation with Rani the other day," she said, upturn of her mouth steady despite the movement. "And it was all about how much you each have grown. How you're all shaping into such handsome men. And how Edy, pretty as she's become, how Edy must incite such jealousy from the girls with the way each of you hover."

Their grins melted. Like icing on a too-hot cake, they thinned and slipped away, until only Edy's mother remained amused. "I wonder, sometimes. Which of you it'll be." Her gaze skated like a stone skipping pond water from one boy to another to another. "So many years together," she said. "Of shared smiles. Secret moments. Memories. *Exhales.* And now this. My daughter, the unexpected beauty. I wonder. Who will it happen to? The moment of realization, of dawning understanding, that the fervor driving your loyalty, your need to protect her has nothing to do with the past and everything with the future you want?"

She tsk-tsked, mirth like a festival in bottomless brown eyes, full of lights and color and joy as her gaze danced from one to the next. Mason. Matthew. Lawrence. Hassan. Hassan, a little too long.

"I could force it from you," her mother said, eyes like two gaping maws of laughter as she pushed away from the table. "But I like a good show. So, we wait. For now."

Her mother nodded toward the invisible staffer in the corner, the one who took notes at family meetings, poured cereal, and wiped her behind, apparently. Together, the two disappeared and the table exploded.

Mason yelling about Hassan's recklessness, about attempting to provoke Edy's mother, Lawrence yelling about the stupidity of having a party in her room, Matt yelling about their endless attempts to protect them and their relationship, while Hassan warned them to stay out of his business.

Edy slipped up to her room, unnoticed, and locked away the shouts. She hadn't known that her mother thought her beautiful.

She hadn't known that she cared either way.

Twenty-Two

Edy sat at the "it" table for lunch. Ushered over with a wave from Alyssa, she sat wedged between the two girls. None of their boys had arrived yet. As she settled in with a leftover bowl of lukewarm curry, the two peppered her for details about the party. Was it true that they hung up balloons? Streamers? True that her mother walked in on them half naked? They guffawed at Edy's weak nods, faces contorting with the pain of reckless laughter.

The news spread up and down their table like a wave, scissoring back again when the boys arrived.

"All of you stripped down? In Edy's room?" Sandra Jacobs said from the other end. Scandalized laughter rippled.

No one answered. And while Edy knew that neither Alyssa nor Jessica thought much of the boys coming to her room, she knew what the others would make of it. Would they whisper it in corridors? Strip it down to its seediest meaning before stringing it up on a flagpole for all to see? Parade her through the streets of Rome, the Cleopatra of South End?

"Only me," Hassan said. "Hoping to get lucky and failed." He shrugged.

And there it was. The silence was something like tendrils of smoke, curling from every pore of Sandra Jacobs, venom as toxic as carbon monoxide

"So, why try?" Sandra spat. "Why grovel behind some homely girl artificially inflated by the company she keeps? Why chase her? Watch her the way you do? You look stupid and everyone says it behind your back. That of all the girls you could have, you pick the plainest, dullest—"

She couldn't see the way he clutched his spork, all five fingers invested in the act. Nor could she see the set of his mouth, set with a line so deep and sealed it could have been tarred.

"Hassan, don't—" Edy reached for him, missing entirely as he leapt from his seat. In two steps he was at Sandra's side. He dropped into the seat behind her, attached to another table.

No one could hear what he said to her. They could only go off the sudden blanching of her skin and the pained pinch of her face. When he withdrew, Hassan met her gaze straight on. "Do we understand each other?"

Sandra nodded once, sharp, and swallowed.

Hassan rose. But instead of returning to the chicken tacos on his plate and back to his friends, he made for the door, picking up speed until he punched it on the way out.

Edy flew after him, down a narrow walkway lined with gaping eyes, under the stare of florescent lights and disapproving adult frowns. A burst through double doors later and she was colliding with his backside like a bike on the tail end of an interstate pile-up.

"What did you tell her?" Edy demanded, taken aback by the desperation in her voice, scalded by the heat of her fears. "That you still had feelings for her? That you're torn? That your summer with her was—was—"

Her mouth wouldn't cooperate. She knew Sandra had been one of the girls he'd had that summer. Would have guessed it if she and her friends hadn't made a point of announcing it anytime they were within a mile of each other. But until that moment, she hadn't allowed herself to consider what it meant: that he'd wrapped arms around her, pressed lips to her, given her the heat and strength of his body, shared himself with her in ways he wouldn't with Edy, even if she had wanted him to.

She turned away from him, eyes flooding.

"Edy . . ."

Her name could have been a sigh, an afterthought; a natural course of his breathing, in and out, in and out, so natural was the sound on his lips.

Still, he'd given others more. Maybe even promised them more.

"Edy," he repeated. "Look at me. I can't . . ."

She turned to see him rake a hand through his hair, grip a fistful, and throw his head back.

"I don't want to do this now. Not like this. I want to—" Hassan hesitated.

And then she knew. Knew that whatever he'd said to Sandra would be a source of tremendous pain, a throbbing ache impossible to heal or mask or alleviate or bear. Impossible to ignore.

"Tell me," she said. "Tell me right now."

His lips parted. "I said I loved you. That I absolutely always have. And that if she opened her eyes, she could see that."

Edy gasped. But she admonished her heart, chided it for leaping with the sudden, unexpected words. Of course he loved her. Mason loved her. Matt loved her. Even Lawrence did. She loved them, too.

"Not like that," Hassan said, breathless. "Not like that for a long time."

Her throat clogged. Disbelief, still, after all that had happened.

He kissed her, gentle as a feather's stroke before sealing it with a fire's brand. She was weightless with him and floating. He backed her to the lockers and pinned, searing her mouth with a groan.

Edy's heart thumped-thumped between her ears as his hand cascaded, first high on her ribs, then low on her waist, until hunger had him squeezing her backside. She pushed into him, marrying their limbs in a tangle of heat shattered as the warning bell rang.

Hassan pulled away with a sigh.

Edy pulled him again. "I love you too," she said softly, shyly.

The hall clogged with students. Guys wolf whistled at them. Girls gaped.

Hassan wrapped his arms around her and they pressed forehead to forehead. "Tell me we can figure this out."

They could. They had to. In the end, growing up worked in their favor. That was their trump card and it meant they could love and marry whoever, no matter the fallout behind it.

"We can figure this out," Edy said. "Together."

~~~

Since they'd been old enough to ride the subway alone, Hassan and Edy had taken to walking the streets of downtown Boston during the holiday season. The mere mention of shopping on Black Friday was enough to make her squeal, but as was the case with all Edy-plus-Hassan traditions, she suspected he enjoyed it more than he let on.

Christmas time between the Phelps family and the Pradhans wasn't as awkward as it could have been. They were Hindu, yes, but as Hindus they believed that God had many names and that all faiths offered truths man should seek. Not only were they not offended by Christmas, but they embraced it, recognizing Jesus as a Prema-Avatar or divine embodiment of love. Nonetheless, theirs was the house that remained dark at the helm of the season, so they embraced the spirit of Christmas without all its trappings—sort of.

Edy made homemade cocoa in a too-bright, starkly gleaming, and freshly remodeled kitchen as she waited for Hassan to arrive. It was the day after Thanksgiving, their day for festivities downtown. What began as a reckless search for presents following Hassan's propensity for procrastination each year eventually became an accepted part of their seasonal plans. On that day, they would purchase gifts for each other apart before shopping for the others together.

When Hassan stepped into the Phelps' kitchen, he wore a black, fitted thermal and blue jeans, which peeked out from an open parka. Even still, Edy saw hints of raw power beneath, contours curving and unyielding in their hardness. She went to him, slipping arms around a dime-sized waist and gliding hands up a broadening back. He was soap. And heat. And everything that was right. She wasn't sure if she could let him go. Maybe shopping could wait.

He pressed lips to her forehead, stole a glimpse at the door, and pressed his lips to hers. He could part her there without trying, with only a hint that parting her was what he wanted. She returned his gentle kiss with a flood of heat, intense and perfect and *right*.

He pulled away with a sigh.

"Parents?" he said.

"Mom's traveling. Dad's shopping."

He returned to their kiss with two hands at her waist, mouth steady, deliberate, thorough its search.

The house escaped her. Breathing escaped her. She was lips and hips he insisted on touching, and oh my, he was too much. Too much of the right thing, of all things, of one thing she rocked hard against him, eager and breathless to have.

He disappeared.

He stood a million miles away from her with his back pressed to the kitchen counter, chest rising and falling.

"What?" Edy said, though she knew.

His gaze slipped over her, memorizing.

"Nothing," he said and went for the cocoa.

Edy couldn't shake the notion that he'd scrambled from her every time kissing got intense and that he scrambled from her now. She wished she had no idea why, but the truth was he was still one of her boys.

"You always make the cocoa so bitter," he said with a wince.

"And you don't make it at all."

She heaped a few weighty spoons of sugar into his cup and turned to fix her own. With her back turned, she knew he'd heap in a few more.

He slurped loudly.

"What do I get your mom?" he asked.

"The election. Can you fix it for her?" She took a seat at the nook. Hassan pulled up nearby.

Edy lowered her gaze to the table's floral arrangement. Nestled into a grooved bamboo vase, the bouquet was an odd assortment of green roses, lotus pods, Kermit mums, and dandelion clocks, none of which she would have known without Rani's green thumb.

Hassan plucked a dandelion from the lot and leaned forward, dog tags dangling from his neck. He blew a gust of flower into Edy's face, white clocks shooting and swirling till she snorted and sputtered from the inhalation.

"Hassan!" she cried, batting in vain.

He watched; face solemn, as if bearing witness to the loss of her sanity. When she stilled, allowing herself but a final giggle, he held out a hand to her.

"Hurry," he said. "I want time enough to take you ice skating."

They spent the day in the stores that dotted Downtown Crossing, shopping, peering in at department store window displays, buying gifts, and, unbelievably, talking with the handful of strangers that recognized Hassan. Afterward, with their bags in the back of his Mustang and a parking ticket that would have given Ali an embolism, they took to the ice on Frog Pond, skating arm in arm until sunset.

~~~

Wyatt stood in an upstairs window, shrouded in shadows, eyes on the pair gathered at the trunk of a perfectly polished Mustang that had magically acquired rims since he'd last seen it.

All day.

Gone all day.

Wyatt and Edy didn't talk like they used to. They spent even less time together. A handful of conversations at school, a few more passed notes, a phone call when it was killing him.

Wyatt was tired of it.

He was no closer to Edy, no better for his restraint, for his harboring hope that she would see him, miss him, yearn for him eventually.

All he'd earned for his troubles was a front row ticket to the Hassan show, tongue kissing included.

Heads gathered, the couple huddle together, close. Wyatt watched as Hassan placed a hand at the small of her back and leaned in. His lips moved, holding a smirk despite speaking. Edy threw her head back and laughed. Joyous, tumbling gusts of laughter wafted up to Wyatt's bedroom, warm and melodious, searing him with envy.

For once in his life, he wanted to have the advantage. He was poor. His parents were uneducated. His father drank too much; his mother was just nuts. They stepped out on each other, had fist fights, and screamed until Wyatt peeled them apart.

He had no risk of being mistaken for handsome, of discovering coordination, of stumbling on money. He worked hard and earned his grades through sweat. He had few clothes, fewer friends, and no one who would miss his absence. Even Edy Phelps was slipping through his fingers.

As he watched his only friend, the girl he loved, toss something up and over Hassan's head, Wyatt leaned in, far too morbid to look away.

She waved a scarf over her head, leaning so that her backside pressed the trunk of his car. Hassan reached for it, body cinched to hers so that they were chest to chest, hard to soft, and stealing Wyatt's breaths.

He'd give anything to be the thing in Hassan's pants.

But just like that, they parted, scarf dropped and forgotten as the Pradhan door opened. And they were odd, natural, just friends and awkward in appearance.

Of course. The truth found Wyatt in a sea of stupidity, snatching him up like a lifeboat with arms. As plain as the decorations that flickered from every house.

Edy was Christian, Hassan Hindu.

The two could never be.

Their families would never accept the two of them together. Never.

And like that, Wyatt Green jumped back in the game.

Twenty-Three

Football season rounded out with a second state championship. Edy's parents, the Dysons, and a few others went straight to a fundraiser in Bellmont Hill following the game. Edy had Hassan, the Dysons, and Kyle in tow for the shindig at Chloe's place.

When they arrived at Chloe's house, it was Lawrence who shoved open the door without knocking. The twins and Kyle followed next, with Hassan and Edy bringing up the rear, fingers laced loosely. She couldn't remember if he'd grabbed her hand or she'd grabbed his, or even whether it was important. But in the face of a packed crowd with dancing girls at the center, she resisted the urge to hold on to him a little tighter.

Chloe slipped between them. The jerk of surprise Edy gave was mirrored on Hassan's face. They'd known each other their entire lives, Edy and Chloe, and the demise to their old friendship had a name: Sandra Jacobs. But this sudden connection they'd conjured, Hassan and Lawrence, was supposed to make them more again. Edy didn't know how to take it, how to trust it.

"He's mad at me," Chloe said. "But he can't stay mad. I know what he likes and how to give it to him."

"I'll, uh, leave you girls," Hassan said. He kissed Edy's cheek, let her hand fall, and disappeared with a look of disgust.

Chloe grinned. "There isn't a girl here that didn't see that."

"See what?"

"Hassan Pradhan not wanting to let you go." She winked and melted into the crowd.

Rap music pierced loud, eviscerating through a speaker to Edy's left, while to the right, a double barrel of kegs earned considerable attention. A second look in that direction revealed faces that Edy didn't know. On squinting, she placed them as Blue Hill Ave football players, officially their rivals.

Hassan and the Dyson twins never took more than a step or three before a clap on the back or a shout stopped them. There were intricate handshakes that differed from group to group, spontaneous bursts of laughter, and an ease that never wavered. This was their scene. Their crowd. In contrast, Lawrence hung back with Kyle, content with a beer, a corner, and a few teammates.

Briefly, Edy considered joining them. After all, both were her friends. But she didn't want them to feel like they were babysitting. Nor did she want to lose progress on the march to adulthood. She didn't want sympathy, or awkwardness, or—

A hand closed around her wrist.

"I love this song!" Chloe shouted. "Dance with me!"

Girls charged the floor with jockeying boys on their heels and clowning Dyson twins among them. But Edy had never danced at a party full of teens, didn't know the latest dance moves. She'd only been instructed in ballet and only managed to mimic Bean's b-boying in her bedroom.

Chloe snatched her to the floor, but hesitated when Edy drew back.

"Can't you dance?" she said with a laugh.

Edy recoiled. Was that how she looked? Awkward? Uncoordinated? Talentless?

Please. She yanked Chloe to the center.

The music shot fast, a wild flow of bass that required more than the lazy hip rocks most were giving it. Edy stepped out with Chloe, imitating her simple lilt, while her body raged at the blasphemy of minimal motion. She didn't know what part of her rebelled first —arms, legs, feet—but she knew it felt right and free, like justice, when it happened.

First, a nuanced pendulum swing of the hips. She rocked through it, surging till it exploded in a complicated pairing of arms, mimicking the motions of braggadocios New York boys in battle. She found a little hop-skip to polish it off at the end; using it to switch directions with an abruptness so sharp she likened it to hitting walls.

It poured in bursts of anger, fueled by what she couldn't tolerate. Of all the things she got wrong: steering away from her mother's wishes, drifting toward Hassan so slow, *so slow*, dance was the one she got right every single time.

"Edy!" Chloe cried. "Remind me not to ask if you can fight."

Edy brushed it off with a grin.

For the next song, something fast and ferocious, Matt shoved through the crowd to join her. Once there his pelvis ricocheted, his fists thrusted, and there was little room for her to respond to his wildness. When that song ended, twin replaced twin, and took up the same hip tossing lunacy.

Done with the forced subjection to their hips, Edy headed for the punch table, where she found a crystal bowl brimming with red liquid. Immediately, her father's words came to her.

"Never take drinks from a stranger, drinks from people you don't trust, or drinks with an origin you can't ascertain."

She scowled. Dancing was thirsty business. And she was having fun. Leave it to her father to muck that up from inside her head. Obviously, Chloe made the punch, though it was possible for a boy to come along and drop something in it. But to what end? He'd be drugging boys and girls alike. Would someone find that fun? Sounded like a really expensive sort of fun. Impractical.

Fingers laced through Edy's, and a body warmed her backside.

"Show off," Hassan said in her ear.

"She said I couldn't dance!"

He played out a little rhythm in her palm.

"Right. Except now everyone's going to want to dance with the girl with gyrating hips. *My* girl, mind you. My love."

He kissed the space behind her ear and vanished.

But his words stayed. His girl. His love.

Edy looked up to spot the twins sandwiching Jessica in that same little horrible hip jerk. Her gaze kept moving, past a cluster of Blue Hill Ave players, a mix of guys and girls, a guy she knew from history, and—

Wait.

The Blue Hill Ave guys were looking at her weirdly. Not even trying to shield it, just staring, unapologetic.

Her eyes widened. *Creeps.*

Edy went for Lawrence and Kyle, her closest, safest bet. When she moved to grab a beer bottle from the table nearest them, however, Lawrence swatted her hand away.

"Chill out," he said, oblivious to the fact that they were the exact same age and that he held one in his own hand.

But Edy was through with the double standard, so she marched around to the opposite side of the table and made a show of assessing the various brands. Budweiser. Michelob. Heineken. Coronas. At the last moment, she decided to join the keg line.

"Hey. Edy, right?"

She turned in surprise. Reggie Knight. Linebacker for Blue Hill Ave.

He stuck out a hand. "Reggie," he said simply.

"I know."

But how did he know her?

"I haven't really seen you around this crowd before," he said. "You must not do the party scene."

It was an odd statement, one that required her to delve into more than she would've liked. She shrugged instead.

"You're not one of the dance girls, or I would have noticed you before." He shook his head. "But I'll tell you this. You should be one."

His dark lips spread into a smile.

"Listen, Reginald—"

"Reggie."

The line moved. They stepped forward together.

"Like I was saying. I saw you. Watched you. Definitely want to know you a little better."

"Well, you've misunderstood." Edy jammed one hand into the other, squirming in some semblance of a disappearing act she'd yet to learn. "I'm sorry, but I'm here with Hassan. Hassan Pradhan."

Reggie held up his hands in a show of defenselessness. "I figured you were with one of them. So, sure. No problem. I understand."

Edy looked around, suddenly wondering where her constant bodyguard service was. She spotted Hassan on the opposite side of the room. Lawrence and Kyle were still near but in a heated discussion about something. Meanwhile, the twins were absent altogether.

Edy turned away. The line moved, she moved, and Reginald moved with it. She couldn't even tell if he wanted beer or not, since he stood adjacent to and not behind her at all.

The twins came in from outside, arms overloading with cases of Budweiser. They dumped them on the table and disappeared. Lawrence and Kyle turned to cracking the boxes open and transferring the beer to coolers of ice.

"Like I was saying, I'm at Blue Hill Ave. A linebacker." Reginald turned as if remembering something. "These are my boys, Will and Jesus. They play, too."

He placed a hand on the back of one guy who appeared to be a seamless part of the crowd, then another. Both turned.

"Oh hey, what's up, baby?" said the taller of the two, Jesus. He had thick, leathery skin and limp black hair pulled tight into a ponytail.

"Nothing," Edy said. She lowered her gaze, put off by the "baby" and torn by the need to show the boys' constant protection of her was unnecessary. She could kill this scene by going to them or she could handle this one by herself.

The line moved again. All three boys went with it.

"Yeah, baby girl was just telling me that she's here with Pradhan," Reggie said.

"Well, that's what's up," Will said enthusiastically, confusing Edy even further.

"So, Edy, how about you and me get together a little later?" Reggie said, gaze dropping to her body.

Edy sputtered, mouth flailing at the audacity of it all. "Did you not just hear me?" she cried. "I'm with Hassan!"

What a stupid, impotent response, like yelling "quit it" when someone pointed a gun at your face. Still, her fists balled.

Reggie touched Edy's arm, just so. "That's what I'm saying, sexy. When you get bored with him, come find me after."

"After what?" Edy cried.

He released her, as if she had somehow offended him. "After you two get done pounding each other. After that, let me get a turn."

Edy swung without knowing she would, fist like a hammer to his eyeball.

Reggie reeled, righted himself, and spat an eclectic selection of profane names as he clutched at his face.

"What did you say to her?" Hassan appeared at Reggie's side.

Lawrence and Kyle looked up.

"Look, your bowwow here—"

Hassan slapped him.

She never knew a man could be slapped that way, with an open-palm of thunder, spittle flying, gleaning a cry of startled pain. The boy plowed into the refreshment table, splashing punch, upturning cups, ice, and beer bottles in the assault. Edy cringed.

"Get up and fight me," Hassan said.

He yanked Reggie to his feet as Lawrence cursed and chucked a beer bottle at Jesus' head, cutting short the fist that swung for Hassan. Glass pounded one side of Jesus' face and sending him reeling with a grunt. Edy jumped back when Kyle and Lawrence lunged in some silent agreement, with the first bringing down a wounded Jesus, and the second sweeping low enough to scoop Will preemptively.

Reggie swung and Hassan ducked, coming up with a crashing fist to the abdomen. He grunted, bent just so, and got an elbow slam to the jaw. Reggie stumbled, and threw a wild fist that Hassan yanked, overextended, and twisted behind his back. He used it to pitch Reggie headfirst into the kegs, where he stomped his back with gusto.

"Hassan!" Edy screamed, fearful for the other boy. She tumbled over as Lawrence and Will crashed into her back and then flew in the other direction, bodies still locked. She couldn't even see Kyle and Jesus in the widening fray.

And then she saw, *really saw*, the scope of what she'd caused.

The twins rushed in. More South End players joined in, then Blue Hill Ave players, before Reggie caught Edy's attention again. Words froze on her tongue, warnings stalled, fears ignited and took flight on wings of frigid foreboding.

Hassan had disappeared into the crowd to help his teammates fight. He'd dismissed Reggie, leaving him to writhe on the floor, bathing in beer and punch. He twisted and maneuvered onto his battered back, where he his neck strained as he struggled to reach into his pants.

No. Hell no. Beat up guys reached into their pants for one reason: retribution with a gun. She knew that from her mother's court cases.

Terror set her charging with gritted teeth, muscles screaming, brain retreating. Edy exploded with a football kick to his face and it jarred her: toe to ankle to calf to knee to hip, all in perfect alignment. Reggie's face exploded with a shift, nose *elsewhere,* before Edy had time to register a scream—her scream. Blood sluiced thick and black from Reggie's nose. People rounded them or maybe backed from them, as he mucked her name and what he would do to her. Oh, he would have her; he promised in gelatinous words, right after he broke her goddamned neck.

No music Edy realized belatedly. She craned around to see why. Still, her boys committed full on to the fight, and oh, Hassan rumbled like it gave him life. Red faced, grinning, and tossing around two boys. He brawled with the best of them.

"Edy!" Chloe shrieked.

The gun.

She turned to find it pointed at her abdomen, Reggie's arm less than steady, his head rested against the wall. Edy swallowed. In fact, while his arm shook, her pulse steadied. She felt . . . calm. Knowing she might die. Understanding he had the upper hand and that this sequence of events had been because of a choice she made. Choices were all she ever wanted.

"Go ahead," Reggie said. "Scream. Beg."

Nothing like that built in her now. For all her indifference, for all the indecisiveness she'd faced in life about Hassan, her future, what she couldn't have and what absolutely belonged to her, what Reggie promised with his gleaming gun and globs of blood oozing from his nose was that nothing, *nothing* laid in her future after he pulled his trigger.

Only death.

And she had no remedy for that.

Reggie guffawed and swung the gun toward the dance floor where the melee continued. His mouth went wide with bloodied glee as he searched, fast, wild, desperate now for his real prey.

Hassan.

A stiletto heel flung past Reggie's face and he canted in Chloe's direction, pissed. Edy popped off the grand battement from hell, kicking his gun arm toward the ceiling. He misfired upstairs. *Bang.* Screaming. Shattering bone breaking shrieking surrounded Edy on all four sides. It overlapped and licked and threatened madness as it tore at the walls in a bid for escape.

The stampede had begun.

A tangle of bodies fell into them, onto them, and Edy plummeted, sandwiched between a cursing Reggie, and another, bulkier than him.

She'd know that body anywhere.

From atop her, Hassan groped for the gun still in Reggie's possession. He closed his hand around Reggie's thumb back and snapped, earning a bubbling howl when it cracked.

"Come on," Chloe cried. "Now!"

She had an arm on Hassan and yanked. While it didn't pull him upright, it did get him moving. He got up, claiming Edy as fast as he could.

Edy shot a questioning look at the front door, still jammed with escapees.

"Back door! Now!" Chloe said and sprinted, joining hands with Lawrence before weaving around a corner and out of sight.

They collided with the twins outside and fled.

~~~

Mirror. Road. Mirror. Road. *Swerve.* With Hassan's eyes uncommitted, his Mustang jerked left into the oncoming lane. No traffic this time, thank God.

"What is it?" Edy said. "Hassan, why do you keep doing that?"

He shook his head. "Nothing. No reason." He exhaled. "Did he hurt you?" Hassan asked, voice delicate as a melting snowflake.

Edy shook her head. "No."

Images rushed her: the crack *back* of a thumb, the *sluicing* of blood, the *skid* of a nose off course. Nausea jolted Edy and she let down the window for air.

"Cake?"

"I'm okay. I—"

She stared down a second bolt of sickness and won.

"Call your mother," Hassan said and then made it nearly impossible by taking her hand and crushing it. His grip juddered as if plagued by a seizure.

As the daughter of the reigning district attorney she had training for . . . mayhem, she and Hassan both did. A rudimentary form of that tried to kick in.

"I'll—I'll call her in a second," she said.

Hassan pulled up to a stop sign, jerked into park, and crushed her in his arms.

"I'm sorry. I'm so, so sorry, baby." He pressed a kiss to her cheek, nose, eyelid, lips, and brushed hair from her face. "I cannot lose you, Edy. Do you understand that? I can't—"

Belated tears stung Edy's eyes. For all his talk, he was the one Reggie gunned for; he was the one that almost died. That image burned the back of her eyelids like an old photo negative: Reggie and his gun aiming for Hassan. It would stay with her always, like acid burns on the heart. No amount of tears could bury that memory; no amount of therapy could soothe it.

The bona fide fear arrived too late. It sloshed through her bloodstream. She saw it flashing in Hassan's too-green eyes. When high beams illuminated the Mustang from behind, he shifted into drive and took off.

"Call your mom," he said.

"Hassan?"

"It's nothing. Just—call your mom."

He exhaled when the car behind them hung a right at the next intersection.

With no answer from her mother, they agreed to head back to Edy's place as discreetly as possible and wait in her bedroom.

They found the house dark, clean, and quiet. Edy knew as they navigated the shadows and climbed the stairs, that they were practiced enough to bump nothing. Not that they worried about being heard. Her father would have fallen asleep with his reading glasses fogged and his academic journals having slipped to the floor anyway. Her mother, if she had occasioned not to have slept in her office, would have tucked into bed with a half dozen assortment of sleep and pampering agents designed for absolutely undisturbed relaxation. How did she know both were there? Because both cars sat in the Phelps drive. Which only *kinda* explained why her mom wouldn't answer the phone, no matter how many times they called.

Once in her room, space evaporated, and they found each other in an instant. Edy melted in his arms, dripping to nonsense, lulled by his heart hugging apologies and a trembling that plagued them both.

She shushed him. Under thin streams of moonlight, Edy stroked the lump on his brow with two shaking fingers. But Hassan claimed the digits in a fist and pressed the tips to his lips with tenderness, gaze on her as he kissed them. Heat bloomed low in Edy, curling and unfurling like a tease.

"I heal," Hassan said and moved his mouth lower, tracing the line of her jaw with kisses, trailing appreciation down her neckline. It felt like heaven. It felt like a thousand chances plus two. "Promise me you're okay," he whispered. "Promise me you're not hurt."

Hurt was the furthest thing from her mind. In fact, she needed a recipe for breathing that second. Edy managed a nod and tilted her head back more, giving him better access. You know, in case he wanted to go a little lower.

He returned to her lips with a smirk.

"Open for me," Hassan said, and Edy *lit*, sure as a match dropped in an inferno.

Their mouths met in a spark of greed, in hunger, in certainty—oh so much certainty *now*, with her giving, validating again and again, until she ached and unraveled, soldering up and into him, leg wrapping his waist, body writhing. She craved what she couldn't even name and willed him impossibly close, bodies tangling till her remaining foot left the floor and his arm tightened. They collapsed into the wall, then the floor.

They giggled from the tangled little knot they'd made, him with his arm still wound around her. Edy had no idea how he'd managed to bear the brunt of their fall, but a glimpse of his lips had her leaning in. The corner of his mouth curled upward, shooting a thrill through her, sure as some drug. They really had waited too long to get together.

His gaze dropped to her mouth, then drew up again, teasing with tender deliciousness, drawing in steady certainty, before a press of the lips had them hurdling toward desperation once again. Slivers of hair trapped in her fingers as she wound him in. They were pulling, arching, not bothering to care; when that trembling whisper appeared in her head, demanding to know how far she'd take this.

"More," Hassan whispered and his lips left hers, first to nibble on her ear, then taste her neck, burning her with roaming hands until she let out a shudder that could have singed. Whispers of love passed between them while air came in great gasping gulps. In their white-knuckled, sweat-ridden embrace he moved, they moved as if entranced. It occurred to Edy; she would have to stop this. Even as she had the thought, she willed him close, closer, with hands that clung and ran everywhere. He had no coat and she tugged at his sweater. In between deep and desperate gasps of air, he managed to get her coat in a series of careful maneuvers.

"Really, Cam. I don't think—" Edy's mother burst into giggles.

Edy and Hassan went still.

"I would tell you it's late," Edy's mother said with a modicum of softness, "but I know how persistent you can be. No one tells you 'no', not even me."

Edy got up and had a hand on the door knob without knowing how it happened. She registered Hassan hissing her name, then him, vice tight on her arm.

"No. Don't even." He shot a hand to the door to block the exit. She knew it didn't look like much, but the odds of her getting out went to zero that second.

"Move," she whispered. "You have no right to keep me here."

"Edy," he said. "We can find out what's up with that call another day. But tonight, we either need to go to your mom or the police."

Edy flinched, hating when he talked sense at her. She started after her mother again.

"Promise me," he said and took her wrists with both hands. "Promise me there's an us when you're done."

Her heart wilted; frail as a bloom past season, too content to be gathered up or undone by the moment. Hassan reeled her in, so that they molded, and pressed a whisper of a kiss into her hair.

"I'm going with you downstairs," he said and drew away from her.

~~~

Wyatt watched as Edy flung herself from the Mustang. Anger goaded her into long and hurried strides until she disappeared onto her front deck.

He hated the tendril of hope that burned in his chest, flickering there where a heart should have stood. Never willing to peter out or dim but scorch to the greatest inferno with the promise of her nearness as his fuel.

Wyatt hated hope.

His stomach bottomed out; pain chafing at his insides in great tangled knots, knots yanking at him always, evermore toward *her*. Every part of Wyatt had been beaten in, chopped off, or scrapped clean; the whole of his body rendered forfeit in a series of high stakes bets.

The driver's side door of the Mustang opened and Wyatt's body tensed. Air escaped his lung's, flattening without the promise of return. With the whole of his will, he ushered Hassan indoors to his home, to his own bed, to his own life.

Hassan eased the car door shut and rose to full height, shoulders tight, tense, weighted. Only when his head snapped counter clockwise did it occur to Wyatt that he was listening. He sprung, slick as a jaguar under moonlight, head low, arms, legs, body, a perfect tandem of obscene gracefulness. He leapt mid-stride for the lowest branch, swung up and disappeared from sight.

Wyatt couldn't understand. Edy knew the truth: that no future existed between Hassan and Edy, that not even their friendship could stand where it did, less all that they cherished rot and fester.

But Wyatt couldn't convince her. Why couldn't he convince her when the whole world stood against them? Why couldn't he convince her of the truth he knew? And his version was the truth. He knew that because of the price he'd paid: the depth of his pain, the wrenching loss he felt every time she chose him, and she chose him every day anew. Wyatt was her faithful friend. Wyatt loved her. There had been no summer of girls him. There had been no cheerleaders to sample first. There would never be another for him. Only Edy. He'd been truest to her.

She'd woven into his soul. Couldn't she see that? How could he make her know?

Time escaped in audible gasps. A fat, mocking moon tip toed across the sky, unapologetic in its creep. Stillness, darkness, nothingness met him in every window of Edy's house, until Wyatt's steady breaths became pants, and his head fell with a thump against a frostbitten bedroom window.

Do. No more thinking. Do something.

Guys like Hassan were men of action. Action accomplished things. Inaction accomplished nothing. Wasn't it obvious?

Wyatt's feet took to the task even as his mind spoke the order into existence. He didn't bother with a coat, crossing the gaping maw of his bedroom—shrunken and mocking on any other day. He yanked on battered Converse and a wrinkled flannel button up, pulled on a ball cap, thundered downstairs, and grabbed his dad's keys as the old man slept in his standard recliner by the door. A plan formed as he moved, quickening his motions, burgeoning confidence, igniting the quivering flame he called a heart until it roared fierce as the fires of hell. On his way out, he kicked over Hassan's untouched donations.

~~~

Edy stood at the top of the stairs with railing and a bit of wall for cover. At her back, Hassan waited for his cue. In the shadows of the stairwell, her mother's slim, jutting silhouette descended at leisure. There'd been such novelty in her voice, such an off putting sense of gratification, of velvet indulgence, of utter bliss. A concept so foreign to Edy's ears it snaked through her, knotting white hot fear with the iciest contempt until nothing but numbness remained.

Buoyancy enveloped Edy on her descent, so she felt nothing. Her hand drifted along the banister with Hassan close behind.

"Now listen to me," Edy's mother said from the first floor hall. "We know all we need to know. You'll ruin our leverage by lashing out indiscriminately. Donations have been coming in, which, as you may recall, was the point."

Edy hesitated, uncertainty gathering like ghost fingers at her neck, ready to seize her by throat, should suspicion prove unsupportable.

She shot a look at Hassan, whose dark brows and thick lashes slipped low, face an effigy of intolerance. A silent conversation shot between the two before she nodded in agreement. He was right. Edy's mother sounded . . . weird on the phone with Cam. Giddy. But Hassan was right. The night of a shootout wasn't the time to tackle that. But tackle that, they would.

Another laugh, one silky as the first, shot a spike straight up Edy's spine. They froze on the staircase and the doorbell rang.

"Cam! Someone's *here*, at this hour. Can you believe it?" her mother said.

Edy cautioned a look back at Hassan. Judging by the stark horror swallowing his face, they'd narrowed their candidates down to the same people: his parents.

"Good evening. Mrs. Phelps?"

"Wyatt?" Edy said.

She shot down the staircase.

"Edy!" Hassan cried and rushed after.

Edy's mother shot them an annoyed glance, phone wedged between her shoulder and ear. "Hold on, Cam. This looks involved." She shot Wyatt an intolerant look.

"Go on, Wyatt. You were saying something about my daughter having boys in her room."

Hassan laughed.

Edy's mouth fell open, hinges dissolved, lost in the wake of this new storm. This friend—this best friend of hers—he'd come to tell on her?

That old fish faced traitor; she'd split him from gut to gullet and leave him on Mass Ave for traffic.

"Whoa!" Hassan plucked her from thin air; the first indication to Edy that she'd gone for Wyatt's throat at all—aside for the whites of Wyatt's eyes suddenly way too visible.

Edy's mother groaned, as if put off by their drama, before slowing at her daughter's appearance.

"I'll call you back, Cam," her mother said. She turned her attention on Wyatt. "I'm glad you came and I'm even more thrilled that you have taken an interest in the company Edy keeps. It's a subject I obsess about, as well, when said company appears out of nowhere. Tell you what. Take a trip with me into the study, will you?"

Edy's mother started off, barefoot and still somehow glamorous, but paused when Wyatt held off, back pressed to the door.

"We could ask Hassan to be your bodyguard if it'll make you feel better."

He followed her, eyes on Edy till he passed.

They returned less than a minute later, with Edy's mother holding a few sheets of paper. Wyatt, on the other hand, had taken on a robust shade of Christmas green, as if Edy's mother had fed him a shovel full of vomit in the interim.

Well, it was a possibility.

"Chaterdee, Rhode Island," Edy's mother announced.

Hassan shot Edy a questioning look.

I'm from Chaterdee. A soot-filled town on the edge of Pawtucket, where steel mills blot out the sun."

Edy wondered if now would be a good time for her dad to wake up. She wondered it, but she didn't dare say it. Not yet. She had to know what was on that sheet of paper.

"225 Willow Lane. Distress call received at 5:10 p.m. Police arrival 5:21 p.m. Incident Type: Assault." Her mother looked up with a grin bearing wisdom teeth before continuing. "White, adolescent male, Wyatt Green, Reporting party. White adolescent female, Lottie Davis, victim, found semi-conscious on living room floor. Breathing is without distress. Multiple blows to the face, torso and legs. Knuckles scrapped. Fingernails torn. Clothes torn and *poorly* rearranged."

Edy's mother tsk-tsked. "So much *evidence.*" She looked from Wyatt, who refused to look at anyone, to Edy, her smile smug.

"Mom," Edy said. "If this is for me, I don't—"

Oh. If looks bore teeth, if looks sprouted fangs, then this one would have clamped down on Edy's neck and sunk its venom deep. It would have taken its time with her.

"The reporting party, Wyatt Green," her mother continued, "initially indicated that there was an accident, though declined to go into further detail regarding the type or location of accident. Closer examination of the reporting party turned up surface abrasions on both hands and a half inch scratch on the left cheek. Green attributes these to difficulty cutting grass earlier in the day."

Edy's mother tossed him a wink.

"Davis regained consciousness before the arrival of the ambulance. She exhibited considerable reluctance to cooperate with treatment or with the identifying of a viable suspect. She indicated that on arriving home, she encountered a masked assailant who attacked her. Her account depicted him as six feet tall with a black shirt and blue jeans, and no other identifying markers. A thorough search turned up no signs of forced entry."

She looked up, at last. "This is what I do, Mr. Green. I make it my business to know your business the second I meet you. *That's* my real trade."

Edy had no recollection of compelling her feet to move, yet the audible *thump* of the back of her head connecting with wall confirmed as much. She'd found Alice's Wonderland bottle labeled "DRINK ME" and guzzled when she hadn't meant to, choking on its contents till she shrunk down and drowned in her problems. She found the cake labeled "EAT ME" and shoved it in her mouth, gouging without hunger. She swelled on her mother's suspected affair with Cam, on what Wyatt might have done, on lips that wouldn't call her father, on tears that wanted to and couldn't fall. The night had no bottom at all.

"I have more ammunition," her mother said and deigned to look in Edy's direction. "Like a knock next door. In case you need persuasion to shut your mouth."

Hassan took a step closer to Edy and placed a hand at the small of her back. Up until then, he'd been a model of indifference for the most part, removed from their spectacle, gathering intel.

"Or what?" he said.

"Quid pro quo. We can all pretend it's yesterday. Friendships for everyone. Or rather, almost everyone.

Cam and Rebecca, Hassan and Edy." Her mouth dragged in an exaggeratedly sympathetic look at Wyatt. "None for you, I'm afraid. All I can promise is that we'll be discreet about your background. I don't think you'll convince Edy to—" a giggle escaped her, and she placed a hand to her mouth to cover it "—date you."

Outside, headlights flashed, illuminating the entire living room.

"What in the world?" Edy's mother murmured, and took on a purposeful stride towards the window.

"No," Hassan moaned.

He shot past her, threw open the curtains, and cursed. "Get down. Get down now!"

He exploded full throttle. Every bit of muscle and mass gunned until he slammed Edy to the ground. The room flashed black, then white, and the taste of bitter metal filled her mouth. Suffocation. With Hassan atop her as if he could shield her from the Earth's existence, she could find no oxygen at all.

"Hassan, please. Let go of my ankle!" Edy's mother shouted as if touching the ankle of an elected official were a serious government matter.

"Please don't move," he whispered.

Numbness toyed with Edy's limbs. Eventually, moving wouldn't be an option.

"What are you playing at?" Wyatt said, from the floor. Though she couldn't see him, trembles laced every word. "Who's outside, exactly? Another girl?"

"Shut. Up," Hassan said. "And stay on the floor."

"He had other girls," Wyatt hissed. "There have *always* been other girls."

He came into Edy's peripheral when he stood and ventured toward the window. "Who's out there that we're not supposed to see? And why? Ask yourself that!"

Wyatt yanked the curtains and crumpled in a hail of gunfire.

Love Edy continues Fall 2014

Sign up at
ShewandaPugh.blogspot.com
for email updates on new releases.

If you enjoyed this book, please review it.

Acknowledgments

Whoa. This novel represented such a group effort that without the help of family and friends, it wouldn't have been possible. First, to my husband, Pierre, who worked out countless early incarnations of characters and plot with me: thank you. Thanks to Nova Southeastern University and Brenda Serotte for shaking out the potential in these characters and in a young, unpublished, writer. Thanks to those in the trenches with me: Ian Thomas Healy, Allison M. Dickson, Tavares Jones, Lashanta Charles, and Leona Romich. Thanks to the members of Scribophile and the Fiction Writers Group on Facebook, the latter of which has a talent for putting up with me. As always, I'm ever grateful for the love and support I get from my parents, Dorothy and Alain Leroy, from my family, and my cherished alma mater, Alabama A&M University. To the fans of *Crimson Footprints* who find themselves here, I have big hugs for each and every one. Trivia for you: I penned *Love Edy* at the same time as *Crimson Footprints,* book one. I must have been insane. In any case, to readers old and new: *Thank you.*

About the Author

Shewanda Pugh debuted as an adult contemporary romance author in 2012 with the *Crimson Footprints* series. Shortlisted for the AAMBC Reader's Choice Award, the National Black Book Festival's Best New Author Award, and the prestigious Rone Award for Contemporary Fiction in 2012 and 2013, she has an MA in Writing from Nova Southeastern University and a BA in Political Science from Alabama A&M. Though a native of Boston, MA, she now lives in Miami, FL, where she can soak up sunrays without fear of shivering.

Made in the USA
Middletown, DE
03 August 2017